THE TREASURE OF MAD DOC MAGEE

❧ ELINOR TEELE ❧

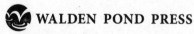 **WALDEN POND PRESS**

An Imprint of HarperCollins*Publishers*

Walden Pond Press is an imprint of HarperCollins Publishers.
Walden Pond Press and the skipping stone logo are trademarks
and registered trademarks of Walden Media, LLC.

ISBN 978-0-06-234513-4

Typography by Carla Weise
18 19 20 21 22   CG/LSCH   10 9 8 7 6 5 4 3 2 1
❖
First Edition

For
Mum

ↄ

The Mountains

ↄ

**And All the Jenny Girls
in My Family**

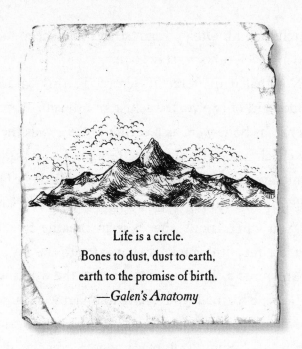

Life is a circle.
Bones to dust, dust to earth,
earth to the promise of birth.
—*Galen's Anatomy*

CHAPTER 1

On the banks of the Arrow, where the gold poplar grew, lived the daughter of Hapless Burns. Her name was Jenny. And if the tale I'm about to relate seems a little far-fetched, then you'll just have to take it on trust. For Jenny had a hand in crafting it.

Course, New Zealand has changed a great deal since the 1870s. These days it's all fat beef farming and "wipe your feet." But back when Jenny was a girl, growing was hard. The Rush for gold had come and gone, the miners had slogged off to the coast, and drought had hit Otago. It got so hot that sheep took to shearing each other to stay cool.

Not that it mattered to Jenny. To this wild, red-blooded girl of twelve, the schist and the gorse and the hills raw as bone were as pleasing to the eye as the fantails chasing flies through the Gorge. The mountains might have taken her mother and befuddled her father, but Jenny was willing to give 'em her body and soul.

"You can't know what it is to breathe free," she once told me, "till you have danced with the sky."

And what a sky it was. To picture the world where our heroine roamed, you'll have to imagine a snug little valley, with pastures like hides and rivers like arteries. This was a living, lively place, where every peak held a secret.

To the north was the Sleeping Girl—a mountain ridge that flanked the edge of the town of Eden. Seen from the side, she had a big, rounded forehead, a pert, pointy nose, and a row of rock buttons down her pinafore. Her dreams, some said, were shooting stars.

To the south were the Wise Women. There's been considerable debate about the origin of that one, for the raggedy furrows look nothing like ladies. But they were said to be the oldest mountains in the territory, and I suppose someone made the mistake of equating age with brains.

To the east was the Crooked Man—Jenny's favorite piece of geology. Romantics claimed the label for this range was inspired by the twists and turns of the Arrow River, where the water swerved sharp through the Gorge before it widened and straightened beside the town.

And to the west were Lake Snow and the frosted Alps. Lake Snow was the site of a famous rescue, where a bloke named Still Hope had died while saving the station owner from drowning. A spiritual man, some said, who spoke of singing trees and sacred spaces. Jenny admired his nerve.

Apart from the Alps, most of these christenings came courtesy of the Rush. No sooner had the gold miners stumbled into an empty space than they filled it with memories from home. The rocks became their family, and the mountains their mates. Though it didn't do much to combat the heat and the heartache, it had the benefit of making the country feel familiar.

They came, they fossicked, and, before you could blink, they were gone, leaving their monikers behind. By the time Jenny was grown, only a few like Hapless and me could recall the characters who had laid claim to Eden. But their ghosts still lingered in the memory.

There was Soapy Jones, who bragged he could smell gold through the ground. Gamblers would often observe him snuffling along Main Street with his nose in a newspaper cone. "The better to focus the scent," he'd say.

There was Kip Two-Fister, who laced his beer with flakes from the Arrow. Drinking your fortune may be a good spectacle sport, but it didn't do much for Kip's constitution. It's no wonder his friends took an interest in his long drop.

There was Lucky Cork and Roaring Sue and Pistol Harry. There was Lazy Bill and Swifty Dan and Tiny Samson.

But I'm sure the character you'll be most curious about was Doc Magee. Having saddled him with the title of this tale, I really can't blame you.

I'd like to satisfy your longings here—to tell you of a man so eccentric he used to stand on his head for breakfast. Of a doctor so crafty he could trick a drunk into using his own bottles for target practice. Of a dreamer who believed in harebrained schemes.

And, of course, of a nugget of gold so bright and gleaming that men compared it to the eye of God.

Only I run the risk of ruining Jenny's story.

What I *can* relate is that Magee caught the same greedy fever that swept through the territory. Some it killed and some it scarred and some it left lonely and broken. For the sake of a shiny thing, folks were willing to torture the ground and ruin their souls.

And maybe, just maybe, murder.

This, at any rate, was the land that Jenny found herself in one scorcher of a Thursday at the beginning of autumn as she scaled the gate toward home. She had been out exploring a goat track and lobbing potshots at the pine trees in the valley below. Her mouth was as dry as a stick and her feet were as sore as cuts, but she was looking forward to an evening on the roof of the shed.

"Help!"

You might think a cry like that would set a kid running, but it was not an unusual sound for Jenny to hear. Hapless Burns was known throughout the territory for being the most ham-fisted, long-winded, foggy-minded bloke you could ever hope to hire. His heart was in the right place, sure. But his work on a sheep station left a lot to be desired.

"Got myself stuck!"

When you're weary from a day in the sun, the last thing you want to see is your father's rump poking out at you from a window two stories up. With his red feet dangling high in midair, and his front half embedded somewhere in the dark of the woolshed, Hapless Burns looked precisely like the tail end of a horse headed north.

"Dad! Why are you in your drawers?"

"Jenny? Is that you? I was trying to climb in the window. Jenny, are you there?"

Jenny stepped back and contemplated the situation. The window was a sticky one—that she knew from personal experience—and lethal when it dropped. If she pushed Hapless out from the inside, she ran the risk of chopping off his neck or breaking his legs. If she pushed him in, he might somersault over the platform and impale himself on a broom handle—she'd seen him pull similar stunts before.

All in all, she reckoned, her father was better in than out. So taking up the ladder that lay by her feet, she scaled the side of the corrugated iron wall. It wasn't exactly cool to the touch.

"Stop kicking, Dad! You'll take my eye out!"

"Oh, lordy, lordy, my calves are burning!" moaned Hapless.

"Then keep your trousers on next time!"

It took a good ten minutes for Jenny to loosen the window, and another ten to shove the remains of her father through the opening. By the time he had gotten around to righting his body and blundering his way back outside, she was practically spitting. Only she had no spit left.

"This has got to be the dumbest trick you've ever pulled," said Jenny.

Hapless sat down on the ground and sighed.

"Guess so."

"Why didn't you go through the door?" asked Jenny.

"I lost the key."

"But Dad, there are *two* doors!"

It was a mark of his character that Hapless had to take a moment to think about this. "Suppose there are."

When you can't say anything nice, the trick is to kick something, hard. Jenny took a swing at the side of the shed and immediately felt much better.

"I spilled paint on my legs," Hapless continued, smiling foolishly. "Took off my trousers because I didn't want to get any on the sill."

Whether you will or no, it can be hard to stay angry at a twig of a man with nought but a wisp of hair on his crown. And if Jenny was good at getting mad at her dad, she was even better at forgiving him. It was one of her finer qualities. So she did the honorable thing and fetched him a drink from the pump.

"I don't know why you're worried about messing up this place," said Jenny, handing him a tin cup. "It's not like it's marble and teak."

"That's as may be," said her father, taking a swig, "but we got our reputations to be thinking about."

A cold rush of worry, like the first surge of a spring thaw, ran through Jenny's veins. "What do you mean, 'our reputations'?"

"Farmer Wilcock has given us a month's notice. Says we have to be up and out of this house before the first frost."

Now, you can infuriate a kid like Jenny in many ways. You can push her over a cliff, or tie her to a rail, or remind her that her mother died of a fever, but the quickest and surest method is to try to wrench her from the mountains of home.

"Why?" cried Jenny.

"Guess I'm no good at my job," said Hapless.

"So get a new one!"

"I've asked. Nobody round here wants me."

For Jenny, this was the end of any forgiving. Her father might have been a hopeless gold miner and a useless stockman, but to give up on being a hand to the slackest farmer in the valley was downright embarrassing.

"Then go right ahead and quit," she shouted, blasting the last wisp of hair off his head, "but I'm STAYING!"

～

It's a shame no one had a thermometer on Jenny that afternoon, 'cause I bet she came as near to busting the mercury as a girl could get. Whenever Jenny hit boiling point—and she hit it fairly often—the first person she ran to was her best friend, Pandora. With the news she'd received, it was a miracle she didn't burst into flames. As it was, she left a fine pair of scorch marks in Farmer Wilcock's paddock.

From the gate of the sheep station, it was three miles north to Eden—an easy enough distance for any country girl to travel, but plenty of time for Jenny to seethe.

What in heaven was she going to do? From the day she first drew breath, she had been as rooted to Eden as the tree of knowledge. The Arrow wasn't *in* her blood; it *was* her blood. The concept of living on some windswept prairie, or a tropical island, was as foreign to her as geometry.

So what would happen if she left the valley? Would she no longer be Jenny Burns?

There was still silver on the ridge of the Sleeping Girl as Jenny came flying through Main Street, but Eden was winding down for the day. Doors were banging, brooms were whisking, and flies were settling down to feast on the blood of the butcher's knife. A lone ray of light was grazing the hills above the Arrow, making the first three letters of the HOTEL sign glow a fine ruby red.

"Jenny Girl!"

In any other circumstances, Jenny would have been

pleased to pause at the vegetable stall and talk to the Lum brothers. They were, after all, her next-to-best friends. But in times of crisis, Pandora took precedence.

"Sorry, can't stop. I'm in a rush."

"Looking for gold?" asked Lok, with his crinkled smile. Jenny knew he was teasing. A prankster to his roots, Lok was fond of pretending to know only a few words of English. It made for a biting reply when passersby took to ragging him.

"Not today," said Jenny, ignoring the laughter lurking in Lok's question.

"What's the hurry?" asked Kam. Around town, Kam was known as the boy with the long, braided queue and a scar through his eyebrow. He was a serious fellow, too serious for a lad of fourteen. But he liked Jenny and her sudden fits of temper.

"It's nothing," said Jenny, reluctant to break the news before Pandora had heard it. "I just have to go."

"You mean pee?" asked Lok, innocent as snow.

"Yeah, pee!"

"I'm afraid we're all out of peas," said Lok with a roguish grin.

He wasn't joking this time. Like everyone who relied on the land for their living, the Lums were struggling with the drought. Market gardens need a lot of water to thrive, and the clouds were drying up. "Those Chinese boys," as the folks of Eden called them, might have earned a certain respect for the heft of their onions and the sweetness of their carrots, but they were only a few weeks away from losing their dreams.

"I'll be back, I promise! See you soon."

"Counting on it!" called Lok.

Chatting to the Lum brothers had brought Jenny's anger into check, but it wasn't destined to stay there long. Within a minute of resuming her run down the boardwalk, eyes down and heart pumping, she was thrown catawampus by a couple holding hands. In less than a trice, she found herself flat on the ground chewing patent leather boot.

"Why, Jenny Burns," cried a coppery soprano from above where she lay, "you haven't been to see me in an age!"

Wherever you roam in this world, I doubt you'll find a woman to compare with Gentle Annie. Rich by the Rush and retired by choice, she was the ugliest, largest, and most bewitching piece of feminine in the territory. Rumor had it she could charm the eggs from a crocodile.

"Evening, Miss Jenny," boomed a baritone. "Enjoying the air?"

Jenny raised her head to glance at the second speaker. There was no denying King Louis was a rake and a ruffian. But it sure takes guts to stick it out in a town that doesn't want you around. When the rest of his mining cronies had upped stakes and scarpered, King Louis had decided to dig in his spurs. According to Louis, panning for gold was the profession of youngsters and fools. A man of fifty owed it to himself to adopt a nobler occupation. Like poker.

"Help her up, Louis."

Up Jenny came, covered in grime.

"But take care with the new dress!" cautioned Annie.

Jenny stepped back. Even she might have guessed that a puffed orange jacket and a tricornered hat weren't the first items a woman would normally choose to wear. Especially if you happened to be square as a chimney, short as a tree stump, and blind in one eye.

"What's the hurry?" asked King Louis.

"I'm going to see Pandora."

Gentle Annie bobbed her wig. That day it was platinum blond, but she tended to switch colors every third or fourth morning.

"A good friend is worth a thunderstorm these days. If she's willing to listen, please give her mother my regards."

"Something troubling you?" asked King Louis.

"None of your business," Jenny shot back.

King Louis grinned. "Careful with that tongue, Miss Jenny. Someone might cut it off."

"Now then, Louis." Gentle Annie tweaked the lobe of his ear. "Girls aren't obliged to be civil any more than boys are obliged to be clean. Just stand aside and give her the chance to go where she's trying to get."

Jenny smiled gratefully. Women who paid attention to motherless children were apt to fuss and smother, but Annie was different. She gave kids the credit of being rational beings with personal privacies. If she figured Jenny was fretting on something, she let her be until Jenny was good and ready to talk. Picking at a scab will only make it worse.

"Whatever you say, Miss Annie," said Louis.

"You come and see me soon, Jenny Burns. After four, of course."

Grasping King Louis firmly by the arm, Gentle Annie pulled her companion away from Jenny's path.

From there, it was only a few doors down and a full flight of steps up to the rooms at the back of Quinn's Sweet Shop. Course, by now the sun had dropped completely behind the hills. The storefronts had turned from a golden yellow to a bluish gray, and the whole town had a look of peeling paper. Jenny paid it no heed.

"Pandora?"

Three solid bashes on wood were greeted with silence.

"Pandora, it's me!" Jenny knew the time had come

to employ the code that only her friend could fathom. "Volcano!"

An odor of sour milk and disappointment came pouring through the crack in the door.

"Want an apple? I ate half." Pandora stuck out a hand. "Oh, and I'm pretty sure Mum's dead."

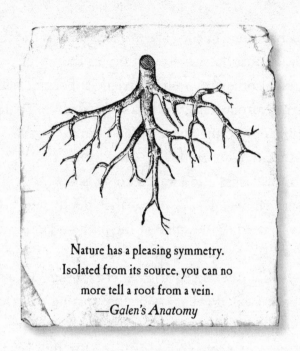

Nature has a pleasing symmetry.
Isolated from its source, you can no
more tell a root from a vein.
—*Galen's Anatomy*

CHAPTER 2

"I'm not dead, Pandora!" retorted Mrs. Quinn from inside. "I was resting!"

"You looked dead."

"Well, sometimes that's what happens when people are ill."

Jenny wasn't surprised by this curt exchange. See, most kids learn pretty quickly to fake their opinions. You get used to saying mutton tastes like lamb and parents know best. It's the quickest route to avoiding trouble. But not Pandora. From the day of her birth, she had never told a lie. If dinner looked like something a dog had done in the corner, Pandora was the first to say it. If pustules were bursting on the tip of Jenny's nose, she could count on her friend to point it out.

"You're covered in dirt," said Pandora, returning her attention to the door.

"I want to come in."

"Okay," said Pandora, stepping aside.

Into the room and out of her depth Jenny went. She was used to the smell of the place—the unwashed sheets and the soot from the stove and the whiff of decay—but the sight of Pandora's mum always set her back a bit. Five years of the wasting disease had stripped her down to skin and bones. When she sat up against a pillow, you could half see through her to the head of the bed.

It wasn't always like this. I'm old enough to remember a day when Lottie Quinn was prettier than a blooming hyacinth. But the Gold Rush was rarely kind to women, and fate is often tough on hopes. In another time and town, Lottie might have been the educated professional she wished to be. As it was, she was simply exhausted.

"Hello, Jenny."

"Hello, Mrs. Quinn."

"You're getting so tall."

"She wouldn't be getting short, Mum," interrupted Pandora. "Unless she was amputated."

Mrs. Quinn sighed. She sighed a lot. She sighed when she filled the licorice jars in her shop, and sighed when she blew her nose, and sighed when she listened to others. Her husband had vanished and her daughter was a riddle, so I grant you she had a lot to sigh about.

"You're out late. I thought you'd be with your dad for supper."

Jenny frowned. She wasn't much for talking to mothers. Perhaps that's because she was lacking the practice. Or maybe she'd decided that ignoring her heartache was as good as treating it.

"He had a job to finish." Mrs. Quinn appeared to be expecting something more, so Jenny added: "Gentle Annie gives her regards."

This time around, Mrs. Quinn didn't sigh. She set her jaw and blinked twice. Then, without another word, she twisted her chin toward the shelves.

"I suppose I could try to find something for you to eat. . . ."

Jenny's stomach was on the verge of crawling out of her throat, but she punched it back down. "I already ate. Can I talk to Pandora alone?"

Mrs. Quinn visibly brightened. "Oh, would you, Jenny? She's been pining for company all afternoon."

"No, I haven't," said Pandora.

"Come on," said Jenny, tugging her friend toward the door. "Remember," she whispered, "volcano!"

On warm, fine nights, the best place to be in the high country was down by the Arrow. There in the shadows lay the pools and mosses and secrets that grown folk seldom bother to find.

As soon as they were old enough to toddle, Jenny and Pandora had staked their claim to every foot of water from the Crooked Man to the edge of Farmer Wilcock's property.

The most coveted of their spots was to be found downstream from Eden, shortly after the river crossing for the road to Reed's Terrace. Tucked into the crook of the bank was an ossified tree. And below it, where a mighty flood had washed the soil from half the roots, was a ready-made hideout.

Jenny liked to call it the Cathedral. Pandora preferred to call it a tree.

"You won't believe what Dad told me!" said Jenny, swinging past the roots and hurling herself into the sand. "It's volcano times a hundred!"

"It's what?"

"Pandora, don't you remember our warning system?"

"No."

"It's a code for saying something bad has happened."

"Why do we need a code?" asked Pandora. To keep

herself occupied, she had begun stacking river pebbles by size and by hue.

"To stop people from poking into our business. 'Paper cut' is something that's sort of bad, like forgetting your lunch. 'Poison oak' is worse, like being in trouble with the schoolmaster."

"We're always in trouble with the schoolmaster."

"And 'volcano' is the end of the world!" finished Jenny.

Pandora pondered this for a bit. "So you're telling me it's the end of the world?"

"Yes!"

"I should have washed my stockings."

When you think about it, it's a perfectly acceptable reaction. Who wouldn't want to be at their most presentable in their final moments? But Jenny didn't have much patience for laundry.

"It's not the real end of the world, Pandora. Only Dad told me we have to leave Eden."

Girls like Pandora don't make it a habit to cry. It uses up water and attracts the attention of old ladies. Instead, if they're feeling extremely unhappy, they tend to get still. In that moment, Pandora grew very still indeed.

"He says he's being sacked," Jenny added after a long and ticklish pause. "Says he's no good."

"He isn't," said Pandora.

"I know!" shouted Jenny. "But I am! And he's my dad, so . . ."

Pandora pondered this conundrum for a while. Finally, she asked, "But why do you want to stay?"

"What?"

"You don't own much. You hate lessons. Everyone at school avoids you." Pandora added a pebble to her stack. "Why do you want to stay?"

Jenny hadn't considered it from this angle. It was true, to be sure, that she was as poor as dirt; her sum of belongings consisted of a bird's nest and three crimson marbles. And there was seldom a day in the year when kids weren't muttering about her mum or her dad or the tint of her skin.

But Jenny was accustomed to all that. Sometime over the course of her twelve years, she had decided that survival meant remaining outside of things, like the husk on a sunflower or frost on a fence. Everyone else in school could worry on names and appearances. She stood apart.

With one exception.

"Well, you're here," said Jenny.

"You'll forget me," said Pandora.

"I'd never. And people will call me names and talk about me in a new town."

"You always say you don't care what people think," noted Pandora.

Jenny's frustration erupted in a shout.

"Fine! Then it's because I'm part of the mountains!"

"You're made of rock?" asked Pandora.

"No. Yes. It's hard to explain." Jenny rested her chin on her hand and stared at the river. How could she spell out to her friend that home doesn't just mean a roof and a wage and the thing men call security? "I suppose it's a bit like when you're lying down on the side of the rise near Lake Snow, and you're watching clouds tumble into the water. And the rain makes the grass smell like clover, and the air taste like chance, and the earth feel like rest. And you think to yourself, if I shut my eyes, I'll be the mountain, too."

Pandora frowned. "I don't get you."

Jenny grinned. "It's okay. You don't have to understand. Except the part," she said, "where I want to stay in Eden."

Here, to Pandora's relief, were words spoke plain. Poetry may be a salve to the soul, but it sure made a mess of vocabulary. "Then you need money," she said.

"Not a lot," countered Jenny. "But it would be nice if Dad could buy his own sheep and a few acres. That way we wouldn't have to worry about him losing his job all the time."

As she spoke, Jenny began to picture it. Old Randolph Scott's place up on Reed's Terrace was for sale, the government desperate to offload the land. She could shore up the foundations on the villa, patch the chimney, build a new shed. There was an orchard in the back—she often picked peaches there in the spring—and a serviceable well. A few months would put it into working order.

"Do you want to rob a bank?" asked her friend.

"What?"

"That's the quickest way to get a lot of money," said Pandora. "We could rob the one in town. I'll need a gun, though."

It took the prime of Jenny's might to stop herself from laughing. The thought of the pair of them, armed to the back teeth and charging up the stairs of the Bank of Eden, was better than a tonic. It made the whole world feel lighter.

"Best not," said Jenny. "We're sure to get caught. But I like the direction you're thinking. We could try gambling—"

"Mum says she'll kill me if I put a foot in the door of King Louis's saloon. Says it's the seventh circle of hell and she burned there for five years. Which makes no sense, because the Bible says you can't get out of hell."

"Okay, then we could try gold mining . . . ," hazarded Jenny.

"Mum says that mining is no better than losing

your mind or dying from fever. Says she's seen too many men go mad trying to suck riches from stone. Which also doesn't make any sense."

But Jenny's ear had caught on a word. "What did your mum say about gold mining?"

"She says too many men go mad—"

"That's it, Pandora!"

"What?"

If Jenny has a vice—and she has a fair few—it's impetuousness. She's not one to wait for the world to turn.

"I have to talk to Dad," she said.

"About what?"

"To see if I remembered something correct!" shouted Jenny.

"What does that have to do with anything?" asked Pandora.

"Tell you about it tomorrow!"

Night was coming on strong as Jenny ran back toward the sheep station. Owls hooted and fence wire hummed in the wind. In the pool of the Milky Way, the tops of the Wise Women rose black as pitch and jagged as sharks' teeth.

Judging by the light in the lower part of the woolshed, Jenny knew her father was working.

"Dad! Dad!!"

"Oh, lordy, lordy, Jenny. Where have you been?"

"Out," said Jenny, her eyes catching the gleam from the shears. A whetstone and an oily rag told her that some long-overdue maintenance was taking place.

"Heaven, spare a prayer for the friendless man and the motherless child."

Since this was an oft-repeated plea, Jenny didn't bother to acknowledge it. "Dad, do you remember a story you told me when I was seven or eight, about a miner named Mike Magee?"

"Sure enough," said Hapless.

Jenny slapped her hand on the bench. "Tell it again."

"Jenny, I'm working."

"I'm sure it'll keep." It was her father's favorite phrase, and Jenny knew it.

Smiling, Hapless leaned back in his chair, took a heel of bread from the box beside him, and handed it to his daughter. "You make yourself comfortable while I marshal the details." He squeezed his hands to his skull. "There now, got it."

Jenny pulled up a seat in the lee of the kerosene lamp and held her breath.

"I first heard of Mike Magee on the day I rode into Eden. I had a nasty sore on my backside and I was hoping to see a medical man about it. You can't be too careful with sores. I had another on my—"

"Dad. The story?"

"Oh, yes. So, I asked around town and everyone said to go see Doc Magee. Mad as a hatter, they told me, but plenty educated. Did his training in a famous medical university overseas, they said. Had a lot of fancy certificates and diplomas on the wall to prove it."

Hapless smiled wistfully. The closest he had ever come to education was his sixth-grade graduation.

"Anyway, I took myself off to his business on Poplar Street and knocked on the door. Nobody there. Went the next day. Nobody there. And my backside was fair aching." With an absence of mind, Hapless patted the spot in question. "So I asked around again. That's when I heard that Mad Doc Magee was a demon gold miner. He and his partner, Silent Jack, had built a place up Moonlight Creek, near the head of the Sleeping Girl. And whenever the weather was favorable, that's where he'd be. Doctoring was something he did to pass the time."

Jenny grinned. She, too, was of the opinion that a day spent roaming the hills with your best friend was a lot more productive than being trapped in an office.

Hapless grimaced. "I tell you, my rear was fair killing me—"

"Dad!"

"So, a few days after I arrive, this rider rolls into Eden and bursts into the Last Chance Saloon. 'Mad

Doc's found the largest gold nugget you've ever seen!' he cries. 'Bigger than a cowbell and ten times as heavy! It's going to bust the Rush wide open.'"

The Last Chance Saloon figured more often than not in Hapless's stories. Jenny had long ceased to wonder why.

"You've never seen a room empty faster. Sixty men went charging for their horses and tools. By nightfall, Moonlight Creek looked like an overturned anthill. I was there myself. A lot of fun if you don't mind the shooting pain in your britches."

"That's fine, Dad, but what happened to Doc Magee?" interrupted Jenny. "And the nugget?"

"Ah, now, that's the real mystery. Because he and his fortune couldn't be found. Any man worth his salt would be over at the saloon celebrating his discovery. But Magee had pulled up stakes and vanished. Along with Silent Jack."

"You mean they both left town? Just like that?" asked Jenny.

"That was the rumor," said Hapless. "Makes sense, I suppose. You wouldn't want to hang around Eden with a treasure like that in your pocket."

This was the point where Hapless's story had originally ended. But Jenny wasn't about to let a sleeping doc lie.

"I don't believe it," said Jenny. "Someone must have

seen Magee leave Eden. Or been in the bank when he exchanged the nugget for money. People can't vanish completely." Revelation arrived as she leaned into the light. "Maybe he was *murdered*."

Hapless winked. "It's funny you should say that, because about nine months after this hullabaloo, a crate arrived in Eden, addressed to the doctor. And when the postman got nosey and opened it, what do you think he found?"

"A body?"

"Near enough," said Hapless. "A human skeleton. To help with the study of anatomy. At least, that's what the note said. Nobody could figure out if the order was late or someone was playing a trick on the town. It was a bona fide riddle."

"What did the postman do with it?" asked Jenny.

"He stored it in Mad Doc's office," answered Hapless.

"Why?"

"'Cause by rights the bones still belonged to the doctor. Granted, it's been a decade or more since he vanished, but there's no one to say that he's actually dead. He might come back."

"Does that mean the skeleton is lying in his office?" demanded Jenny. "Nobody's moved it?"

A speck of guilt became lodged in Hapless's eye.

"Well, you see, most of us had already scoured the

place from top to bottom before the postman arrived, wondering if Magee had left anything of value there. We didn't find much but books. Why? What were you thinking?"

What Jenny was thinking was what Pandora would say. When a skeleton arrives on the doorstep of an eccentric medical man, there's more to the story than a study of anatomy. There was a mystery attached to Magee's disappearance—that she was sure of, deep down in her spine—and this box of bones had something to do with it.

"I wasn't thinking anything, Dad. Except that it sounds puzzling."

"You never said a truer word." Hapless rose from his seat and extinguished the lamp. "Now, then, we'd best to bed."

Jenny was willing to oblige. The sooner she slept, the sooner she could determine the next stage of planning with Pandora. Tomorrow was figuring to be interesting.

"Okay, but you didn't tell me the end of your story."

"I didn't?"

"How did you heal the sore on your butt?"

"Oh, that." Hapless grinned. "I rubbed earwax on it. Amazing what the body can do."

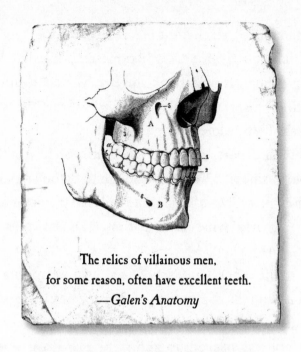

The relics of villainous men,
for some reason, often have excellent teeth.
—*Galen's Anatomy*

CHAPTER 3

On the list of Jenny's dislikes, going to class was right up there with tooth extraction. There was only one schoolroom in Eden—a shed of rough-sawn wood next to the church. Desks and ink were for the rich and mighty. Eden kids sat on old pew benches and scribbled on slate. In the summer, you sweated; in the winter, you froze; in the spring, your chilblains erupted one by one. On bad days, Jenny used to bleed half a pint a day through the cracks in her fingers.

All this might have been sufferable with a good schoolmaster at the helm. But Mr. Grimsby was the worst kind of teacher—the kind that doesn't believe in childhood. To Eden's schoolmaster, kids were lowly grubs, sluggish and slow. Sure, now and again you might discover a butterfly, but the best method was to squash them before they could grow.

For her part, Jenny did her utmost to avoid the whole business. There was enough to do on the station without having to trudge three miles to purgatory each morning. And what use is arithmetic when you're trying to birth a lamb?

On the other hand, school was where Pandora was. Come drought or high water, Mrs. Quinn was set on her daughter getting some book learning. Every day, Pandora was packed up and shipped out the door. If Jenny was intent on seeing her friend, she would have to take the stings with the honey.

"Miss Burns. How kind of you to favor us with your presence." Mr. Grimsby peered at Jenny through the lenses of his round spectacles. "And what are we wearing this Friday? Sackcloth and ashes?"

It was whispered around Eden that the schoolmaster had learned his way of speaking from an early career on the stage. Someone had seen a poster billing a man named Grimsby as the second sailor in *The Barbary Pirate*, a lost play by William Shakespeare. It was a sound-enough theory. Acting is not a profession that lends itself to survival.

"No," said Jenny, regretting her decision already. She could have met up with Pandora after school.

"No, what?"

"No, Mr. Grimsby."

Mr. Grimsby sniffed. "Though I am aware we are suffering from inclement climatic conditions, this should not prevent you from applying water to your face, now should it?"

"No, Mr. Grimsby."

Jenny has a clever trick of hinting at insolence. You know you're being mocked, but there's little you can do to determine the cause.

Mr. Grimsby sniffed again. "Well, if you must be here, be seated and be silent."

It was Pandora's general custom to keep to corners in the schoolroom. Most of the kids in Eden didn't like or care to understand a person who stripped the varnish from talk. More often than not, Miss Quinn could be found in the back row, reading on her own. Squeezing herself past three sets of disgruntled knees, Jenny shuffled into a seat beside her friend.

"Morning," she murmured.

"Miss Burns! What did I just say?"

"Sorry, Mr. Grimsby," said Jenny.

❧

The hours dragged on. It wasn't until tea break, when the rest of the class was playing tag among the elms, that Jenny felt it was safe enough to relate the story of Mad Doc Magee.

"So," said Jenny, "all we have to do is find the nugget."

This was a clear-enough statement in itself, but you'll remember that Pandora had a ruthless approach to facts. "No, it's not," she said.

"What do you mean?"

"We have to find out if Doc Magee is dead. We have to find out if he left the nugget somewhere in Eden or took it with him. We have to find out what happened to Silent Jack. We have to find—"

"Pandora!"

"What?"

"I grant you," conceded Jenny, "that we have many things to do. But the most important thing, in the end, is to find Magee's gold."

Pandora nodded. "Yes, you're right."

"With all the questions, where do we start?" asked Jenny.

"Doc Magee's office," said Pandora. "We should see if the skeleton and the crate are still there. And the note that came with them. That might tell us more about the doctor."

Jenny nodded.

"You said your dad and his mates searched the place right after Magee disappeared," continued

Pandora. "But adults miss important things. I want to go over it again."

"I can meet you tomorrow," said Jenny, thinking of Hapless's regular schedule at the Last Chance Saloon. "Dad's always asleep on Saturdays."

"I suppose we can wait one day, especially since nobody except your dad knows you've been asking about the nugget." Pandora, like everyone else in Eden, was aware that Hapless had the memory of a stretched sieve. "But what if the door is locked?"

"I guess we'll bust through a window?"

"Instigating an insurrection, ladies?"

With the sun standing at ten, Mr. Grimsby's shadow didn't have long to stretch. It might have been cut as a silhouette, it was that sharp and clean. You could see a strand from his long, stringy hair, a thread from his frayed cuff, and the willow switch in his right hand. All that was missing were the spectacles, the nose, and the slash of his lip.

"What were you two doing?" queried the school-master.

"Talking about paper cuts," replied Jenny, hoping Pandora would have sense enough to recognize the code word for mild danger and say nothing.

The right hand twitched.

"I thought I told you to keep quiet," said Mr. Grimsby.

"And I thought different."

It twitched again.

"Miss Burns, if I hear one more word out of you, I'll—"

"Mr. Grimsby! *Mr. Grimsby!* Attention, please."

Saving graces come in a variety of forms, but Jenny was not expecting hers to be Mr. Polk. For Eden's banker was a sour old man with a pickled personality. Years of bickering with farmers about mortgages had reduced his interior to bile and greed.

"How much do you think the schoolmaster heard?" Jenny whispered to Pandora as Mr. Grimsby walked away to greet the visitor. "Do you reckon he knows that we're interested in Magee's office?"

"Dunno," Pandora whispered back. "But we better be careful that we're not being followed when we start our search."

"Let's muster at dawn," muttered Jenny.

"Mr. Polk. How kind of you to visit," fawned the schoolmaster as he escorted Eden's banker across the schoolyard. "And to what do we owe the honor?"

"Letter from the district superintendent," said Mr. Polk, working his jaw side to side. "Asked me to pay a visit. Report back. Observe the workings of the higher mind in Eden. Didn't bother to consult my schedule."

Jenny noticed that Mr. Grimsby had assumed what

King Louis called the rictus grin. It's a look he had seen on many a man who cheated at cards.

"How splendid," said the schoolmaster. "You will be here for the whole afternoon, then?"

"Long as this sad-sack pony show takes. Have to put 'em through their paces. Watch 'em run. Stifling nuisance." Mr. Polk snorted.

"Then we shouldn't waste your valuable time," said Mr. Grimsby. "Miss Burns, go ring the bell."

Taking Pandora by the hand, Jenny headed off for the schoolroom. But Mr. Polk caught her by the shoulder after two steps.

"Hey, missy! Manners first! What do you say to your betters?"

When fate provides you with a gift, it's best to enjoy it. Jenny turned and smiled her sweetest smile.

"Why, of course, Mr. Grimsby. I'd *love* to help you out."

◡

"Today, class, we will be exploring the wonders of enigmata. Here I will illuminate how the grammar of the ancients can provide a window into a forgotten world. Open your primers to page thirty-four."

Everyone in the schoolroom knew this request was pure malarkey. Mr. Grimsby's normal method of instruction was based on grind and repetition. Endless drills were the usual order of the day, seasoned with a pinch of corporal punishment. Exploration had naught to do with it.

"Land sake, Grimsby, do we have to have grammar?" Mr. Polk thrust his jaw to the fore. "That sort of thing gives me heartburn. Bring one of the senior students up. Let me quiz 'em. If they know their stuff, I can go. Full pass for the class. All done and dusted."

By Mr. Polk's calculation, this was an excellent offer. But Mr. Grimsby apparently failed to see it that way. There were only two senior students in class that day, and their names were Jenny and Pandora.

"I'm not sure I can pick—"

"Oh, acorns!" Nuts were the closest Mr. Polk ever came to a curse word. "You. Fat girl at the back. Stand up."

Pandora stood up.

"Come here."

A man on his way to the gallows would have had an easier time of it. Jenny knew her best friend was petrified of speaking in public. But short of lighting her primer on fire, there was little she could think of to do to help.

"Face the class."

Pandora faced the class. Her big eyes blinked twice and stopped.

"What's your name?"

Something akin to the sneeze of a fly whisked through the room.

"Speak up, girl! Can't hear a word."

"Pandora, sir."

"Pandora? Mr. Grimsby, what fool kind of name is that?"

"I believe Mrs. Quinn thought it sounded 'poetic,'" said Mr. Grimsby with a smirk.

"Mrs. Quinn's daughter, eh?" Mr. Polk sniffed. "Should have guessed. Right, Miss Quinn, tell me. What's the capital of the territory?"

"Don't know, sir." Pandora's words were soft and slow. Jenny was certain her friend knew the answer, but your brain can do funny things when you're frightened.

"No? Tsk, tsk, Mr. Grimsby. Can't have children that don't know their own country. Next question. What's five into seventy-five?"

"Don't know, sir."

Mr. Polk crossed his arms with an irritable slap.

"Disgraceful. I run a bank, Mr. Grimsby. Need mathematics to do that. No use teaching them grammar if they can't balance their figures."

The sweat on Pandora's forehead was signaling panic. Jenny was on the verge of vaulting the pews and dragging her friend back when she caught the eye of Mr. Grimsby. Very slowly, he extended one lily-white finger. Jenny followed the line to the switch on the desk in front of him. And stopped.

"Right, Miss Quinn. One last time. I'm gonna give you a hard one. See if you can redeem yourself."

Pandora blinked.

"A woman and her daughter are seated on a bench. A man walks past and both ladies say, 'Hello, Father.' How is this possible?"

A flea scratching his nose might have made more noise.

"Speak up, girl!"

"The father had a baby with his daughter."

A girl gasped. One of the boys in the second row sniggered. Mr. Polk clasped his hands to his heart and toddled sideways. "What did you say?"

"First he had a daughter. Then he had a baby with his daughter. So he's the father of both of them."

Pandora's logic was as sound as a new copper bowl, but logic and copper appeared to be wasted on Mr. Polk.

"Revolting."

Pandora blinked again, this time more in confusion than fear. "I didn't say it was a good thing. It's horrible. But it's the right answer."

"No, Miss Quinn, it is not." Mr. Polk's jaw was positively churning. "The correct answer is that the two women saw a Catholic priest. The title for a priest is 'Father.'"

"What if they weren't Catholic?"

Skepticism was the last spin of the penny for the banker of Eden. If this was what folks meant by modern education, then Mr. Polk was having none of it. He wheeled away in disgust.

"My apologies, sir," said the schoolmaster, tagging along after the departing banker. "I'm certain Pandora was dropped on her head as an infant."

"Unacceptable, Mr. Grimsby. Unacceptable." Mr. Polk gave Jenny a vile look as he strode past her. "Just the kind of filth we tried to get rid of after the Rush."

"But what can one expect from the daughter of Lottie Quinn?" pleaded Mr. Grimsby.

Mr. Polk paused at the entrance of the schoolhouse. "Mr. Grimsby. Happen to have a dictionary?"

"We have Latin, Greek, and English dictionaries," said the schoolmaster, craven and low. "Donated to serve as the start of a town library. The English dictionary is leather bound in two volumes."

"Then find the word 'teacher'!" Mr. Polk opened his mouth and screeched. "Means to bloody well TEACH!!"

❧

For a small man, Eden's banker sure could rouse a storm. The dirt cloud that he left behind him cloaked half the kids in sandy gloom. When it cleared, Jenny was aghast to see that Pandora had remained standing at the head of the class.

Where Mr. Grimsby was caressing his switch.

"In ordinary circumstances, I am a peaceful man," he said, running the switch through his palm. "But in times of tribulation, my temper can be roused." Here he tapped the tip of the switch three times on his desk.

There was nary a fidget from the room. Every kid in Eden had felt the lick of that venomous snake.

"When a gentleman reaches the limit of his tolerance, there is an expectation," said the schoolmaster, flashing his pearly whites as he bent the switch to test its strength, "an expectation that justice will be served."

He paused to kiss the willow wood. Jenny could have skewered him.

"Pandora," said the schoolmaster, "hold out your hands."

Pandora held out her hands. As slow as he was able, Mr. Grimsby reared his switch high, and higher, ever higher, till it was touching the tip of the rafters.

"O justice," said the schoolmaster, "thy will be done."

With an almighty crack, he brought the switch down hard across the side of his desk. Pandora's eyes shot open as she realized she hadn't been hit.

"But you see," said Mr. Grimsby, ignoring the shock on the faces in front of him, "justice can work in mysterious ways. Billy, bring me the slate on the wall."

The schoolroom's slate hung on a nail by a short loop of twine. It was in regular use for announcements.

"Place it over Pandora's head."

Billy did as he was told.

"Since you obviously enjoy the limelight, Miss Quinn, I think we should indulge your fancy." From the corner of his pocket, Mr. Grimsby plucked a piece of chalk and turned his back to the class. "You shall stand *here*, and only *here*," said the schoolmaster, "for the rest of the day. By then, perhaps, you will have discovered a better answer for Mr. Polk."

With a final flourish, he turned. Jenny told me you could have read those letters from the moon, they were written that big.

"There now, students of Eden. Look that up in the dictionary."

Pandora's eyes were blank and cold. Her mouth was grim as granite. And below her chin, on the front of her chest, was the word: DEGENERATE.

No one was sure what it meant. Everyone was sure it was bad.

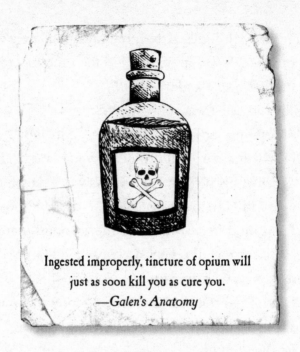

Ingested improperly, tincture of opium will
just as soon kill you as cure you.
—*Galen's Anatomy*

CHAPTER 4

When you live in the mountains, dawn has a quality all
its own. The air is thin and spare. Strangers become
giddy. Old men grow young.

On Saturday morning, Jenny got up an hour before
sunrise and dressed in the dark. Miles to the east, light
was pouring over the beaches and drowning the shells.
But in the hills, the sky was a sheer layer of gray. It
would be quite a while before the blue settled in.

As any kid can tell you, it's easy enough to avoid
men at that time of morning. Those who could man-
age it were still in bed, snoring off a hard night. Those

who weren't were out in the paddocks, tending to stock. Jenny walked the three miles to Poplar Street with birdsong as her sole company.

It was an uneasy walk, for Jenny was fretting about seeing Pandora. On the surface, her best friend was seldom one to show emotions. But inside, Jenny knew, Pandora must be feeling as vulnerable as spring earth. Nobody in the territory deserved that shame.

The thing was, Jenny was feeling a mite shameful herself. Instead of racing forward to destroy the slate, she had let the sight of the switch intimidate her. Instead of risking her neck like Still Hope and saving Pandora from drowning in embarrassment, she had simply ducked out at lunchtime and headed for the river. She had wanted to help, but she had failed to act. So it was with a hitch in her step that she turned the corner into Poplar Street.

Mad Doc Magee's office was a strange, knockabout cottage, more miner than medical. The walls were whitewashed cobbles and the roof was rippled iron. It appeared to have paused under the shade of a scraggly pine and never had the energy to get back up.

"Hi, Pandora."

"Hi, Jenny."

Pandora was standing on the doorstep, staring at the Wise Women. Avoiding the eyes of another was one way she had of avoiding a fight.

"I brought lots of tools," said Jenny, unpacking her school satchel in haste. "Chisel, knife, hammer, pick. And if the window doesn't work, we can try the chimney."

"What are you going to do?" asked Pandora.

"Break into the building."

"The front door is unlocked."

Jenny paused. You may recall that she'd found her father firmly lodged in a window because he'd neglected to think of the door. It struck her that someone above was having a good joke at her expense. "Oh."

"I checked it as soon as I got here. But I decided to wait for you before I went in," said Pandora.

"Thanks."

Pandora waited. And waited some more. "Do you want to go in?"

"Okay," said Jenny as Pandora turned the handle.

Jenny yelped. Pandora frowned.

Mad Doc Magee's famous skeleton was reclining, comfy as sin, in an old doctor's chair. His left hand was tucked under his head, his right hand was resting on his heart, and his feet were planted on the floor. He was sitting as natural as a wired pile of bones could sit.

"He looks like he's laughing, doesn't he? As if someone's been tickling his spine?" asked Jenny, trying to quell her fear with silliness. Her best friend was silent. "Pandora?"

"The skeleton came in a crate, right?"

"That's what Dad said."

"Then where's the crate? And who put him in the chair?"

No sooner were the words spoken than the sun rose far enough above the ridge to strike the side of the cottage. A shaft of light bored through the window and hit the glass of the framed diploma on the opposite wall. From there, it pinged off the brown leather textbooks and the blue ointment jars and the brass spittoon on the floor. In the split of a second, the room was dancing with gold dust.

"Maybe the postman did?" hazarded Jenny, uneasy as sin.

"That makes no sense," said Pandora. "It would take forever. Plus there's a bone missing," she said, pointing to the skeleton's right shoulder.

"How do you know?"

"Because it doesn't match the other side."

Jenny studied the skeleton. She'd seen a lot of calcium in her time—the remnants of rabbits and sheep were rife on the station—but she was taken anew by the beauty of creation.

A line of symmetry ran clear and clean from the tip

of the skull down to the spaces between the toes. The whole of it, from the balls of the feet to the ends of the fingers, was balanced for use. And Pandora was correct. There *was* a bone missing.

"Jenny, look."

On the wall above Magee's desk was the faded drawing of a man. The artist had sketched him two ways. In the first pose, he was stuck inside a square, standing with his arms stretched parallel to the floor and his feet turned slightly to the side. Lop his head off his body, and you'd be viewing a T.

On top of that drawing, the artist had made another sketch, putting the man inside a globe of the earth. Now his arms and legs were stretched into Vs, straining to touch the edges of the planet. Lop his head off the same, and you'd be viewing an X.

At the edge of the drawing was a fine piece of print:

Nature is the source of all true knowledge. She has her own logic, her own laws; she has no effect without cause nor invention without necessity.

"This place is very odd," said Pandora.

Jenny was inclined to agree. Perhaps it was the staleness of the air, but creeps and jitters seemed to be multiplying faster than lice. She was reminded of her talk with Hapless. It's much easier to chat about murdered men in the dark than shake hands with them in the light of day.

"Pandora, do you think this dead bloke could be Doc Magee?"

Bless Pandora, she refused to be worried. "How do you mean?"

"If Magee was stabbed or shot for his gold, then the killer would have to get rid of the body. Maybe he fled the territory and shipped the Doc back as bones." Jenny had a vision of what it might take to strip the flesh from a corpse and shuddered.

"It could be a she," noted Pandora.

"Who? The skeleton?"

"The murderer," retorted Pandora. "But it would be a funny thing to do, to ship a man back to the place where you killed him. Anyway, we don't know enough about Magee to tell." She returned her gaze to the room. "You keep asking questions. I thought we were going to search for the letter that came with the crate."

Here was Jenny's salvation. Perhaps an hour or so of riffling could distract her from fancies. "Okay. You look through the desk and I'll investigate the shelves. See if you can find anything that seems suspicious. Then we'll try the books. Blackwell, Gray, Doyle . . . ," she said, running her glance over the names in the bookcase. "Lordy, lordy, this is going to be duller than dull."

~

As expected, the search went slower than Jenny would have liked. It was the first time she had set foot in a doctor's office, and it was tricky to tell if the items on the shelves were normal for a medical man to own.

For instance, she might have guessed that Mad Doc Magee would need a magnifying glass and a spirit lamp, but she wasn't sure what the accordion of sharp metal files was for, or the curved silver picks. Neither seemed crafted for comfort.

On the second shelf she came upon a hollow ebony stand, like something you might use for flowers. It was nestled beside a tray of glass eyeballs in twelve different hues. These eyes were made truer than life, and they seemed to follow Jenny wherever she twisted.

A scrape of old wood told her that Pandora had finished clearing the first drawer.

"Anything?" asked Jenny.

"A lot of receipts."

Most folks find that contrition takes the better part of a day to come to maturity. Jenny had been so surprised by the skeleton that she had neglected to acknowledge that her best friend was still refusing to look her square in the eye. It was high time for repentance.

"Pandora?"

"What?"

"I'm sorry I left you lonely yesterday."

Pandora fixed her sights on the drawer. "Okay."

"No, it's not," said Jenny.

"You couldn't help me. You would have been switched."

"I could have at least stuck around," insisted Jenny. "Sat in the front row."

"I don't like people staring at me," said Pandora.

And that was the end of that. When you've tried an apology and haven't heard what you wanted, the best you can do is wait. Resigning herself to the present, Jenny resumed her attack on the shelves. From eyeballs and picks, she moved to vials and jars, running her fingers down a row of bottles covered in symbols.

"Ewww! This one has a real frog in it." She turned to Pandora, holding the jar up for inspection. "I think it's in brine."

"Frogs soak up water through their skin," said Pandora.

"How do you know that?"

"Mum told me."

This was a surprise. Whenever Jenny thought of Mrs. Quinn, the words "nervy" and "ailing" were foremost in her mind. It was hard to picture a fussbudget like that at home with amphibians.

"I wonder where—" But Jenny didn't get around to finishing her wondering. "Holy cow!"

"What cow?" asked Pandora.

"I think I found the envelope that came with the crate."

"How do you know it's the right one?"

"It was sent from a hospital. It's addressed to Dr. Magee!"

Pandora stumbled out from the drawers and Jenny ran in from the shelves and they knocked heads in the middle.

"It was wedged under that bottle," Jenny continued excitedly. "The one with the skull and crossbones on it, next to where the frog was sitting. Maybe it's a poison bottle. Maybe that's the way the murderer killed Mad Doc Magee!"

"*If* he was murdered," corrected Pandora. "Is there a letter inside?"

Jenny unfolded the paper and spread it on the edge of the desk.

Dear Dr. Magee,

Please accept, with my regards, your order of the third, lot #129: a complete skeleton displaying

key natural features. I'd like to draw your
attention to the particularly fine quality of the
hands—I believe the specimen was a scholar.

It has been a long time since we discovered
the secrets of bones at our university. Do you
remember the trouble we had deciphering the
names and assigning them to their earthly places?
And what pains we had determining where to
start? Life would have been much simpler if
anatomists had stuck with words like "wishbone."

Regarding your proposal, it's kind of you to
invite me to roam the rocks and ridges of Eden
with you, but I don't believe that fortunes can be
found so easily. Are you still brewing your soporific
poppy concoctions in Moonlight Creek? Might I
recommend a strong pot of coffee instead?

Sincerely,

Dr. Galen

In the annals of letter writing, this was hardly going
to win the prize for composition. Jenny was reminded
of Kam, and his unhappiness when a new seed failed
to sprout. It might seem a little thing now, he often told
Jenny, but every seed holds a promise. Staring at those
dull lines of text, Jenny was beginning to understand
what he meant.

"It doesn't say much, does it? Maybe it has nothing to do with the nugget."

Pandora was tugging on the end of her plait. "This place is very odd."

"You said that already," replied Jenny.

"No, it's not right. It's fake. The skeleton and the drawing and the tools being tidy. Your dad said that the place was ransacked by miners before the crate was delivered. So why is it all organized now?

"And the letter," she continued. "It makes no sense. It's *not* a complete skeleton. You don't drink poppies. And you write the month with the day. You don't just say 'the third.'" Pandora stuck her thumb on the signature. "He says they were friends at university. Why doesn't he use his first name?"

Jenny squinted at the paper. "Maybe he was trying to be polite?"

Pandora had begun to pace. It was a precise kind of pacing, two steps forward and two steps back. It was her usual routine when burrowing into a difficult problem.

"I've seen something in this office. Something I read . . ."

Jenny stood to the side. As Mr. Grimsby had yet to learn, when an active mind is working, it's sensible to keep your mouth shut.

"Holy cows . . . wishbones . . . the third . . ." Pandora stopped and raised her head. "Gold."

Without a word to Jenny, she walked over to the bookcase and took out a massive textbook embossed in gold lettering. Then she twirled it around:

GALEN'S ANATOMY
VOLUME 3

Jenny's heart missed a thump.

"It's the only book on the shelf with his name," said Pandora.

"Order of the third," said Jenny. "Volume Three."

"Lot 129," said Pandora, turning to page 129.

As she did, a scrap of an object floated out from the seam and slipped to the floor. Jenny bent down to pick it up.

"What is it?" asked Pandora.

"A dried red poppy."

Jenny had seen Pandora smile three times in her life. The first was when she had observed lightning fork. The second was when Jenny had told Mrs. Quinn that Pandora was her best friend.

And now.

"Look," said Pandora.

Page 129 of *Galen's Anatomy* was a detailed

Clavicle

Scapula

Humerus

Radius

Ulna

Xiphoid

Ilium

Coccyx

Phalanges

Trochanter

Femur

Patella

Tibia

Calcaneus

Fibula

Talus

diagram of a skeleton, drawn with meticulous care. Yet it appeared that someone had been messing with the page. Every major bone had been labeled in a hand-written script, from shoulder to toe and back again.

"Pandora, remember what the letter said?" Jenny ran her eyes over the paper. "'Key natural features' . . . 'secrets of bones' . . . 'deciphering the names' . . . 'fortunes can be found' . . . The words on the skeleton have got to be connected to the gold nugget!"

"And here's the bone that's missing," said Pandora, pointing to the diagram. "It's called the clavicle."

"But what does that mean? Do you think it's a clue?"

"Dunno," said Pandora.

"Breaking and entering is against the law, kiddy-winks," said a voice from behind them.

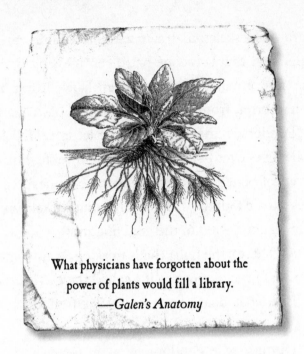

What physicians have forgotten about the
power of plants would fill a library.
—*Galen's Anatomy*

CHAPTER 5

"But," said King Louis, sauntering in from the doorway, "the law and me have never been bosom companions. So I wouldn't be worried."

Louis wore clothes like milk wears its cream. On this day and date, he was sporting the sharpest of trousers, sliced through with stripes. Above these lay a coat of fine wool in a shade of deep green. Across the crease of his waistcoat was a long, golden chain. In the palm of his hand was a crisp walking stick.

"Morning, Miss Burns," he said. "Miss Quinn."

Pandora appeared to be hoping the earth would

crack beneath King Louis's feet. She backed herself up against the wall.

"Morning," said Jenny, primed to fire. Pandora was holding the book, and Jenny was holding the letter, and it was even betting that Louis had observed both. Like Pandora, he was an observing kind of person.

"Saw the door was open on my way into town," said Louis. A thin crest of sweat crowned the top of his black goatee. "You looking for something?"

Jenny shrugged. "Us? No, we only were . . . checking to see if there was any medicine left for Mrs. Quinn. She gave us a list of what she was after." Jenny shoved Dr. Galen's letter down deep in her pocket. "And we came for a hunt." Out the side of her eye, Jenny saw Pandora start to tear the skeleton drawing from the book. "Besides, the door was unlocked."

"So you *was* looking for something."

You'll remember that Jenny had given Louis the sharp side of her tongue two days prior. But that was before he was standing between her and a fortune.

"Why, King Louis," said Jenny with a sly wink. Pandora was taking forever and an age. "Anyone would think you weren't a trusting man."

"Why, Miss Burns," said King Louis, wry as old whiskey. "What would make you think such a thing?" He smiled and perched himself on the desk.

It was a friendly enough gesture, but it had the

result of blocking Jenny's view. She could see the shelf, but not Pandora. After a few hairy seconds, Volume 3 finally slid back into place.

"Oh, nothing. Words I've heard round the saloon," said Jenny, swatting at air. "Pandora, any luck finding the name of that medicine?"

King Louis swiveled. Pandora shook her head.

"Then we'd better be off," said Jenny.

"I might accompany you," said King Louis. Pandora crossed her eyes. Jenny shrugged in dismay. "Beauty before wisdom," added Louis, pushing them gently into the light.

～

Out on the road, the morning was proving to be another killer. Heat rolled off the ground in transparent waves and settled in hollows and holes. You could hear the leaves gasp as the last of the moisture was yanked from their veins. It was a day for lying in the river, not walking through Eden under watch.

"I'm sorry you couldn't find what you needed," said King Louis, strolling along beside them. "Was it important?"

Jenny glanced at their companion. King Louis had always been a hard lake for her to fathom. He was charming and dapper and smooth, and crafty and canny and tough. One minute he might be telling her the truth; the next he might be lying to line his pocket. And joking all the time.

Though Jenny didn't have the word for it, Louis was what folks would call an opportunist. Instead of acting on his morals, he politely declined to have them. Instead of inciting a riot, he tended to take advantage of the effects. He wasn't a bitter soul by nature; he was simply out for himself. Even at her age, Jenny understood you gotta be wary of folks like that.

"Oh, no," said Jenny. "Not at all important." Pandora was vibrating with nerves beside her. "Funny we should meet you here."

"Why?" asked Louis.

Jenny smiled. "You don't live anywhere near Poplar Street."

It was a brave attempt at fishing, but Jenny wasn't going to catch Louis with an amateur cast.

"Sure enough," drawled Louis. "But I told Gentle Annie I'd keep an eye on the place now and again. As a favor to Mike."

"You knew him well?" asked Jenny, trying to keep the excitement from infecting her vowels. The more they could learn about Magee, the better off they'd be. But she needed to keep the conversation frothy. Any hint of seriousness might lead Louis to suspect a motive.

"We were best mates." Louis grinned. "Craziest son of a gun I've ever met. He'd footrace rabbits and coast down glaciers and drink concoctions that no sane man would touch. Even me."

"Dad said he was book smart, too," prodded Jenny.

"And loved to show it," noted Louis. "That's how I got my title. The day I met him, he put a tin crown on my head and gave me a coronation by dunking me in the river. Said I was vain enough for the Sun King."

"You didn't mind?" queried Jenny.

"Not when I dunked him back. Oh, we had grand times together, him and me and Gentle Annie." The corner of Louis's mouth twitched sideways. "Though none that I can relate in polite company."

"He sounds like fun," persisted Jenny.

"Humor," mused Louis, "is an intoxicating thing. Course, he sobered up a good deal when he started going around with Silent Jack."

Something in Louis's tone made Jenny pause. "You didn't like his partner?"

King Louis frowned. "Always kept himself to himself, did Jack. Suspicious of everyone. He seemed to prefer skulking around Moonlight Creek to hobnobbing with me and Magee in the back room of the saloon."

"Did Doc Magee have a big head?" interrupted

Pandora. It was the first thing she had said, and Louis was startled. He might have forgotten she was there.

"No more than the next man."

"Did he have any enemies?" asked Pandora.

King Louis raised a waxed eyebrow. "No more than the next man."

There was a taut air of tension to this exchange, like a trap that's yet to be sprung. Pandora was watching Louis and Louis was watching Pandora, and neither was willing to cede an inch.

"Hey, Jenny! Over here!"

In the shade of the elms, about a quarter of a mile off, stood Lok. He was waving his arms so hard he'd taken to levitating.

"Hallo!" yelled Jenny, waving back.

"You know that boy?" asked Louis, his gums curling.

"Yes. So do you."

King Louis tipped his hat. "Well, I must be off, ladies. Enjoy the rest of your day."

Using his cane as a pivot point, King Louis rotated ninety degrees to the east. Then he descended toward the riverbed.

"I don't think he likes the Lum brothers," said Pandora, watching his back retreat.

"No," ruminated Jenny.

"Does he know where your mum came from?"

Jenny paused. Though she realized King Louis had a habit of objecting to certain men and religions, he had never been nasty to her. Abrupt, yes. Scolding at times. But perfectly happy to converse. Perhaps Gentle Annie had instructed him to be civil.

"It's pretty clear—he must have guessed. Still, he hasn't said anything about it." Jenny shrugged her shoulders back. "And I don't think we should bring it up."

Pandora nodded. On the subject of adults, her vote was ever for silence. "Lok keeps waving at you."

"Give us a minute!" shouted Jenny down the road. She pulled Pandora in close and dropped her voice to a whisper. "Did you get the diagram of the skeleton?"

Pandora tucked her fingers under her cuff and extracted page 129. She glanced behind them. "Mum says tearing up books is a crime."

"You didn't tear it up," said Jenny, peering at the names. "You staked a claim."

Metaphors were a slab of cold comfort to Pandora. "I don't understand why you're excited," she groused. "We still don't know why the bones are labeled that way or why the clavicle is missing. Or what it all means."

"Tired of waiting!" called Lok.

"No," said Jenny. "But maybe there's somebody we can ask."

"We can't help you, Jenny Girl," said Kam, "if we don't know what you're talking about. Please pick up your feet—you're slopping the bucket."

"You want trotting," teased Jenny, "buy a horse."

In the parlance of Jenny's day, Kam's market garden was called Little Eden. Before the Lum brothers took it over, it was a small scrap of nothing down by the north end of town. Now it was ruled as a kingdom of earth. There were long mounds and furrows for the crops in demand. There were herbs in their beds and berries in their bushes. And at the edge of the garden, in a pocket of sunshine, there were apples and plums, peaches and quinces. In the spring, you'd catch lovers under the blossoms.

To Jenny, Kam's garden was pure revelation—she had never encountered so many varieties of cabbages in all her life. On her first visit to Little Eden, she had come away with a hundred and one questions. On her next visit, she had brought three jars of jam made with the fruit Kam had gifted her. Jam led to supper and supper led to talk. Children of wanderers have a talent for finding each other.

But it was a parched paradise that morning in autumn. The tributary that ran down the hill had slowed to a trickle. The irrigation pond was half mud, and the water channels had little to spare. Everybody who was able had been called to shoulder the yoke. After an hour of hauling, Pandora and Jenny were baked dry in sweat.

"Please put your water on the broccoli, Pandora." Kam stood by his crops like a mourner at a grave. "We'll have to hope that we can save this year's harvest."

"And if you can't?" asked Jenny.

"Lok and I must think about the next step."

Jenny didn't want to ask what the next step was. She was half afeared that it meant Kam would be leaving the country.

"I'm tired," said Lok, chucking his bucketful next to Pandora's. "And it's lunchtime," he added. "Plums?"

"They're meant for the stall," said Kam.

"Tough," said Lok, taking the basket in hand. "We have guests."

Together, the quartet sat down by the herb garden, in the crook of the hill. Pandora stared at her feet and Kam gazed at his creation. To liven the mood, Jenny and Lok ate eight of the plums and played "hits" with the pits.

"Please," said Kam, finally lifting his head, "explain your problem a little more."

"There's this word," said Jenny, attempting to ask a question without asking a question. As much as she wanted to tell Kam about the clavicle and the skeleton drawing, she was thinking of Old Randolph Scott's place up on Reed's Terrace, and how much money she might need to purchase it. "We think it's important."

"An English word?" asked Kam.

"It doesn't look like one," said Jenny. "I've never heard of it."

"Then how did you learn about it?"

"It came from a medical letter. Or near enough," clarified Jenny. It was hard to know what to say. Pandora was blinking in a way that urged caution.

"And why do you think I can help?"

"Well," said Jenny, "you're smart. You learned English when you came here. How did you decipher what a word actually means?"

Kam hugged his knees to his chest. It was a trick of his to pause before speaking. Jenny was always tempted to bowl right over his thoughts.

"That's a difficult question. The meaning often changes with the name."

"Come again?"

Kam smiled and prodded his brother. "Lok, what does *wong kei* mean? In English?"

Lok yawned and stretched out on the rocks. Chat of linguistics was not to his liking.

"Yellow elder."

"*Wong kei* is a small flower," said Kam, "part of the pea plant."

"Fresh out of peas," murmured his brother.

Jenny flicked a pit at Lok's head. It wedged in his hair.

"The inside of the root is yellow, and it's a root that grows in yellow earth," said Kam, ignoring the interruption, "so the first character we use for this plant is *wong*." He drew a symbol in the dirt: 黄 . "The color of the bright fields."

Jenny did her best to look interested. In her mind, a lecture was a lecture, no matter how personable the speaker. Pandora, she noticed, was paying close attention.

"The second character is *kei*. This means a few things. Leader, venerable, aged. Or if you pronounce it a different way," said Kam, demonstrating his point, "it means energy, a force."

"Or to eat," said Lok.

"Or to eat," said Kam, drawing the second character next to the first: 芪 . "So, what do the two characters mean together? Eating the yellow root will help you feel less tired and old."

"Kam," said Jenny.

"Yes?"

"No offense, but this is dull as ditchwater."

Kam smiled again. A simple enough smile, quiet

and sure. It gave Jenny the feeling of feathers brushing her skin.

"Oh, Jenny Girl," said Kam. "Always leaping mountains." He drew a pea-shaped flower next to his characters. "What I wish to say is that you must discover the language of your word before you can understand its true meaning. For example, when I showed wong kei to farmers, they didn't know it meant yellow elder. They said in English it was called milkvetch or goat's-thorn. And when I needed to order seeds from the catalog, the storekeeper said, no, it was called astragalus."

"Why on earth would you call a flower goat's-thorn?" interrupted Jenny.

"Because when goats eat it they make more milk," replied Kam.

"Maaaaaa," said Lok. Jenny chucked another pit. It glanced off his cheek and winged Pandora in the ribs.

"I can see I'm not helping," said Kam, prim as a picket fence. Up he rose, brushing the dust from his trousers. Up Jenny scrambled after him.

"Sorry, Kam, we were only having a bit of fun."

"I understand."

This was the second apology Jenny had given that day, and her temper was rising. Was it her fault that words were a right royal mess? And how come she had to be the one asking questions? Pandora had been sitting right there next to her.

But Pandora was focused on loose ends. "You didn't finish. What does 'astragalus' mean?"

"I don't know," said Kam. "The storekeeper told me scientific names are almost always in Latin or Greek, and I have not met anyone who speaks those languages."

If bones could twitch, Jenny's bones would have twitched! As it was, her muscles had to do the work. Courtesy of Mr. Polk's visit to the schoolroom yesterday, Jenny knew exactly where she could find a mind that spoke in scientific tongues. Or, at least, a couple of dictionaries that listed Greek and Latin definitions!

She was about to hurl this idea at Pandora when she hesitated. Even if the words on the skeleton were in Latin and Greek, and they could find a time to decipher what each label meant, they still didn't know how the names of bones might apply to a missing nugget. It was downright perplexing.

Perplexing, sure, but one step farther along than they had been a few hours ago. Jenny felt the urge to share her good humor with her instructor.

"Come on now, Kam, don't be gloomy." She tossed him a plum. "That was very helpful." Jenny swooped up a water bucket. "And not to worry—we'll soon have Little Eden to rights."

She began prodding the trio toward the irrigation

pond. Despite the heat, her mood was improving with each stride. First she'd find the nugget, then she'd buy the land on Reed's Terrace, and then she'd ask Kam to help her graft some peach trees. The fact that Jenny hadn't yet puzzled out a sizable proportion of the moves before that didn't bother her. Being near to Kam always made her feel airy.

Pandora, on the other hand, appeared to be feeling the weight of the world. She had her feet in a lock and her eyes fixed oddly to the ground.

"I don't understand how you've laid out this garden—your vegetable rows look exactly like udders," she noted, pausing at the brink of the herbs. "Did you plan it that way?"

Lok roared with laughter and swatted Kam on the arm. "Udders! Brilliant!"

"No," said Kam, pushing his brother away with a gentle shove. "I was thinking of a famous emperor and my father."

Jenny was surprised by his willingness to answer, for the Lums seldom spoke about their home country. Kam had told the story of Little Eden only once to her, and that with great reluctance.

"When the emperor was laid in his tomb, he wanted to be surrounded by all his lands. So he had craftsman create rivers from quicksilver and mountains from bronze." Kam plucked a sprig of thyme and rubbed it between his fingers. "But I wanted something living to honor my father—a garden instead of a tomb." He hesitated. "So I decided to plant a tiny version of his birthplace. A mound for a mountain and a pond for a sea."

"And in a forest of fruit trees," said Jenny, encouraging him, "there is snow in the spring . . ."

". . . warmth in the cold," finished Kam.

Pandora rubbed the tip of her sunburned nose. Truth be told, she couldn't care less for the romance of opposites. But she recognized that an important truth lay buried beneath the couplets.

"You mean Little Eden is meant to be a map? Every section is supposed to resemble some part of your father's country?"

"Yes," replied Kam. "Or at least the key natural features."

Whhhiccoip!

Pandora's cry was a cross between a hiccup, a belch, and a full screech of joy, and it set Lok rolling on the ground in hysterics.

The thing was, at that moment, Jenny knew exactly what her best friend was thinking. And she was half tempted to *whhhiccoip* herself.

"What's the matter?" asked Kam, staring at his friends. "Have you gone mad?"

Jenny wasn't listening. Pandora wasn't listening.

They were both jumping up and down with their arms locked together. Well, Jenny was jumping up and down. Pandora was being hauled along with the force of her friend's enthusiasm.

Though she had no way of knowing it, Jenny was exhibiting the first signs of a famous malady. Gold fever is a canny devil, and it strikes the youngest the hardest. It's unfortunate that this should be so. Children have everything to look forward to, and even more to lose.

"The secrets of bones!" shouted Jenny at Pandora. "Nature is the source of all knowledge! Decipher the names and assign them to their earthly places!"

Lok stared at the girls for a long while. Then he looked up at his brother and shook his head mockingly. "Too many plums."

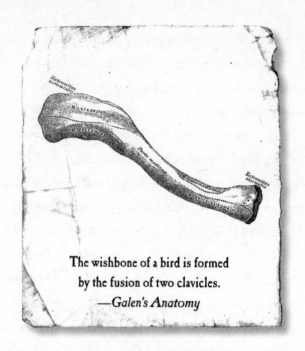

The wishbone of a bird is formed
by the fusion of two clavicles.
—*Galen's Anatomy*

CHAPTER 6

"Are you done?"

"Give me half a breath, Pandora!"

To Jenny's discerning nose, the school's Latin dictionary smelled a lot like Mr. Grimsby—sickly and sweet, wormy and worrisome. But it was only by dint of shoving her face in the pages that she could see clear enough to make out the definitions of the words in the skeleton diagram. The schoolroom at dusk was rarely a place of illumination.

"Is anybody coming?" asked Jenny.

"No. I said I'd tell you."

Jenny redoubled her efforts to decipher the names of the bones. On a normal Saturday, she and Pandora would have been in there hours ago. But an endless church meeting and the rites of Eden's sewing circle had prevented their entry. It was lucky they could snatch an hour before dark. And what torture that long afternoon had been. Knowing they had the clues to a treasure hunt, and not knowing what they meant!

"How do you think Dr. Galen came up with the idea of using a skeleton as a map for the valley?" asked Jenny.

"Dr. Galen was only a clue to finding the title of the book where the skeleton was located," corrected Pandora. "We don't know who labeled the diagram. But it's very clever," she added. "Most people wouldn't think of connecting parts of the body with natural features like mountains and streams."

"We have to start with the clavicle," said Jenny. "That has to be the first clue. The missing bone. I bet the ribs are all the roads crossing Main Street. And maybe the head is Kam's garden. Which part of Eden do you think is the shoulder?"

"Dunno. But first we need to understand what the scientific names mean in English. Then we'll know a lot more."

This was the hope at noon, but hopes at noon often give way to sorrows in the evening. Latin can be a troublesome language, and Jenny was busting her brain cells trying to make sense of the medical.

"Pandora, psssst! I need your help."

"I'm watching."

"Please?"

In came Pandora, trailing a cloud of righteousness. It had been her idea to stand guard at the schoolroom door. Being caught twice by snoops was twice more than she enjoyed.

"What?" asked Pandora.

"I think I've got definitions for most of the others, but I'm stuck on the meaning of clavicle. Do you think this could be it?"

Clavus: A nail, a rudder, a spike, a purple stripe. Cognate with Ancient Greek κλεις

Pandora swung her plait around to the front and began to chew on the end. "Why would you start a treasure hunt with a nail?"

"Maybe we begin at a spike," hazarded Jenny, "like a spike in the ground?"

"What does 'cognate' mean?" asked Pandora.

"Hang on a tick, let me check the other word," said

Jenny, catching hold of the Greek dictionary. "It's a lovely sort of writing, isn't it? Like Kam's."

"Kam fancies you," said Pandora.

Now, you may think you've seen red before—blood from a cut, the juice of a cherry, a stain left by rust. But I'll tell you for certain that naught could compare to the blush that fired on Jenny's cheeks.

"He does not!"

"He does." Like sarcasm, teasing was absent from Pandora's philosophy. This was a pure statement of fact. "He calls you 'Jenny Girl' and watches you walk away and always smiles when you talk. That's what happens when a boy fancies someone. Did you find it?"

Jenny ducked her head to try to suck dull thoughts from the dictionary. "It says . . ." She stopped.

"What?"

Words having failed her, Jenny pointed to the definition:

κλεις: kleís: something used to lock and unlock; a key.

But that wasn't the most important part. No, the most important part, if you were searching carefully enough, was a tiny drawing scratched out in pencil to the left of the κ.

Which looked precisely like a poppy in bloom.

"Oh," said Pandora. "You know, that definition makes sense."

"Of course it does!" Jenny leaped off the schoolmaster's chair. "Remember that Mr. Grimsby said these dictionaries were donated to the school? Someone in Eden is trying to tell us where to begin! Look." She pulled Dr. Galen's letter from her pocket. "See this bit about drinking the poppies and making coffee up at Moonlight Creek?"

"Yes."

"I bet that's where we'll find a key! At Mad Doc's hut. Remember what Dad told me? Moonlight Creek is where Magee discovered the nugget."

"But a key to what?" asked Pandora.

"The buried box with the gold inside," said Jenny.

"How do you know there's a buried box?"

With a touch of dramatics, Jenny slid the diagram under Pandora's troubled eyes. "Guess what's next to the clavicle in a skeleton?"

Pandora squinted at the scrawl.

"Your handwriting's crap."

"Pandora!"

Pandora studied the words.

Clavicle
Key

Scapula
Shovel

Humerus
Shoulder

Radius
Ray, Spoke

Ulna
Elbow

Trochanter
Wheel

Femur
Thigh

Tibia
Flute, Pipe

Fibula
Pin, Clasp

Xiphoid
Sword

Ilium
Groin

Coccyx
Cuckoo

Phalanges
Infantry Ranks

Patella
Pan, Dish

Calcaneus
Chalk

Talus
Die

"Scapula means shovel and clavicle means key, and we're going to Magee's hut at the creek," burbled Jenny, dancing a jig. "It's a perfect place for starting a hunt!"

Pandora switched her plait from left to right, right to left, and back again.

"I s'pose it makes sense. But I . . ."

"Avaunt, villain!" came a voice from outside. "Begone from my abused sight."

Jenny hit the floor harder than horseshoes. "Oh, God," she hissed, cantilevering herself under the desk.

"You see?" said Pandora, gathering the dictionaries and skeleton map in her arms. "This is why I was standing at the door . . ."

"Yes, yes," whispered Jenny, hauling Pandora in after her, "I'm wrong, you're right, now shhhhh!"

Luckily, Mr. Grimsby's stage voice had the full support of his diaphragm. He must have been haranguing the hills, for it took him five minutes to reach the door of the schoolroom. By that time, Jenny and Pandora were firmly wedged in the dark.

"Oh, what a peasant slave am I, to labor for the unwashed masses. Deny me not my birthright, capricious gods! Make me not mad, ye heavens, not mad!"

Leaning forward, Jenny risked a peek at the speaker. He was bent double over the side of a school pew, pounding his fist on the back of the wood. Acting, it seemed, involved a fair bit of force.

"No," said Mr. Grimsby, straightening up. "Too soon. In all good drama, one must hint and withhold." He turned toward the end of the room, and Jenny attempted to imitate a pancake. "Now, where did I leave my spectacles?"

Fortune was smiling on youth that afternoon. Mr. Grimsby was almost blind without his glasses. Slicker than oil, Jenny reached around the lip of the desk and slipped the schoolmaster's specs into Pandora's hands.

"Alas, I am but a poor fool," said Mr. Grimsby, rummaging through the papers. He was so close to the girls that Jenny could have drooled on his shoes. "Whither shall I wander when I am old and addled?"

The Arctic would be nice, thought Jenny.

"Blast this cursed country and all the people in it. A switch, a switch, my kingdom for a switch! Toil and trouble, where are my spectacles?"

With a petulant sniff, Mr. Grimsby took his documents in hand and stumbled out of the schoolroom. A rush of air swept through the aisle and caught itself in an eddy near Jenny's feet. The door slammed shut.

For safety's sake, the pair of them waited until the first stars were beginning to puncture the sky. After untying herself from a knot of limbs, Pandora rose to her feet and placed the spectacles on the desk.

"That," said Pandora, "was very annoying."

"Let's filch his specs!" said Jenny. "Then he won't be able to see anything."

Pandora shook her head. "Then he would know someone had been here." With care and intent, she put each dictionary back in its place. "Now he'll never be wise."

"I guess you're right," said Jenny. Mr. Grimsby was already alert to their alliance. The less attention they brought to themselves, the better. "Anyway, it's too dark to go tonight. Can you meet me tomorrow after breakfast? Around eight?"

Pandora nodded.

"Tomorrow morning, then. At the foot of Moonlight Creek."

～

Conventional wisdom decreed that Moonlight Creek was named for the dappled rays that fell on its waters. From its head at the peak of the Sleeping Girl to its end, where it joined Lake Snow, the stream was dotted with pools and waterfalls.

That was the official line. But according to old-timers like me, the creek got its moniker from a miner called Pete "Moonlight" Shay. He was so smitten with nights in the sylvan woods that he took to running up and down the rindle with his bum as bare as a newborn babe's.

When the gold ran out, the creek lost its luster. Pete sailed away on a ship bound for wrecking, men vanished into the ether, and the warblers returned to their nests. The sounds of swearing and sluicing were replaced by a gurgling calm.

Taken together, it was a good place to be walking on a Sunday morning. For Jenny, the quiet felt like a gift from above. There had been so much happening in the past two days—so many discoveries and uncoverings—that she'd barely been able to sleep. The mystery of Doc Magee's nugget seemed to have more pieces than a vulture's insides. She was glad for the opportunity to think things out.

At times like these, a girl like Pandora was a comforting person to have around. She didn't fuss with her blisters or clutter her talk with guff about the weather. Sure, she was slow-moving, but she always looked a challenge square in the eye and set her feet to conquer it.

They were on the right track, Jenny was certain. The missing bone and the skeleton and the letter and the poppy drawing next to the definition all pointed to a plan. Someone had staged the office with a whole lot of thought. But who?

To avoid the sin of making no sense, Jenny attempted to work it through in her mind. Doc Magee was a medical man. So he was probably the one who came up with the idea of a skeleton map. But why would he do that? You don't discover a gold nugget and then create a convoluted way to find it.

Unless, she thought, Magee was in deadly danger. Maybe he was so nervy about being murdered by thieves that he buried the nugget and ran away across the sea. Then he created the treasure hunt as a sneaky way of remembering where he'd put it. Something only he would be able to work out.

If that was true, Jenny reasoned, then Doc Magee still had enemies living in local parts. Maybe that was it! Maybe someone in Eden was waiting to wring his neck for the secret of where the nugget was buried. There were a number of dodgy characters who hadn't left town after the Rush. Maybe that was why Magee had stayed away so long.

Jenny was just congratulating herself on solving the puzzle when another thought came to her. What if the nugget had already been found? What if a practical joker had knocked off Doc Magee, pocketed the gold, and dreamed up the hunt as a nasty prank? He— or she—could have snuck into the office and set up the skeleton. So maybe those bones really were Magee after all!

"It's not Doc Magee," said Pandora.

"What?"

"The skeleton. It's not Doc Magee."

"How did you know I was pondering that?" demanded Jenny.

"I didn't. I was working it through in my mind." Pandora employed her trademark brand of logic. "King Louis said Magee didn't have a big head. The skeleton has a really big head. So it's not Doc Magee."

Jenny sighed. Syllogisms can be awful hard to beat. "Then who else could it be?" she asked.

"Anyone who's been dead for a long time," answered Pandora. "But that's not important right now. What's important is reaching Moonlight Creek and finding a key and figuring out the next step on the skeleton map before it gets hotter. I'm sweaty."

After an hour or so of hill climbing, the pair hit the remains of an old mining camp. Dented pots and pitted knives, blackened campfire stones, and rusty spoons— the site was a rubbish pit.

Jenny might have pardoned laziness, but the miners had also chopped down scores of mountain beeches to make the clearing. In a place where native trees were rare, this was sacrilege.

"Men are idiots," said Pandora.

"You said it."

Jenny kicked over one of the pots.

"Pandora, will you be mad at me for asking another question?"

"No."

"Do you think Doc Magee was the one who created this hunt?"

"Probably," her best friend answered. "He's the only medical man I can think of."

"So if he's alive, he's bound to come back for the nugget."

"Maybe," said Pandora. "Or maybe he wants one of his mates to find it instead."

Altruism was a factor that Jenny had never thought to consider. Sure, Louis had mentioned that Magee was good at forging friendships. And a trained doctor had the benefit of a steady and well-paying profession. But could any man from the Rush be unselfish enough to give up a fortune?

It was what the bookish among us might call a conundrum, and it puzzled our heroine for quite some time. Jenny slurped at water from the creek. She patted a severed stump. She leaped rocks, enlarging the minutes. And she kept right on thinking.

"Pandora?"

"I'm next to you."

"What would you do with the gold nugget? I mean, if you had it all to yourself?"

For once in a blue moon, Pandora was flummoxed.

Instead of barging forward, she sat plumb on a stone and stared at the water. She sat there for some seconds.

"Pandora, are you okay?"

"I'm considering."

Jenny found a perch beside her friend and attempted to snag a glimpse of the valley through the leaves. By her calculating, they must be a mile below the head of the Sleeping Girl and far above Lake Snow. This was higher than she had ever come up Moonlight Creek, and she was furious at what the drought had done. Falls were now dribbles and pools were bare puddles. Her whole world was drying up faster than a dewdrop in a desert.

"I guess I'd pay for Mum to go to a fancy clinic," said Pandora finally. "And then I'd buy a zebra."

"A zebra?"

"Zebras sleep on their feet," stated Pandora.

"Did your mum tell you that?"

"Yes. She wanted to be an animal doctor before she came here."

Jenny rested her chin on her palm and pondered the image of Mrs. Quinn shoving her hand up a cow's bum. Adults were a funny bunch. You'd expect a person to pick a goal and stick to it. Instead, everyone she knew over the age of twenty appeared to be blundering in six different directions. Only Gentle Annie looked like she knew which way was north.

"Is she really bad enough to need a clinic?" asked Jenny.

"Yes. She'll probably be dead before New Year."

Now, before you get to judging Pandora's bluntness, you have to remember the way of the time. These days, we've got potions and procedures and nurses all starched. You can't sneeze without someone trying to microscope your hankie. That wasn't the case right after the Rush. Back then, the undertaker was a very busy man. Drinking, eating, coughing, sleeping—you took your life in your hands just getting out of bed. Not a day passed without an acquaintance falling by the wayside. Get a good epidemic raging and you might lose half the territory.

So you'll understand why Pandora, who lived her loves in the moment, would take a practical approach to Mrs. Quinn's prognosis.

"Even if she dies there, I think they'll have cherry pie. Mum loves cherry pie."

Jenny nodded. "They will probably have lemonade, too."

"Yes," said Pandora, "at the fancy ones."

Lemonade, cherry pie, and a zebra, thought Jenny. There were worse things to wish for in a fortune.

"C'mon," she said, tugging at her friend. "We must be almost there."

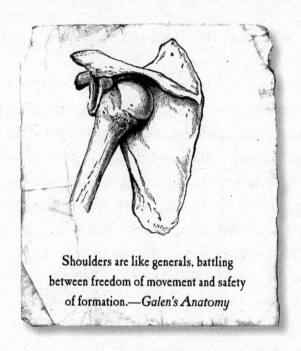

Shoulders are like generals, battling
between freedom of movement and safety
of formation.—*Galen's Anatomy*

CHAPTER 7

"I bet it has rats," said Pandora, examining their quarry. "Huts like that always have rats."

"They gave it their best," said Jenny, feeling a spot of tenderness for the heap in front of them.

Doc Magee's hut was a ramshackle affair surviving on orneriness. The bulk of it was built with flat river schist, with walls stacked a mite higher than a man's top hat. One side was a chimney pipe, supported by a fat wad of rocks. The other side was simply a higgle and piggle of stone. Two slabs of corrugated iron met in a peak above the weathered wood door. You'd find more beauty in a wart.

"It must have been a haul bringing in the roof. And it's got a veranda." Jenny patted one of the sapling poles that supported the edge of an overhang. The roof shivered in protest. "Though I think it wants keeping up."

Pandora picked up a stick and made for the entrance. "It's okay. Mum says I'm pretty good at killing rats."

That was assuming the rats had something to live on. Jenny didn't expect the inside to be much better than the outside, but she was still sorry to see how stark the interior appeared. This was hardly a room crammed with clues. It was hardly a room at all.

"Silent Jack must have been a very patient man," said Pandora, groping her way through the gloom. There was only one window to the hut, and it was an inch thick in grime. "Or deaf."

"Why?" asked Jenny.

"Because I wouldn't like to sleep this close to someone who snored," she said, poking her stick under one of the two cots in the corner. A table by the window and a piece of calico balled up over a curtain rod were the most that could be said for the rest of the furniture.

Jenny sighed. "Do you see anything that resembles a key or a shovel?"

"No. But I doubt they'd be lying around in plain sight." Pandora jabbed her stick at the ashes in the fireplace. "There's probably a hint in the letter. The writer wouldn't have left us without directions."

Into her pocket Jenny went. Out on the table fell a ball of twine, an apple core, two nails, and the scrunched-up skeleton map. Into her pocket she went again—and came up clutching gullyfluff.

"I don't have it!" cried Jenny. Panic was none too fine a word for her feelings at that moment.

"What do you mean?" asked Pandora.

"The letter is supposed to be with the skeleton map," said Jenny, clawing at lint balls. "But it's not!"

Pandora poked her stick at the contents of Jenny's pocket. "Did you leave it at home?" she asked.

"No. I haven't changed since Thursday."

"Well, that explains the smell," said Pandora. Before Jenny could react to the insult to her hygiene, her friend began pacing. She took two steps forward, stopped, and stepped back.

"It's okay. Mr. Grimsby will have it."

"What?" screeched Jenny.

"You took the letter out in the schoolroom. That was the last place you had it. You must have left it on the desk."

"This is a disaster!"

Pandora cocked her head to the left. "Why?"

"Because now he knows where we've been!" cried Jenny. "He'll spoil everything."

It was one of Pandora's quirks to stick out her tongue when she wanted to express an objection. She had many a scar from the schoolyard to prove that it worked.

"What's the tongue for?" demanded Jenny.

"A disaster is the town burning down and my mum chucking me through the window to save me and rams stampeding through the street and bashing out my brains."

"So?"

"So this is a *problem*," explained Pandora. "Mr. Grimsby has Dr. Galen's letter, but he doesn't know what it means. He may make a guess about Moonlight Creek, but he probably doesn't realize what we're after. We'll just have to be careful that he doesn't see where we're going."

Jenny breathed a deep breath. Somehow she expected a treasure hunt to be more daring and less debate. "So what do we do now?" she asked.

"First, you should give me the skeleton map," said Pandora, "so you don't lose that, too." With a hitch of reluctance, Jenny handed it over. "And then I guess we need to search everything in the hut and see if a key appears."

"And if it doesn't?" demanded Jenny.

"Then we might have to give up."

At that time, with her stomach growling, this was

not a conclusion Jenny was willing to allow. Her dander was up, and when Jenny's dander is up, it's best to keep your head down and your netherparts covered. "Fine. I'll start near the cots." She stomped into a corner.

"Okay. Then I'll start near the table," said Pandora, oblivious to the fury that was rampaging through the room.

Sitting down with a thump on the cot by the wall, Jenny began running her hands along the stones. The only other place someone might consider hiding a key was under the earth floor, and she wasn't keen on grubbing around in the dirt.

After she'd covered a good portion of the wall, a sticky mass of gunk was Jenny's sole reward. She was about to succumb and shove her head under the cots when her fingers caught on something in a crook of the corner. She eyed Pandora across the room, and when she saw that her friend had her back to her, she pulled it out.

It was a small metal box wrapped in an oilcloth. Catching her breath between her teeth, Jenny carefully slipped the box from its covering, removed the lid, and examined the contents.

Her heart dropped. It was nothing. Or next to nothing. A lot of tintypes of women in their undergarments. Jenny could never figure why men liked to collect such things. You'd do better to spend your money on a haircut and a shave. Then you might stand a chance at getting near to the reality. But each to his own, or so Hapless would say.

Puzzling a little at her impulse to hide her discovery from Pandora, Jenny pulled the box farther into the light. She was on the verge of showing her best friend what she had found when she spotted a familiar face amongst the tintypes. Studying the picture in question, Jenny realized that there was only one person in Eden it resembled.

Mrs. Quinn?!

"What did you find?" asked Pandora.

"Nothing," said Jenny, shoving the tintype of Pandora's mother into a crack in the wall. Some family secrets are best left to cobwebs. "Pictures of girls dancing around in their bloomers." Jenny rattled the box for proof.

"That's an uncomfortable thing to do in your underwear."

"Have you got anything on your side?" asked Jenny.

"Not much. A few unopened cans. I was hoping to find food bins, but there aren't any."

The idea of chowing down on twelve-year-old camp bread garnished with moth maggots drove Jenny's hunger far into the hills. "Yick and yuck. Do you really think any food lying around would be worth eating?"

"No, but Dr. Galen wrote to Doc Magee about drinking coffee." Pandora frowned at the dead flies on the table. "Which makes me wonder if that was a clue."

For once in her short and eventful life, Jenny was a step ahead of her friend's observational powers. "Pandora, that's what I forgot about! The coffee!" Dashing to the fireplace, Jenny rammed her skull into the deep and the dark. She emerged with her head covered in ash and her hand clutching a black pot.

"How come I didn't see that?" asked Pandora.

"It was up on a shelf on the side." Jenny tried her best to keep from crowing. "You chuck your coffee grounds in the pot, boil off the water, and let the stuff settle at the bottom. I've seen some of the roustabouts make it."

The lid of the pot was almost rusted shut, but with a great deal of twisting and banging, the two friends finally succeeded in wrestling it off.

Inside, rolled up neat in a tight wad of paper, was a clavicle bone.

"We found it! We found it!" screeched Jenny. She took a running leap off the wall, as if she was going to dance a two-step on the ceiling. "I was right! It *is* a treasure hunt! Lordy, lordy, Pandora, we're going to be richer than Egypt!"

Ducking her head to avoid being clonked by her flying friend, Pandora fully unwrapped the paper and spread it out on the table. A faint odor of stale coffee clung to the print. The bone wasn't the only clue in the pot. For there was writing on the paper as well.

MOLDY PEAS

Lying by the campfire, propped up on my fleas,
Dreaming of my sweetheart, eating moldy peas.
When I turned a soldier, I could lift a barn,
Now I need a pulley just to raise my arm.
Peas, peas, peas! Eating moldy peas!
Goodness, how nutritious, eating moldy peas!

Marching is a puzzle, as you muddle through,
First you turn in circles, then you split in two.
Oh, to find a general pointing to the fore,
Then I'd hide behind him, safe forevermore.
Peas, peas, peas! Eating moldy peas!
Goodness, how nutritious, eating moldy peas!

"Garters and guts," said Jenny.

"It's a song, right?" asked Pandora.

"Yep. From one of those wars they keep fighting. Dad hums it when he's docking lambs." Jenny warbled a few off-key bars. "The words aren't quite the same."

"You shouldn't really sing unless you have to," said Pandora. "But," she added, civil-like, "I did ask the question."

Taking the apology with the intent that was meant, Jenny studied the lyrics. For a few moments there was silence. The echo of a woodpecker came riffling down the chimney.

"Pandora, do you think . . . ?"

"I'm always thinking. Otherwise I'd be dead."

"No, I mean, do you think this song is supposed to lead us somewhere else? Like the letter from Dr. Galen that brought us to the hut?"

Pandora yanked on her plait. "I guess that would make sense."

"So instead of finding a real key . . . ," began Jenny.

". . . the clavicle and song are the *key* to the map," finished Pandora.

"See this part?" said Jenny, pointing to the lines of the song.

"About lifting?" asked Pandora.

"And this bit . . ."

"About the circle?"

"It's all the bones in the arm!" shouted Jenny.

Pandora laid the skeleton map alongside the "Moldy Peas" lyrics. "The radius or the ray—that must be the part about the circle."

"And see how the arm splits into two bones in the lower half?" Jenny pointed to the skeleton. "Plus you have to use your arms to haul things, and your elbows to prop yourself up!"

Pandora nodded. "It's pretty simple when you look at it."

Jenny let out a peculiar sound.

"Do you need to visit the outhouse?" asked Pandora. "'Cause I don't think they have one."

"No," said Jenny. "But I just realized where we're standing."

Pandora glanced at the packed earth and back at Jenny. Heavy weather was riding across her brow.

"We're at the dip that leads to the top of the ridge," Jenny exclaimed. "We're on the *shoulder* of the Sleeping Girl!"

In the split of an instant, the clouds of confusion turned to sunshine. "Oh, I understand," said Pandora. "It's . . . it's a bit like when you were talking to me about lying on the ground and becoming part of the hills. The bones of a skeleton are supposed to be like the rocks in the hills. That means to follow the "Moldy Peas" song, we need to start at the shoulder of the Sleeping Girl—which is one of the biggest mountains around town—and go down the ridgeline of her right arm toward Eden."

Jenny slapped her hand on the table. A plume of insect parts scattered to the four winds. "Gimcrack, what I wouldn't say to Doc Magee if I had him here! Hauling us all the way up to this stink hole. We could have climbed the ridgeline straight from town."

"A treasure hunt isn't supposed to be easy," said Pandora. "Otherwise you'd call it a treasure find." She studied the skeleton map. "What's at the end of the Sleeping Girl's arm?"

"Brush and rabbits, as far as I know."

"That makes no sense—there must be something to do with the song or the phalanges and the finger bones. But I suppose we'll have to figure it out when we get there." Prudent as pennies, Pandora refolded the map and tucked it into the bottom of her shoe. Then she picked up a ratty woolen blanket from one of the cots and laid it on the floor.

"What are you doing?" asked Jenny.

"Packing our lunch," Pandora replied, placing the unopened food cans in the center of the blanket and gathering the corners into a makeshift bag. "I've got a couple of biscuits, but you didn't bring anything. Unless you want to eat your apple core." She handed Jenny the sack. "It will take most of the afternoon to walk the ridgeline. And we can use the two nails from your pocket to punch the tops of the cans."

"How come I have to carry everything?"

"You're stronger."

It was a rational enough reason, if not exactly fair. Jenny had slung on the bag and was on her way out the door when Pandora paused.

"What's wrong now?" asked Jenny.

"We're forgetting about the shoulder bone."

"I told you," said Jenny. "We're *on* the shoulder bone."

"No, I mean the scapula. The shovel in the skeleton map."

"Oh, that old thing," said Jenny, her impatience getting the better of her sense. "I'd imagine it's outside. We'll have a search around the lean-to."

SQUEAK!

"What did you say?" asked Pandora.

"I didn't say anything," said Jenny.

SQUEAK!

"That's very interesting. Your blanket is moving," said Pandora.

Jenny held the bag out in front of her. The cans inside had every appearance of writhing. "Oh, my—"

"Don't drop the—"

But Pandora's warning arrived a hair too late. The sack hit the ground with a bump and a colossal brown creature came streaking out of the center.

"Get it, Pandora, get it!" screamed Jenny, breaking for the safety of the cot.

"I can't find my stick!" said Pandora, scrambling for the table.

Furious at having his day of rest disturbed, the rat

was ricocheting around the hut's interior, baring his pointed teeth and hissing blue bloody murder.

"Holy son of a rodent—he must be two feet long!"

"I wonder what he eats," speculated Pandora. "He's much bigger than most of the ones in town. Carcasses, maybe?"

"Pandora!"

"What?"

"He's climbing the cot!"

There are times in a young woman's life when the forces of instinct overpower any qualms of character. Even now, when she's grown, Pandora still talks about her act of heroism that day.

Seizing hold of the calico, she ripped the curtain rod from the wall and grabbed one end. Like a soldier waving a flag for glory, she let off an earsplitting yell, leaped off the table, and brought the rod down hard upon the edge of the cot. The rat screeched in terror and raced toward her toes.

WHAM! went the rod.

SCREECH! went the rat.

WHAM! SCREECH! WHAM!

Finally, after one last thump of the rod, the rat streaked through the open door and into the woods.

Jenny stepped down off the cot.

"Thanks, Pandora. I don't think Still Hope could have done it any better—you were very brave."

"Yes," said Pandora, in a wondering kind of way. "I was, wasn't I?"

She bent to pick up the curtain rod. Spotting the shine of metal, Jenny seized her arm. "Look!"

And there, half buried beneath the calico folds, etched with a poppy flower, was the small blade of a shovel.

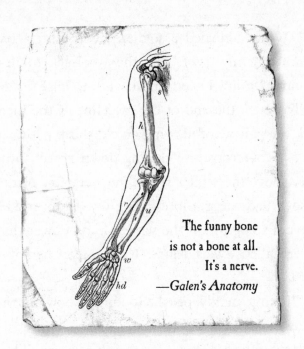

The funny bone
is not a bone at all.
It's a nerve.
—*Galen's Anatomy*

CHAPTER 8

Folks who have been in Jenny's neck of the wild often find it hard to express their joy. On a clear day, with peaks in front of you and peaks behind, the world of sorrow shrinks to a fleck in the dirt. There's no taint of past to a walk in the mountains. Just the sky and the wind and the scent of the black honey bush.

Jenny was a happy girl by nature, and happier yet on this Sunday above Eden. The path might be crumbling, and the grass sharp as swords, but the glint of gold could be seen in every ray of sun. A few of them had caught in Pandora's hair.

"'When I turned a soldier, I could lift a barn,'" hummed Jenny, switching the woolsack to her left shoulder. "'Now I need a pulley just to raise my arm.'"

To get to the end of the ridgeline of the Sleeping Girl, the pair was following an old sheep path, climbing over outcrops and skating down gravel slips. Up here, above the winter snow line, very few plants but tussock had the gumption to grow. Jenny tried hard to avoid stepping on the white alpine flower that her father called Sweet Mary. It reminded her of Mrs. Quinn.

"'Eating moldy peas! Goodness, how nutritious, eating moldy peas!'"

It was an ideal hour for seeing mirages. The idea of fixing up Old Randolph Scott's place and living the quiet life in Eden was becoming a distant memory. It would be a grand adventure, mused Jenny, to ride through the prairies of her father's childhood, or roam through canyons of red. Who knows? She might buy herself a ship and sail it to the ends of the earth.

The first bout of gold fever was taking a firmer hold. The more Jenny fixed on striking a fortune, the less she remembered her connection to the country. It's a shame—as her mood would suggest, the land was the thing that made her whole.

"How you doing, Pandora? Loving the air and everything in it?"

"No."

Jenny paused to let her friend catch up to an outcrop. Having spent most of her time in the must of home or the dust of the schoolroom, Pandora was struggling with the altitude. Her nose was peeling and her breath was short. She dumped the shovel on the ground. "I'm hot."

With a smile, Jenny picked up the shovel and leaned it, careful as she would a baby, against the rock. "Pandora, I've been thinking. We've got to be sure we're not being followed. Keep an eye out, like."

"You're worried about Mr. Grimsby? Because he has the letter from Dr. Galen?"

Jenny nodded. "And King Louis. What reason did he have to be loitering about Doc Magee's office? I bet he's after the nugget, too."

Pandora stuck out her tongue.

"What?" asked Jenny.

"King Louis has more money than the government," said Pandora.

"How do you know that?"

"Mum told me. He's rolling in it. That's why he has so many fancy suits. He's the best gambler in the territory. Mum says he's bankrolled a quarter of the businesses in Eden."

"Then what was he doing on Poplar Street?" demanded Jenny. "Maybe," she said, recalling her earlier theory, "King Louis is a *murderer*. He said himself he likes practical jokes—maybe he knocked off Magee, stole the nugget, and came up with the idea of a skeleton map!" Jenny paused, already seeing the holes in her theory. "Of course, putting together a fake treasure hunt is a lot to do after you kill a man. Especially if he's your best friend."

Pandora grunted. "We shouldn't speculate until we have all the facts. And I'm hungry."

"Fine," said Jenny, untying the sack. "But our motto from now on is 'Don't trust anybody.'"

~

Doc Magee's mystery meat proved to be canned pork and beans. It's wholesome enough grub, but somewhat tricky to eat with bare hands. Jenny held her nose and drank half the liquid from the can. Then Pandora did the same. They were unlikely to find fresh water at this elevation.

"That was disgusting," griped Pandora, "and now my shoulders ache."

"Mine too," said Jenny, soothing-like. "We'll rest a few minutes until it gets cooler."

Stretching back under the welcome shade, Jenny laid her head on her hands and let her attention wander for a while over the valley. Her gaze roamed from the tussock to the trees to the bumps of the Crooked Man in the east. Quite suddenly, she laughed.

"What?" asked Pandora.

"This is just like the day when I pretended to have scarlet pox at school. Remember? I wrapped a hot stone in a rag to warm my forehead. Then I dotted myself all over with red ink . . ."

"I used blackberry juice to dye your tongue black . . ."

"And then I started flapping around on the floor like a bug on a griddle. Ooohh, grooble, Mr. Grimsby, cooble wooble!" Jenny gave an encore of her original performance. "Scooble, rooble, I've pooped on the floor!"

"I've never seen Mr. Grimsby run that fast before," said Pandora.

"God, what a funny day," said Jenny, wiping away her tears.

"I wish I knew how to be funny."

Jenny twisted sideways and examined her best friend. Pandora's face was the same as ever, forehead creased and mouth dipped down. But there was a longing in her eyes that Jenny had seldom seen, even in her own reflection. "Why do you say that?"

"Funny people have friends," said Pandora.

Jenny had to acknowledge the truth of this statement. Pandora could be comic in moments, but it was usually by way of something she accidentally did or said. A joke or two would go a long way to making her life easier in the schoolyard.

"That's simple enough—I'll teach you," said Jenny, sitting up and brushing off her hands. "Try this one. Why couldn't the miner ever find gold?"

"What miner?"

"It's the start of a joke," said Jenny. "You've got to answer the question."

"How am I supposed to do that when I don't understand which miner you mean?"

Jenny sighed.

"It's just the way a joke works." She cracked her knuckles speculatively. "Tell you what, you ask the question."

"What question?"

"The one I asked about the miner," said Jenny.

Pandora appeared to be thinking of asking Jenny a question about her question, and then thought better of it.

"Okay. Why couldn't the miner ever find gold?" quizzed Pandora.

"Because he looked and looked," Jenny said with a grin, "but searched in vain."

"So?" asked Pandora.

"So, it's a pun! He searched in vain *and* he also searched in the vein of a rock."

"But if he searched in the vein of a rock, he'd be sure to find gold."

When Pandora turns to logic, your sole course of action is to admit defeat.

"Never mind," said Jenny.

If Jenny thought this was the end of the matter, she'd forgotten her friend. As was her wont, Pandora was revisiting every word of the conversation. Eventually, after a few minutes, she came to her own conclusion.

"Then I guess that's why the song about peas is supposed to be funny."

"What are you on about now?" asked Jenny.

"'Moldy Peas' is a humorous song." Pandora paused for Jenny to cotton to the meaning. She didn't. "Because we've been walking down the humerus bone."

"Jiminy, Pandora," groaned Jenny. "That's terrible."

Her best friend shrugged. "I said it was *supposed* to be funny. I didn't say it *was*." With a firm step and determined thrust, Pandora got to her feet and handed the shovel to her friend. "I feel better now. I'll carry the cans."

Jenny was tempted to note that the bundle was considerably lighter than before, but it wasn't worth the debate. Anyway, she was determined to get Pandora to the tip of the ridge before her best friend ran out of puff. She swallowed her pride and shouldered the burden. "Okay. But I'm going first."

It was tough to pick up the trail. From its height in the afternoon, the sun beat down like a hammer on the Sleeping Girl. As soon as they hit the ridgeline again, all Jenny wanted to do was burrow under the skin of the earth and find a sweet place to nap. But there was nothing to do but keep at it. Treasures were in want of finding.

"How far do you think we've come on the map?" asked Pandora, when a parched and weary hour had passed.

"We must be well beyond the elbow. See?" Jenny swung her shovel in a circle to the south. "There are the peaks of the Wise Women. Beyond that knuckle of rock."

Pandora wiped her pink cheeks with the edge of her sleeve. "This part seems far too easy."

"Which part?" asked Jenny.

"The song. And the arm," said Pandora. "It doesn't feel hard enough."

"Hard enough? We're hotter than cast iron."

"That's because we didn't come prepared. On a regular day, this tramp would be simple to do." She sniffed. "Dr. Galen's letter had more challenging clues."

"Pandora," said Jenny, "why do you *always* go looking for trouble?"

"Because it's usually there." She turned around. "Like that man who's following us."

"*What* man?"

"That one," Pandora said, pointing to the black silhouette that was approaching from the north. Framed as he was by the circle of the sun, it was impossible to tell what manner of beast he was—friend or foe.

"Why didn't you tell me about him sooner?" yelled Jenny. "I told you to keep an eye out!"

"I only noticed him now," retorted Pandora. "You were distracting me."

All manner of horrors were sprouting in Jenny's mind. It could be Mr. Grimsby, following the clues in Dr. Galen's letter and finding their trail. It could be King Louis, crafty and keen to see what was happening where Magee had lived. It could even be a mysterious murderer after the secret of the nugget!

Fortunately, thanks to years of rescuing Hapless from various perils like swollen creeks and mad-dog ewes, action was the one reaction Jenny had down to an art.

"We'll have to run for it."

"You can't run on a ridgeline like this," said Pandora. "You'll break your neck. Or your arm. Or your ankle if you land on the wrong—"

"Then we'll walk really quickly! C'mon!"

Despite what the storybooks would have you believe,

the sight of two sweaty girls haring over a mountain-side is rarely romantic. There were tongues flapping and knees grinding and clods of dust flying in every cardinal direction. Then and again, grunts would be joined by an *oww!* or an *oomph* as a foot hit a stone or a hand scraped a thorn.

"Why," panted Pandora, "don't . . . we stop . . . and ask him . . . what he . . . wants?"

"Because we're likely to be switched or stabbed! And I like my skin as it is!"

You know the uncomfortable feeling you get when you burp the wrong way? Now imagine that plus the addition of warm sloshy beans and pickled pork. Jenny was fair bursting with the effort of keeping her lunch in her belly.

"Aim for that rock!"

"Which rock?" cried Pandora.

"The one that looks like a pea!"

They both reached the formation at around the same time. Pandora was still holding the woolsack with the grip of a dead man.

"Here," said Jenny, pushing Pandora to the safety of the shade. "Keep low to the ground and don't say a word."

"What are you going to do?"

Jenny wedged herself in front of her friend. "I'll

wait till he comes round the corner and crown him with the shovel."

Pandora's jaw dropped. "You'll kill him."

"I won't put my back into it," said Jenny, trying to ignore the lumps in her throat. "But if we're going to negotiate, I want the upper hand. Now, shhhhhhh!"

It's rare to find real silence in the mountains. If there isn't a glacier creaking or a river pounding, there's the snap of schist cracking or a bud bursting or the wind tickling the grass. Jenny stood with the blade of Magee's shovel high in the air and listened with all her might and main.

Shick, wick, shick, went the soles of a pair of boots over the dust. From the weight of the walk, Jenny was certain it was a man. And a cautious one at that.

Shick, wick, shick. With her heart beating faster than a grasshopper's leg, Jenny crouched beside the rock and waited. And waited. And when she thought she could wait no more, the man finally shuffled his toes around the corner. Jenny hiked the shovel—

And promptly puked.

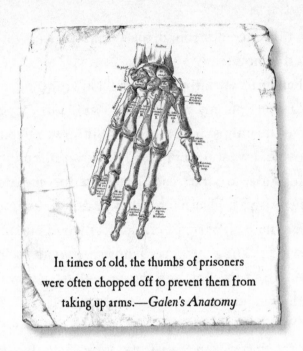

In times of old, the thumbs of prisoners were often chopped off to prevent them from taking up arms.—*Galen's Anatomy*

CHAPTER 9

"Lordy, lordy, daughter, what *have* you been eating?"

Hapless Burns stood with his hands in a position of surrender, his boots immersed in chunky brown goo.

"I've never seen that much sick," said Pandora, rounding Hapless to get a full measure of the hurl. "You must've spewed it six feet."

Jenny was feeling a little like she had being chugging on Doc Magee's poison bottle. Her teeth were bathed in acid and her lips were lined with slime.

"We had pork and beans," said Pandora to Hapless. "They weren't very good," she added.

"I can see that," said Hapless, flicking a piece of chewed pork from his calf. "Oh, heaven, spare a prayer for the friendless man and the motherless child."

"What are you doing here, Dad?" To settle her stomach, Jenny was trying to keep her body bent at the waist and her gaze fixed on something other than goo.

"It's Sunday," reminded Hapless. "You promised you would help me move the flock off Mount Lister and down to the Arrow. Farmer Wilcock says if we don't get moving, he'll dock my last month's pay. And I'll need that to cover my debts before we leave town."

"I'm sorry," said Jenny, straightening up. "I forgot."

Cautious as a fawn, Hapless lifted one skinny leg out of the spew and planted it on clean ground. Then he followed it with the other. His pants were stained to his calves, but the upper half had escaped calamity. "I don't suppose there's any water round here?" he asked.

"Not until Moonlight Creek," said Jenny, taking a breath. "And not much there, either. How did you find me, Dad?"

"I came up the dried streambed by the cemetery. Lordy, Jenny, half of Eden saw you walking along the ridgeline from the dip of the Sleeping Girl. You're plain as a pimple."

Well, if that wasn't the straw that broke the skeeter's back, thought Jenny. There they were, thinking they were so smart to have found a secret path to the nugget. Now everyone and their grandmother would be talking about their journey.

"What's so important that you'd take to bashing a bloke on the head?" joked Hapless. "You hiding a treasure chest back there?"

"Poison oak!" said Pandora.

Hapless lifted his hat and scratched a few scales of skin off his scalp.

"Poison oak?"

Jenny regarded her friend with wonder and awe. For the first time in their history, Pandora had remembered one of the code words for danger. Only problem was, she didn't understand what to do with it.

"Poison oak," repeated Pandora, helplessly.

"We're searching for poison oak," said Jenny, charging to the rescue. "Mrs. Quinn wants to use some of the leaves to make medicine."

"Isn't poison oak"—Hapless paused for a second to find the right descriptor—"well, poisonous?"

"Only for some," said Jenny, leaning into the lie. "But in the right mixture it can cure pretty much anything. I'm surprised you didn't know that, Dad."

Hapless leaned against a rock shaped like a half-moon and shook a few beans from his bootlaces. "Beats me to a pulp. I'm so dumb, you see."

There are men in this world who are born to be babies, no matter how often you try to wean them.

Jenny had spent most of her twelve years playing parent to her father and was used to his moods. This time around, Hapless was verging on tears. If they were going to get rid of him, they would have to humor him first.

"It's gonna be okay, Dad. Truly it is. Here, take a seat and dry off a bit." Jenny dusted the crumble from a tricornered stone and sat Hapless upon it. "I'll help with the sheep tomorrow, when it's cooler."

Hapless smiled his slight, crooked smile. "You sound like your mum when you say that. She was always after me to take things in steps."

Jenny kept quiet. It hurt like a pistol shot when her dad spoke of her mother's memory. Like many I know, she preferred to keep the past buried deep in the bedrock of her mind. I suppose she figured the longer she kept it there, the more chance she had of forgetting the pain.

Hapless might have been clueless, but he wasn't completely deaf to his daughter's silence. He caught Jenny's mood and changed the subject.

"Well now, it's been a month of Sundays since I was up here. A view and a third, they always said."

Jenny took a gander around the valley of home. With the sun giving way to the afternoon, new shadows were creeping into the folds of the Wise Women. Far off to the west glowed the blue of Lake Snow. To the east lay the Arrow Gorge and the Crooked Man, gloomy and deep. And right in front of them was a small row of schist pillars, like four friends in a line. If you had to pick a place for the end of the Sleeping Girl's arm, this would be it.

"Are those pillars pretty well known?" asked Jenny, her eyes fixed on the rocks. The tallest of the four, and second in line to the left, was leaning over the first. Somehow, the whole row felt vaguely familiar.

Hapless slapped his leg. "Why, to be sure! This is the place where a surveyor first caught sight of the valley. Gabriel Andreas was his name. He came from the coast, trying to find a good source for timber, and stumbled into an empty paradise."

"Was he the one who found gold?" asked Pandora.

"Nah. He put his trust in sheep. Figured they were the best stock for a land prone to heat. He was right there," said Hapless, shedding his hat. "You'd be stuck with seared steak today if you were a cattleman."

Jenny had a vision of Eden, heavy with beef, rivers brown with manure, and roads trampled by hooves. She made a secret wish that she'd never live to see the day.

"Nah," burbled Hapless, "the first man to find gold in this area was Still Hope."

Jenny raised an eyebrow. The stories she had heard about Hope were all to do with his piety, not his pleasures. Along with the parable of rescuing a station owner from drowning, Eden's minister often mentioned in sermons how Still Hope was kind to wild animals or patient with sinful men. It seemed unlikely that such a saintly creature would go grubbing for gold.

"Hope was resting his horse at the river when he saw that his shoes were speckled with stars." Hapless regarded his feet with despair. "Two weeks later there were a hundred men in the territory."

"Did they find gold as well?" asked Pandora.

"Find it? They hauled it out by the barrow," said Hapless. "Men who had spent their whole existence believing that hard work and penance were the keys to success found it was all a lie. There wasn't any rhyme or reason to getting rich. You might be a lowdown, dirty son of a dog with a gunfighter's twitch and you'd be a millionaire by morning. In the first season, it was a dream to be living."

"But you weren't here in the first season," said Jenny.

Hapless twitched. "Nah, I came later, with the rest of the suckers and the saps. Do you know what I did the first minute I stepped off the boat? I bought me a tin of gold grease. The shop owner said I should spread it all over me and roll down the hill picking up flakes. Easy as that, he said."

Jenny passed a look to Pandora, who passed it back.

It was ever a trial being the daughter of a man who believed in gold grease.

"Easy as that," Hapless repeated, ruefully. "He didn't tell me what it was like to stand in a freezing river, with my back crippled and my fingers flash frozen to the pan. Didn't mention the cold and the muck and the wind howling through your eye sockets. Didn't say what it was like to live in the society of a thousand greedy men, worrying your throat would be cut for the sake of your tea. Easy my—" Hapless paused. "Aunt Sally."

Jenny grinned. Her father used a stronger and more evocative word at home.

"I should've stayed where I was and tended to the crab apples," said Hapless. "Could've sold the family cider and bought myself some bear fat."

"Bear fat?" asked Jenny.

"You stick it on your scalp. For healthy hair growth," said Hapless.

Pandora might be cautious of most adults, but Hapless Burns was always an exception. She was tired of his ramblings, weary of the heat, and bored with old stories. "You shouldn't do that."

"Do what?" asked Hapless.

"Go over what might have been in your life. The past is past; you can't fix it different. Besides, Jenny wouldn't be my friend if you hadn't come to Eden.

And why would you waste your money on bear fat? You're balder than a new possum."

Hapless rubbed his skull wistfully. "You never know what might happen with time."

Jenny plucked her father up by the arm and set him on his stinking feet. "Pandora's right, Dad. You'd better be getting back down to the valley."

"Pandora didn't say that," said Hapless.

"Yes, she did," said Jenny, giving her father a firm but gentle shove. "You've got to listen to the words more carefully."

"What about my hat?"

Sighing a little, Jenny raced back to the tricornered rock and fetched her father's hat. By the time she'd returned, Hapless was on to another ramble.

"A view and a third, yes, sirree." He plunked his lid on his pate. "You can see why Gabriel would call this place God's Army."

Pandora paused in the midst of handing Hapless the empty cans. Jenny froze in the act of prodding her father off the ridge. "What did you say?"

"God's Army," said Hapless, gesturing to the pillars of schist. "Gabriel decided the rocks looked like a row of soldiers doing battle with the clouds. Course, the middle one wasn't leaning over as far as it is now."

"'Oh, to find a general pointing to the fore,'" sang Jenny, repeating the last stanza of "Moldy Peas."

"'Then I'd hide behind him, safe forevermore,'" muttered Pandora.

"What are you two on about?" asked Hapless.

"Nothing, Dad, nothing," said Jenny, giving her father a hearty push. "You get yourself going."

"But when are you coming home?"

"In a while," said Jenny. "We've got some digging to do."

❦

"You shouldn't say that," called Pandora after Hapless had stumbled off down the mountain. Jenny was running toward the pillars. Pandora was trotting at a brisk pace.

"Say what?"

"That we've got digging to do. Your dad will probably talk about what we're doing to King Louis at the saloon."

"Who cares?" shouted Jenny, skidding to a stop before the left-hand pillar. "By that time we'll be filthy rich!"

She stood beside the stone, shovel in hand, and took a long, pure breath. Around her rose the peaks and before her shone the quartz. She offered a silent prayer of thanks to Doc Magee.

"I still think this part is too easy," said Pandora, catching up.

"What are you on about? The skeleton map says

that phalanges are the bones in the fingers. The Greek dictionary said 'phalanx' means an infantry formation, and Gabriel called these rocks God's Army. We're staring straight at the fingers of the Sleeping Girl! That's a choice puzzle, no matter which way you parse it. What more do you want?"

"A challenge," grumped Pandora.

"Then decide where we should dig," said Jenny. "The song says the treasure is hiding behind the pointing general."

"The index finger," corrected Pandora.

"But does that mean the side of the pillar facing the valley and the Wise Women, or the side facing the mountain behind us?"

"The side facing the mountain."

"How do you figure that?" asked Jenny.

"Because we're looking at the back of the Sleeping Girl's hand," said Pandora, holding out her right arm and sticking her fingers up. "And the soldiers are facing the clouds. You hide behind a man's back, not his front. Unless he's blind. Or standing in heavy fog. Or wearing a mask—"

"Okay, okay!" said Jenny, beginning to dig. "I understand."

Roasted for weeks by the sun, the first layer of earth was tougher than steel. But once Jenny had cleared an inch or so, the dirt became as fine as talcum powder. A plume of dust rose from the hole and settled as grit on her clothes. Jenny didn't care. She was so close to the nugget she could almost smell it.

"You should probably take more off the sides," commented Pandora. "The ground could have shifted with settling."

The last thing Jenny needed right then was a critic. She was on the verge of making an obscene gesture, had her right hand staking the shovel and her left hand primed, when metal hit metal.

Pandora peered into the hole. "What was that?"

Tender as touch, Jenny pulled out a tin. It looked like a larger sibling to the one in the hut, the box full of dancing girls.

But this box wasn't full of dancing girls. It had only two items within it.

A large piece of paper. And one little key.

It was quite an ordinary key, smaller than most that Jenny had encountered, but serviceable enough. What marked it from the run-of-the-mill was the tag—a circle of copper with an X etched into the middle.

"X marks the spot," said Pandora.

"But to what?" asked Jenny, annoyed with her find and understandably so. It's hard to reconcile the promise of gold with the shine of a lesser metal.

"To this," said Pandora, handing Jenny the paper.

Decimus (fl. 70)

Be it known: Each low Roman soldier takes his equable place about a just Rex.

"And what in an owl's hoot does that mean?"

"Probably instructions," said Pandora. "For where the treasure is locked up."

"Oh, wonderful," said Jenny, whacking the shovel against the second pillar. "Because that's what we need after a day walking through hellfire. An unbreakable code."

Luckily for the tale we've been telling, Jenny's best friend refused to be cowed.

"It's all wrong again," said Pandora, beginning her pacing.

"What's wrong?" asked Jenny.

"The sentence is talking about Roman soldiers."

"So?"

"We found 'phalanx' in the Greek dictionary," noted Pandora. "It doesn't make sense."

"Nothing makes sense," grumbled Jenny.

"Yes, you're right," said Pandora, missing the point. "That's why it's so important. It's a nonsense sentence. Like the letter from Dr. Galen."

"Except this one is written by Decimus," grumped Jenny. "Who's probably some nutty Roman general who didn't know his ABCs from his 123s."

"Say that again."

"A nutty Roman . . ."

Pandora wasn't listening or pacing anymore. Instead, she was on her knees, the paper in front of her, counting. "One, two, three, four . . ."

"Pandora, what are you doing?"

"Shhh!"

Jenny waited in anxious suspense until Pandora had finished her task. "Well?" she demanded.

Pandora righted her spine. "The gold nugget is in the bank, in a box with the number ten."

"What?"

Pandora pulled her best friend down to her level and pointed at the paper. "How many times does seven go into seventy?"

"Ten," replied Jenny.

"How many fingers—how many digits," Pandora corrected herself, "are on your hands?"

"Ten."

"What does the Roman numeral X mean?" asked Pandora.

You'll remember that Jenny didn't waste much time in the schoolroom. "Dunno."

"It means ten," said Pandora. "Now look at this sentence and count to the tenth letter, each time."

Slower than syrup, Jenny started her count.

"I've got seven—"

"No, you ignore the number—that's only to tell us how many letters are in the clue." Using her finger, Pandora drew a grid of seven by ten squares in the dirt. "Read it like this."

D	E	C	I	M	U	S	F	L	B
E	I	T	K	N	O	W	N	E	A
C	H	L	O	W	R	O	M	A	N
S	O	L	D	I	E	R	T	A	K
E	S	H	I	S	E	Q	U	A	B
L	E	P	L	A	C	E	A	B	O
U	T	A	J	U	S	T	R	E	X

Pandora leaned back and admired her work. "It's a good clue. Much better than the song."

But Jenny wasn't in an admiring frame of mind. Maybe it was the effect of the sun, or the beans lodged between her teeth, or the gravel in her shoes. Or maybe it was the fact that Pandora had solved the puzzle so quickly. Whatever the reason, she was no longer disappointed. She was angrier than a fire ant.

With a lurch, Jenny rose to her feet.

"Why are you mad?" asked Pandora, fumbling to a stand. "I got the answer. Now all we have to do is pick up the gold."

"Oh, is that it? You think Mr. Polk is going to let

two twelve-year-old girls waltz right into his bank under his nose and claim a nugget? You've been sniffing too much of your mother's smelling salts."

Since this was a piece of pure logic, her best friend had to agree.

"Yes, you're right. It'll be hard to get into the bank. But you're good at that kind of thing," noted Pandora. "The planning and the sneaking and persuading friends to do what you want. Gentle Annie says you have winning ways."

Whenever you receive a word of praise from Pandora, you can be pretty darn certain it's on the level. Jenny felt a new well of confidence rise in her soul. She *was* good at sneaking.

What's more, the mention of Gentle Annie had sparked an idea in her overheated mind. If they couldn't get into the bank without an adult, well, then, an adult it would have to be.

"What are you thinking?" asked Pandora.

"I'll tell you about it on the way down to the cemetery," said Jenny, filling in the hole and holstering the shovel. She wanted to be ready for surprises, whatever they might be. "I've got my hands full. You better hold on to the Decimus paper."

Together they set off for low ground. They were almost to the point where the dried streambed met the peak of the ridgeline when Jenny stopped short in her tracks. "Oh, mother of Moses," she groaned.

"What's wrong?" demanded Pandora.

"I just recalled something."

"What?"

"The skeleton in Doc Magee's office," said Jenny.

"So?"

"Remember where his right hand was resting?" asked Jenny.

"Yes," said Pandora. "On the place where his heart would be."

"Don't you see the joke?"

"No."

"We're going to the bank to use a key to unlock a box full of gold."

"Yes?"

"Dad was right—we are after a treasure *chest*."

"Oh," said Pandora. "You know, I don't think that's very funny."

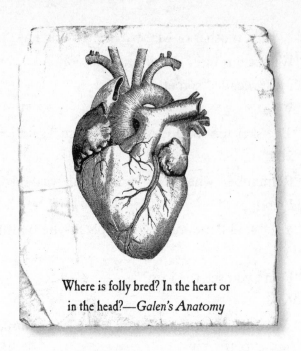

Where is folly bred? In the heart or
in the head?—*Galen's Anatomy*

CHAPTER 10

"Fashion," said Gentle Annie, tweaking the tilt of her bonnet, "is the best form of camouflage. People seldom bother to look past first appearances." She glanced at the couple beside her. "You're doing just fine with your petticoat, Pandora. Hold the hem a little, lest it catch in the dust."

Bystanders on their daily rounds the afternoon after Monday's bank holiday could scarcely believe their eyes. Seldom had they witnessed such a cataclysm of finery. Every soul in Eden lurched back in awe as a tidal wave of feathers and fur, buttons and bows, and one tremendous bustle swept through the center of town.

"And who would have guessed, Jenny Burns, that lilac and lime green were your colors? They go so well with your pretty brown hair."

Jenny wished she could spare the breath to protest. She was cinched into a corset as tight as a straitjacket.

Not that she had any right to complain, for it had been remarkably easy to finagle Gentle Annie's assistance. A chance meeting on Main Street on Sunday, a nip and tuck of sewing at Annie's favorite dressmaker during the holiday, and by three on Tuesday the girls were ready to storm the citadel of finance. Even Pandora was willing to skip a morning of school to have her flounces adjusted.

You may wonder at the speed of these proceedings, but you have to remember that Jenny was playing on her friend's sentimental side. Since the day of her birth, the wild and wandering Burns child had been lodged like a bulb in Gentle Annie's heart—as welcome as snowdrops in spring.

So to get at the bank box, all Jenny had to do was tell Annie a story about hidden family heirlooms and mother ache. Tintypes were in the box, said Jenny, and love letters, and locks of her mum's hair—things that would heal her wounded soul. You may have noticed that like King Louis, our girl of the mountains was not above manipulating others for her own gain.

The result of Jenny's little white lie was a red-letter date in the annals of Eden. It was the first afternoon in nigh on a decade when Gentle Annie had forsaken her usual teatime hour.

"Hey there, Annie, what's the big occasion?" bellowed the postman.

"Planning my wedding," cooed Annie.

A chorus of whistles rose from the sidelines.

"I thought you forfeited your love in the Rush. Who's the lucky man?"

Gentle Annie smiled coyly and winked her good eye. "Ah now, that would be telling."

Whistles became whoops.

"It'll be hell to lose you, sweet Annie," said the butcher. "What shall we do without our lovely lass?"

Taking this as his cue, the melancholic owner of the livery started playing a poignant air on his harmonica. Most of the men in Eden picked up the refrain:

"Oh, Annie, sweet Annie, where have you gone?
Come back and love me, now don't you be long."

"I appreciate the sentiment, gentlemen," said Gentle Annie, dropping a veil of lace over her rouged cheeks. "But you're making us late for our appointment."

"Step aside now, lads," said the postman, "step

aside. Let the procession through."

The sea of faces parted to let the Queen of Eden promenade her two hundred pounds down the boardwalk. Her hips were wide and her steps were dainty, and the whole of Eden was hers for the taking.

Like any good ladies-in-waiting, Jenny and Pandora followed up with the train. Pandora, who hated to be watched, had shot past her mum's seventh circle of hell—where men roasted in the flames of King Louis's saloon—and was writhing somewhere in the tenth.

But Jenny, who had a prime view of Gentle Annie's generous backside, was worrying. They were so very . . . bold. Was her plan really going to work?

Gentle Annie seemed to believe so. A few minutes later, on the parched bit of grass that ringed the Bank of Eden, she stepped aside to review procedures.

"You just let me do all the talking and we'll be in and out in a trice. Pandora, can you give me a little smile? We're supposed to be celebrating."

"She doesn't like to smile," said Jenny.

"Oh, sure enough. But I thought it would make it less likely for people to ask questions of her."

And with that, Pandora smiled for the fourth time in her life.

"Jenny, so I don't make a muddle when we're in the bank," continued Annie, adjusting her bustle, "your mother's possessions are being kept in box number ten, correct?"

"Yes," said Jenny, glad to hear how believable her fib sounded coming from another person's lips. "Only we can't let Mr. Polk know that's the box we're after," she insisted, "or he'll tell Dad that we've been looking into it."

"Yes, I understand," said Annie. "Sometimes, the ones we love best we would rather forget."

There was a plaintive echo in Gentle Annie's voice. Jenny remembered the postman's comment about her forfeiting a man.

"Have you been trying to forget someone from the Rush, too?" she asked.

Gentle Annie smiled poignant-like, but she took a skirt to the question. "A word to the wise, girls. Avoid the mad and the bad when you're thinking of courting. They always lead to trouble."

Jenny nodded. Though Annie was admirable in most respects, she had often noticed that Eden's favorite lady had a habit of favoring sly and cunning men. As she saw it, Annie's fondness for King Louis only went to prove one thing: in matters of the heart, logic need not apply.

"If you're feeling sad, maybe we should do this some other time," said Jenny, suddenly experiencing an ache without cause.

"Keep your chin high, Jenny," said Annie, buttoning the last mother-of-pearl button on her right glove. "If I've remembered the dimensions of the boxes correctly, we have little to fear."

Walking toward the steps of the Bank of Eden, Jenny wished she felt near as confident. She had forgotten the building's thick central dome and the cold granite slabs and the carving of the armored knight that stood by the door. Even from a distance, she could feel the suspicion in his glance. Did he know of her lies? Would he raise his sword and lop off her head as she went by?

"Just cast your eyes on this stone," said Gentle Annie, tightening her grip on the balustrade as she walked up the stairs. "Would you believe, girls, in the first year of the Rush, men left their gold lying around in saddlebags with one lonely cook to guard them?"

"Yes," said Pandora. "Because most men are idiots."

Gentle Annie threw back her head and roared with laughter. It was fortunate she was wearing a hat; otherwise her wig would have leaped off her head.

"Oh, Pandora, how right you are." She wiped a tear from her eye and elbowed the knight in his ribs. "But give Mr. Polk credit for being a crafty idiot. I was here the day he laid the foundation for this building, in the third year of the Rush. Whatever you think of his methods, he's made his mark on Eden."

In Jenny's mind, Mr. Polk had done more than made his mark—he'd built a temple to his own self-worship. What with its tall, fluted columns and colored inlays, the Bank of Eden was easily the flashiest structure in the territory.

She was on the lip of saying just that when someone came bashing out the front door and slammed straight into her.

"Kam?"

"Hello, Jenny Girl."

Kam had the appearance of a boy who'd been told he had five days to suffer and six days to live. The rim of his hat was frayed with rubbing.

"What the dickens are you doing here?" demanded Jenny.

Kam shrugged. "Bank business."

"Was it good business?" asked Jenny, fearing to look into his eyes.

"No." Kam touched his fingers to the lock on his brow. "Good-bye, ma'am."

Jenny watched her friend slump down the steps. It hurt her heart to see him so dispirited. Judging by his tone, she was guessing that the drought was biting hard into his harvest. Perhaps he was asking for a loan to see him through the next few weeks. Or maybe he was thinking of mortgaging Little Eden. Whatever it was, he hadn't been successful.

In a few moments, Kam had lost his edges in the shimmering heat. In a few minutes, he had dissolved completely into the blaze of the sun. Say what you will about the supernatural; I say a ghost is only a man who has given up trying.

～

Now, then—over the years it's been my experience that banks delight in setting you in your place. Shameful of your parentage? Worried about your prospects? A lobby filled with wax-polished floors and high vaulted ceilings is sure to remind you of the fact.

The Bank of Eden was a prime example of this phenomenon. Almost everyone who stood in the center of its atrium, under the light from its dome, felt a swift surge of panic. It was a feeling that Jenny observed her schoolmaster was in the midst of experiencing first-hand.

"Mr. Polk, an educator's mind requires a steady supply of nourishment!" pleaded Mr. Grimsby. "How am I supposed to retain my skills when I cannot sustain myself?"

"Don't know, Mr. Grimsby. Don't care." Behind the safety of the marble-topped counter, Mr. Polk was working his enamel like a millstone grinds chaff. "I'm a bank, not a charity. Have to stand on your own two feet."

"But that's hardly equitable!" the schoolmaster

exclaimed. "This is the only bank in the territory, and I require a loan to survive!"

"Busy man, Mr. Grimsby. Clients to serve, money to make." Mr. Polk took a hasty step back and jerked his thumb. "We've had our talk. Take yourself off."

Red in the ears and long in the mouth, Mr. Grimsby turned toward the center of the atrium and froze. Jenny told me she'd never seen such a look from a man.

It was fear as well as loathing; shame as much as venom. The schoolmaster seemed to be funneling every ounce of his embarrassment into a bullet shot straight at her heart.

"Jenny Burns," he hissed.

"Mr. Grimsby, how very nice to see you!"

Into the fray swept Gentle Annie, taking out bystanders with her bustle and sending stacks of correspondence scurrying across the floor. "I wanted to thank you for the lecture you gave on drama and the supernatural at the Lyceum. Who in the tarn hill knew that witches could spawn locusts?"

Mr. Grimsby was one of the few men in the territory immune to Annie's charms. He aimed his next shot directly at her frilly pink blouse.

"Go to blazes."

"Mr. Grimsby! Manners!" Mr. Polk scurried out from behind the counter. "Miss Annie is one of my best customers."

Feeling the eyes of Pandora upon his back, Mr. Grimsby twirled. "And I see Pandora Quinn is here. Always the supporting player. I spied a tintype of your mother yesterday." He smirked. "Quite the varied career she's had."

The schoolmaster's remark occasioned a notable change in Annie. From being all laughter and larks, she went to being all muscle and might. With her hands on her hips and her bosom thrust forward, she began driving Mr. Grimsby toward the entrance.

"That's quite enough of that, young man. You take the advice of one who knows better and keep your trap shut unless you have something useful to say."

With one swift, roundhouse turn, Gentle Annie swung her bustle at Mr. Grimsby's hollow chest and launched him through the door.

"Which will be never," she added, daintily dusting her palms.

"Pandora!" whispered Jenny as Gentle Annie made her way back through the applause. "Poison oak! I'm pretty sure Mr. Grimsby has been up at Doc Magee's hut!"

"How do you know?" asked Pandora.

Jenny paused, then shrugged. "A hunch," she whispered. After all, to explain her conclusion would require mentioning how she had seen a picture of Mrs. Quinn in her bloomers. And she wasn't keen on giving

Pandora conniptions just at this time.

"Apologies, Miss Annie." Mr. Polk twisted his liver spots into a fawning pout. "Disgraceful behavior. Man is diseased."

"That's all right, Mr. Polk," said Gentle Annie. "Poverty is enough to drive angels to despair." She brushed a lock from her brow. "Now then, if you have a moment, I'd like to pay a visit to my box in the vault."

"Yes. Well. I'd be happy to, but do we have to bring"—Mr. Polk cast his eyes over the two unusual girls before him and clenched his jaw in an attempt to avoid a nut-laced profanity—"the other members of your party?"

Gentle Annie pulled herself up to her full height of five feet. "These are my trusted friends and nuptial attendants, Mr. Polk. Need I say more?"

"Course not," said Mr. Polk, giving them one last glance before spinning around. "Righty-way!"

In that moment, Jenny knew Eden's banker must also be hopelessly in love with the bride to be. Why else would he be willing to tolerate the so-called "filth" of the Rush?

Lacing his arm through Annie's substantial silk folds, Mr. Polk led his favorite client toward the door at the back of the bank.

"Isn't this a lark?" He squeezed her wrist fondly. "Like walking down the aisle. 'A suit of the same I will put on, your wedding I'll prepare. . . .'"

Jenny had her heart in her mouth and Mr. Polk had his key in the lock of the door when a sharp baritone voice cut through the sap.

"Something you've been neglecting to tell me, Annie?"

Jenny nearly leaped out of her skin.

"Why, Louis," called Annie across the lobby, "whatever brings you here?"

"Came to deposit my winnings from the weekend," said King Louis, stepping lively toward the group and eyeing Pandora's scarlet and yellow stripes with mistrust. "Like I always do. What the deuce are *you* doing here?"

Mr. Polk cackled. "Secret's out, Miss Annie. No hiding things now!"

King Louis drove his walking stick into the floor. "Hiding *what*?"

Mr. Polk crunched on his molars nervously. "The plans for your upcoming nuptials."

King Louis turned pale as driftwood, clutched at his cravat, and buckled at the knees. Gentle Annie stepped in and started patting his pompadour.

"That's it, Louis, breathe nice and slow. I can't go losing my husband before the deed is done! I was hoping to keep the jewels from your sight, but now that you're here, you should come along and help decide.

After all, you won't be seeing me in the dress." She giggled. "I'm saving that surprise for the wedding day."

King Louis was still suffering from congestive pains.

"Both of our bridesmaids are favoring diamonds," continued Annie, "but I had a mind to use colored gems. Didn't you once say that my love was more precious than rubies? You might change your tune when I show you my mother's earrings."

Gentle Annie's allusion to bridesmaids had the effect of diverting King Louis's attention to Jenny and Pandora. His breathing seemed to settle as he raised his eyes and scrutinized them with a gambler's ken.

"Miss Burns and Miss Quinn. Nice to see you again. And so soon after our meeting on Poplar Street."

Jenny cursed the dome and the marble and the fancy lettering on the bank teller's glass. The day was turning into a disaster. First, there was the strong suggestion that Mr. Grimsby had been fossicking around Magee's hut, and now there was King Louis observing her at the door of a bank vault. You'd have to be a dimwit not to realize that something was up concerning the nugget. And how was she supposed to get rid of Louis once they found the bank box?

There was no use fretting about it; by the time Jenny had finished cursing, the five of them already through the door to the vault and into the room beyond. This was a smaller atrium, lit by a lone tunnel of sun from the roof. It was a stark and unwieldy place, chilly as an icebox and nigh on as dark.

"Now," said Mr. Polk, locking the door behind him. "Do you have your key?"

Gentle Annie removed a key with the tag "IV" from her handbag. "Right here."

Mr. Polk scuttled over to the far wall, which was arranged in stacks and stacks of cubbyholes. There must have been fifty metal boxes. Jenny nudged Pandora's foot. All of them were labeled with Roman numerals.

"One of my bank's first contributors," said Mr. Polk, removing the fourth box from the bottom row and bringing it to the table in the middle of the room. He took the key from Annie and tenderly worked it into the lock. "You, my dear, proved my idea of safety deposits would be profitable."

From the interior of her bank box Gentle Annie pulled out a heavy necklace of amethysts. "Here we are, Louis. These will go perfect with my apricot-and–polka dot pelisse on the honeymoon."

Jenny ran her attention around the room. King Louis was saying nothing and seeing everything. Pandora was sucking fierce as a baby on her plait. Gentle Annie was swinging the amethysts at Mr. Polk's nose. For Jenny, it was act now or kiss the future good-bye.

"Oooh," she said, grabbing at the stays of her corset. "Oooooh!" she cried, falling to the floor.

"What goes on?" asked Mr. Polk.

"Oooh," moaned Jenny, "cooble wooble!"

Gentle Annie pushed King Louis to the forefront.

"Get that restrictive jacket off her, Louis. She must be having one of her fits. She takes to them occasionally. Ever since that encounter with scarlet pox."

"Good golly," gasped Mr. Polk, flinging himself toward the door. "Is it catching?"

"Oh no," said Gentle Annie, maneuvering her sizable backside toward the wall of boxes. "But fiendishly painful."

"Rooble!" yelped Jenny.

"And sometimes quite messy," added Annie.

If Mr. Polk had been paying more regard to his ladylove and less to the twitching heathen on the tiles, he might have noticed that Gentle Annie's fanny was sporting a moving hump. He might also have noticed that the girl he'd decided to humiliate in the schoolhouse the previous week had upped stakes and vanished. But he didn't. Unlike Louis, Mr. Polk was not a noticing sort of a person.

"There, there," said King Louis, pinning Jenny's flailing arms to her side. "You're doing no good by acting this way." His gray eyes bored into her brown.

"You'll put yourself in real danger."

"*Scrooble!*" screamed Jenny, straight into his eardrum.

"Ah!" said Gentle Annie. The growth in her tush had subsided, the bank boxes were in their rightful slots, and Pandora was once more chewing on her hair. Only the keenest of observers would have spotted that bank box ten was now one shade lighter than its neighbors. "I remember what we're supposed to do with a fit. Louis, tap three times on her forehead."

"What?"

"You're trying to trick her brain. Go on, the poor girl's in agony."

With one manicured index finger, King Louis reached down and tapped three times on our heroine's skull.

And, just like that, Jenny felt fitter than a six-string fiddle.

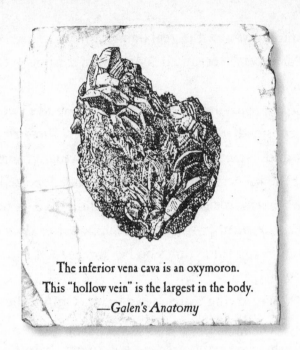

The inferior vena cava is an oxymoron.
This "hollow vein" is the largest in the body.
—*Galen's Anatomy*

CHAPTER 11

If you ever take it into your head to visit Gentle Annie's establishment on the second floor of Main Street, above the general store, I'd recommend a stop by the bathhouse first. You can't spit in Annie's rooms without winging a gilded mirror.

To tell you true, you can't spit in Annie's rooms at all. She's covered the walls in a red, rippled silk, and she's most particular about keeping it pretty. You'd better be sure to mind your spurs and boots as well. Her parlor is stacked with tippy wee tables and plush velvet sofas. It's not a decorating style that I particularly care for, but the company more than makes up for the inconveniences.

Jenny and Louis were regular visitors to Annie's, so the plaster cherubs on the ceiling held no surprises. Pandora, on the other hand, was shocked to her core. Mrs. Quinn's idea of gracious living was a day without fleas. This kind of luxury, with doilies for saucers and silver for spoons, was akin to a trip to the moon.

"Well, now, Jenny," said Annie, whirling her bonnet onto the hat shelf and pinching her cheeks, "let's fetch you your box."

Jenny squirmed. From the bank to the door, she'd been doing her best to push off King Louis. But Louis had stuck stronger than dried molasses. Her only hope now was to get the safe-deposit box away from his sight to search it in private. It was useless relying on Pandora for assistance in this task. Her best friend was fixed on tracing the roses in the carpet.

"Pandora, come help me with the fastenings. Louis, lay out the tea cakes."

Pandora got to her feet and headed off with Gentle Annie into the next room. Jenny had a glimpse of brass and puffed eiderdown before the door swung to.

Without a word, King Louis walked over to Annie's sideboard, took an array of apple cakes, and arranged them on top. Striking a match on his teeth, he lit the burner under the kettle and tossed the stub in a saucer.

Then he sat down on a chair and stared at Jenny. Willing her eyelids to stay still, Jenny stared back.

"Here we are!" said Gentle Annie, barreling back into the room and laying the box with the X on a side table. "The Burns family treasures." She patted her bottom. "It's fortunate you thought of hiding the substitute box in my bustle, Jenny. It's the one place large enough to hold such a thing."

Jenny looked for the option to bolt, but King Louis was stationed between her and the exit.

"Well, aren't you going to open it?" demanded Louis.

"Shush your mouth, Louis," said Annie. "There are things of a private nature in there."

"You're not wrong," said Louis, grinning. "Because that's not her bank box."

Jenny gulped. Pandora flinched.

"What are you talking about?" asked Annie.

"It belongs to Mike Magee."

Gentle Annie crossed her arms over her substantial bosom. "And how do you know that?"

King Louis leaned his chair back, dug into his waistcoat pocket, and tossed a metal object into Jenny's empty teacup. It ricocheted a few times around the side before coming to rest in the middle. "Because I was ordering mine at the exact same time he was ordering his."

Jenny took her time looking down, predicting from the start what she'd see. And, sure enough, there it was.

A brass tag with the letters "IX."

"Jenny? Pandora? Do you have something to tell us?" asked Gentle Annie.

The lie on Jenny's tongue never got past her teeth.

"We think we've found Doc Magee's missing gold nugget," said Pandora. "The one he fetched up at Moonlight Creek."

This was a gunpowder blast and no mistake. Gentle Annie's eyes bloomed to the size of melons. King Louis's chair returned to its four feet with a thump. Jenny glared at Pandora.

"We might as well tell them," Pandora said to her friend. "Louis wasn't going to let us leave the room with Magee's box. And I want to see what's inside."

"*That* explains why you were nosing round his place of business," said King Louis.

Jenny interrupted before Pandora had the chance to reveal anything more about the skeleton map and their journey and the clues.

"Yes. And we found something in the office that led us to the bank."

She paused and waited for the response. King Louis was petting his goatee. Gentle Annie was playing an invisible melody on the tabletop. The kettle started to scream. Gentle Annie rose without speaking and quenched the flame in the burner. With an ease born of practice, she poured boiling water over the tea leaves and into the pot. "It will need a few minutes to steep," she said, placing the porcelain in front of them.

"So?" asked Jenny. "Are you going to let me open the box?"

"Well," said Louis, "legally speaking, it's not yours."

"Why do you care?" countered Pandora. "You already told us that the law and you have never been bosom companions. And Mum says you're the trickiest gambler in the territory."

"You got me there," said Louis. He began twirling the ring on his pinkie finger.

"Louis, we haven't heard from Mike for years," said Annie. "He could be dead."

"Could be," said Louis. "Or hiding. We don't know for sure."

"No," said Annie, tapping her fork on her cup. "We don't know for sure."

"Oh, for the love of Peter and Paul!" yelled Jenny, her temper finally finding its voice. "Can't we talk about it after?"

Louis rapped the table. "Who's got the key?"

Pandora knelt down, unlaced her shoe, lifted up the inner sole, and pulled out her prize.

"Ah," said Annie, smiling. "Clever girl."

Jenny was too ginned up to notice the compliment. Snatching the key from her best friend's hand, she shoved it into the lock. The lid sprang away.

The first thing she saw was another box. A wooden one with a curved lid, the grain laced with red and the sides composed of triangular panels. It was resting on what appeared to be a bed of wilted petals. She caught it up and laid it down on the table. A faint scent of roses floated through the room.

"It *is* a chest!" said Jenny. "And it's heavy."

"Gold is weighty stuff," said Gentle Annie. "That's how you can pan for it. It sinks to the bottom of gravel and silt."

"That's some fancy-looking wood," noted Louis. "Tropical, I'd bet."

Willing herself to keep from cackling, Jenny cracked open the chest and peered inside. "Holy troves!" Laughing maniacally, she grabbed hold of the nugget, vaulted the table, and began springing from chair to sofa and back again. "I'm rich, I'm rich, I'm *rich!*"

"Jenny Burns, sit down! You're grinding dirt into my velvet!"

But Jenny was not to be sat. She'd forgotten Pandora, and Annie, and the bend in the road that led to home. She was gripped in the fever that was the bane of this country's existence.

She might have been jumping all day if Louis hadn't

started laughing along with her. And that's when she knew something was awfully awry. Louis only laughed like that when the occasion was to his advantage.

"What?" asked Jenny, leaping off her perch.

"You do realize you're holding iron pyrite."

"What's that?"

Louis grinned. "Fool's gold."

Jenny was of a mind to weep. She was of a mind to wail. She was of a mind to chuck herself through the window and let the devil take the dismount. But instead she sat down on her chair and clamped her mouth shut. Beside her, Pandora gave a miserable moan.

"What is it?" asked Gentle Annie.

Pandora raised her right hand toward Jenny. "Remember how the second pillar on the Sleeping Girl was leaning over the first?"

"Yes."

"I thought it was for luck—crossing fingers." Pandora crossed her middle finger over her index finger to form a narrow X. "But it's also for backing out on a promise."

Gentle Annie sighed and poured herself a cup of tea. "I think we'd best hear the whole story. From the beginning."

The last thing Jenny felt like doing was explaining herself to Louis. On the other hand, she'd run out of options. She could almost hear that fool piece of iron pyrite blowing raspberries at her.

"We discovered a map—" started Jenny.

"A diagram of a skeleton," interrupted Pandora. "And we realized the bones on the map were pointing to rocks and places in the mountains. So we went to Doc Magee and Silent Jack's hut, where we found a shovel and a humorous song that led to the end of the Sleeping Girl. That's where we dug up the key with the X on it and another clue. It pointed to the gold nugget being in bank box number ten."

Disregarding any talk with her mother or Hapless, this was probably the most sustained bit of speech that Pandora had ever had in the presence of adults. Jenny put it down to Gentle Annie's winning ways, but you never can tell. Perhaps Pandora was beginning to realize that in order to make your voice heard, you need to exercise it.

"Phewwww," Louis whistled through his teeth. "That sure as heck sounds like one of Mike Magee's larks. But I'm surprised about the ending. He usually kept his promises."

"Someone else could be involved," noted Gentle Annie.

"Yes, that's what I was thinking!" said Jenny, recalling her earlier guess. "See, one of my ideas is that a killer in Eden knocked off Magee and found the nugget. He could have figured out the clues about the hut and bank box, took the gold, and substituted iron pyrite. Or he might even have made up the hunt himself!"

The words were no sooner out of her mouth than she realized to whom she was speaking. Louis was one of her chief suspects. He was close with Doc Magee, he was cleverer than sin, and his pursuit of wealth knew no bounds. You don't go and tell a potential murderer that you've discovered his cool and cunning plan. It's an invitation to getting your throat cut.

Fortunately, King Louis didn't seem to believe he was capable of slaughtering his best friend. And he looked much more intrigued than amused by the fool's gold.

"Sounds like a pie-in-the-sky theory to me. Despite your antics today, I can't believe Polk missed someone lugging a great big rock out of the vault. Annie, can you peg anyone in the past ten years who's gotten rich unexpectedly?"

"Just you and me," said Annie. "And I can account for all the men at the poker games who made it so."

"Which brings us back to the notion that it was Mike Magee who planted the pyrite," noted Louis.

"But why would he go to the trouble to create a fake treasure hunt?" asked Jenny.

"Darned if I can figure," said Annie. "One last laugh?"

"That'll be it," said King Louis. "I'll lay you ten to one Mike cashed in that nugget as soon as he fished it up. He's probably lounging in a hammock somewhere in the South Seas."

"And nobody talked about a man exchanging the biggest piece of gold in the territory for money? I don't believe that," said Pandora, sticking out her tongue.

"Well, bully for you," retorted Louis.

"I wish Magee was here now," said Jenny, gripping the iron pyrite so hard that blood leached from her fingertips. "I'd show him what I think of jokers."

Gentle Annie laughed. "Even you, Miss Burns, with your fiery ways, would have a hard time losing your temper." She smiled at a secret memory and sipped at her tea. "Do you remember the first time I saw the both of you, Louis?"

King Louis chuckled. "Sure as the corn grows."

"I was just come to Eden," said Gentle Annie to Jenny, "and didn't know my top from my tail. Someone told me that the miners were celebrating the end of snow with a dance over at Mackenzie's barn."

"Keep in mind there were very few females round these parts in the early days," said Louis. "So we had to make our own entertainment."

"He means that men were dancing with men,"

interrupted Gentle Annie. "And pretty poorly, too."

"Except for our Mike!" laughed Louis, slamming his fist on the table and making the cutlery quiver. "That man could waltz with a polka and still have breath for the gallop. Everybody wanted to be his partner."

"He was jigging a mazurka on the top of two beer barrels when I met him," said Gentle Annie. "And juggling potatoes."

Jenny had seen enough of Eden's parties to picture it. The kick of the hay dust and the wheeze of the harmonica and one hundred beards twirling in unison. In spite of her fury at being tricked, she was beginning to develop a liking for Mike Magee.

"Louis told us about being dunked in the river and given a coronation," noted Jenny.

"That's right!" Annie smiled. "I'd forgotten that! Do you remember, Louis? Mike was also the one responsible for turning poor old Victor Jones into 'Soapy.'"

"Sure I do. The Crooked Man range is one of his babies."

"And the Wise Women," added Annie. "I reckon he must have given a title to half the places in the territory." She sighed. "Lord, I do miss him."

With the sigh came a thought. Jenny wondered if the love Annie lost in the Rush might have been Doc Magee. That was probably the reason she liked having children to visit and Louis to joke with. It must have been very hard to picture the promise of a life and a family, and then have it taken away.

King Louis uncorked a small bottle and tipped some of the liquid into his tea. "I blame Jack. We were all fine and dandy until Mike's twit of a partner went and ruined our good times."

"Louis, you know how I feel about medicinals."

"Keep your garters on, Annie; it's just vanilla." He waved the bottle under her nostrils. If Jenny noticed that the bottle near Annie's nose wasn't the same as the one being deposited in Louis's pocket, then she wasn't going to waste her time on it.

"I don't know why you took against Silent Jack," said Gentle Annie. "He seemed pleasant enough."

"Shifty," said King Louis. "Like those Lum brothers."

"Louis!" exclaimed Annie. "Kam and Lok are as honest as can be!"

"Rubbish. Look how they stick to themselves, don't bother to learn good English, pick over the remains of other men's diggings. I'm willing to tolerate a variety of folks, but a man has to draw the line somewhere. My father always said you can't trust an Oriental, and I believe him."

Though Louis's loathsome creed was typical of the era, and worse besides, there's a reason Jenny asked me to repeat it. Folks who follow the twists and turns of character might find it a point of interest that our heroine stayed silent. Jenny wanted to leap up and tell Louis he was plumb ignorant of everything to do with Kam and Lok's history and their family and their country. She wanted to scream that his statement was as ludicrous as saying you couldn't trust a European. She wanted to scrub every hateful racial slur from common speech.

But she knew that to speak out now would mean putting herself in the line of fire. So instead of rising from her chair and smiting King Louis with her wrath, she merely gnawed on her lip and stared at her reflection in the mirror. For a girl who prided herself on loyalty to her friends, it was not an edifying spectacle.

"Enough!" said Gentle Annie, whacking the round of her spoon hard over Louis's knuckles. "Say one more word against the Lum brothers and you can find another nest to feather. Their father was from away; I'm from away; you're from away. In fact, the only people who have a right to claim a patch of Eden are the two girls in front of us. At least they've got the blood of the land in their veins."

"Silent Jack must have been from away, too," piped Pandora. "Where was he born?"

Her scalp crackling with sparks, Gentle Annie rubbed her powder-gray wig from side to side.

"You know, that's a funny thing. I don't remember. He spoke so little that it was hard to get a noun out of him. He had a growl, that I recall, and a habit of pronouncing his *w*'s like *v*'s. Further than that I wouldn't like to say."

"Do you know where he lives now?"

"Oh, I see," said Gentle Annie, bustling out of her seat to refill the teapot. "You're thinking that Silent Jack may know more about the iron pyrite. I guess it's possible."

"But I don't fancy your chances of getting anything out of him," said King Louis. "He's liable to eat you for dinner."

Gentle Annie caught Louis by the tip of his goatee and yanked it hard.

"Louis, stop frightening the children." She turned to Pandora. "As far as I know, Jack's been roaming the territory since the Rush ended. Turned into a bit of a wandering hermit. You can ask around, but you'll have a hard time pinning him down."

Abrupt as an adder, Pandora tucked the wooden chest under her left armpit, stood up, and thrust her right arm toward Annie's stomach. "Thanks."

Realizing, slightly late, that Pandora was attempting to shake hands, Annie smiled and touched her fingers to Pandora's.

"Don't mention it." She paused. "Truly, I mean

don't mention it to anyone."

Pandora pulled away and punched her fingers into the folds of her dress.

"We won't. And I want to keep the chest with me."

Gentle Annie nodded. "You're welcome to it. We can always put it back in the bank if the need arises."

"What are you going to do now?" asked Louis. He might have been curious; he might have been making idle conversation while he calculated the future of wool prices. In the haze of Annie's red parlor, it was difficult to say.

"Nothing," said Jenny. "We're going to do nothing."

King Louis leaned back in his chair and sugared his next cup of tea. "Fair enough. But mark my words, kiddywinks. You're begging for trouble with Silent Jack."

The syrup of rose hips can be used to relieve dysentery, digestive issues, scurvy, and bad temper. —*Galen's Anatomy*

CHAPTER 12

"Why did you have to go and tell Gentle Annie and Louis about the skeleton clues?" groused Jenny.

In the pink of a mountain sunset, the two girls were on their way back to Quinn's Sweet Shop. Main Street—for once in its sordid life—was quiet. Houses were puffing gently on their chimney pipes, and the scent of burned tobacco lingered in the air.

Jenny was in no mood to appreciate the scenery. There was a gnawing, twisted feeling in her gut that was wrenching its way toward her heart. She knew she should have acted. She knew she should have spoken. But she hadn't.

Having recovered from her first bout of gold fever, Jenny was seeing her world with cold and cynical eyes. Men were cruel, dreams were silly, and money was king. As a young girl, you might as well accept you'd been given the bum steer.

"I like Gentle Annie," said Pandora. "She's got grit."

"It was a private quest," insisted Jenny. "And why did you keep harping on about Silent Jack? He's none of our business."

Pandora wrinkled her nose. "Course he is. He might have important information."

"About what? Fool's gold?" Jenny slapped the side of the sign for Boz's Miracle Cough Syrup. "The hunt is over, Pandora. We got played liked suckers, and I'm leaving town. And that's the end of it."

Pandora paused on the foot of her stairs. "You're giving up?"

"Yes," said Jenny.

"Because of iron pyrite?" asked Pandora.

"No," snapped Jenny. "Because I want to."

"Well, that makes no sense."

"Oh, to heck with it, Pandora!" yelled Jenny, venting her spleen. "Not everything in this world makes sense!"

Turning on her heel, Jenny bolted for the hills. She wanted to be away from teacups and bankers and keys. She wanted to be back at the top of Reed's Terrace, before the dry and the drought. Before her father had lost his thousandth job and put them in this position.

But if you've been paying attention to my rambling, you will have discovered that mountains don't care much for the troubles of humans. Year after year, they sit and wait for the earth to turn, and their bones to freeze, and the snow to fall. In the past week, when no one was watching, autumn had come to the valley. And it was promising to be a hard season.

So Jenny went home.

~

Home wasn't much to speak of—a patchwork of corrugated siding attached to the sheep shed—but it was all Jenny wanted. A good, quiet night and a sleep without end. She ought to have recalled one little thing.

"*Owwwwww!* Oh, Jenny, my skin is on *fire!*"

Stripped to his waist, Hapless was hopping around in the middle of the room. From his wrists to his chest, he was covered in patches of vicious red welts. Some were cracked like volcanoes; some were oozing with lava. In less than a day, he had become an atlas of eruptions.

"Dad! What on earth have you done to yourself?"

"I was fetching poison oak for Mrs. Quinn's

medicine like you suggested," he moaned. "Oh, lordy, lordy, Jenny, my skin is fair crawling! I took to scratching my arms and it seemed to make it spread. Is it very bad?"

What could Jenny say to such haplessness? She could hardly tell her dad he appeared to have been boiled in hot oil. Besides, it was her fault in the first place for devising the code words for Pandora. Her day went from desperate to dire.

"Dad, stop *itching*!"

Hapless dropped his hands to his side.

"You stay right there while I get you a bath. And don't touch anything, you hear me? You've probably got the stuff all over your clothes."

You're unlikely to encounter a more pathetic sight than your scrawny excuse for a father trying to pick at his wounds without moving his fingers. Jenny didn't know whether to scream or cry.

Instead, she took a trip to the pump, heated the cooking kettle, filled a tin bath with warm water, strung up a modesty curtain, and instructed her dad to soap himself down.

Then she took another trip to the pump, put on her working gloves, picked up her father's clothes, and stuffed them into a stew pot. She'd have to soak them with lye, she reckoned, to strip out the poisonous oil.

Hapless emerged from his bath with his long johns

damp and his rashes shining. Jerking with agony, he sat down on the floor and stuck his hands under his butt.

"I don't know what kind of curing Mrs. Quinn was expecting, but I don't think plants are going to do her much good."

In lieu of a direct reply, Jenny stirred his socks into the pot with a rod. "Sorry, Dad. I should have told you to wear gloves."

"Lordy, Jenny, I should have realized. I'm hopeless at brainwork, that's the trouble."

That was always the trouble with the Burns family, thought Jenny. No brains and no luck. She stared at the murky water and pondered where the two of them might be headed next. Someplace wet, most likely— wet and swarming with sandflies. Kam had told her of places on the west coast with mud eight feet deep. She hated mud.

"Something bothering you?" asked Hapless.

Without knowing quite where the desire came from, Jenny felt the need to hear that there was good and truth to life. That her presence on the planet might still have some uncharted meaning.

"Dad," said Jenny, looking up from the water, "can you tell me again how you met Mum?"

"You sure?" Hapless sniffed. "Talk of your mum always makes you growly."

"Please," insisted Jenny.

"Well, now," said Hapless, grinning his grin and clamping his hands ever tighter, "I first met your mum on a fine summer's day in the port of Tooray. I'd come from the prairies, and she'd come from the islands. We were both looking to earn enough money for a new life. And we fell in love." Hapless sighed happily. "Just like that."

"Where did you meet her?" asked Jenny.

"She was tending counter in one of the supply shops next to the water. Prettiest girl I'd ever seen. I must have bought eight pounds of flour that day to have the pleasure of conversing with her."

Absent of mind, Hapless slipped his hand from his seat and scratched at his neck. Jenny slapped his arm away.

"You'll only make it worse. Wait." She pulled two rags from the bucket next to her and wound them around her father's fingers. "Keep these on for a while."

Hapless gazed at his bandages. "I look like a crab wearing mittens."

"Could be worse," joked Jenny. She was softened to see him so helpless. "You could be a trout."

The tops of her father's words were tinged with longing. "Your mum used to talk about fish on her islands. 'Creatures of every color of the rainbow,' she said, 'striped and spiny and bug-eyed and starry. Like a bed of living flowers.'" Hapless sniffed. "She had a way of picturing things that stuck in your mind."

Jenny hesitated slightly before asking the next question. "Did she miss her family?"

"Seldom spoke about 'em," mused Hapless. "When we got married, and she came to live with me here, in secret-like, I got the impression she was running away from something. But I didn't want to ask."

This was the point that Jenny had been working herself up to ever since the argument between Louis and Annie in the parlor. "But *why* didn't you ask, Dad? Why didn't you want to know about her family and her people and where she'd come from?"

Hapless stared at his daughter. "I loved her. What did it matter?"

What did it matter? Oh, lordy, lordy, how could Jenny make her dad understand? For how can you describe what it's like being caught between heaven and hills? How do you explain what it means to be the daughter of a question mark?

And how could she ask someone to live in her skin? Jenny knew that one of the reasons folks ignored her was because her dad was pale and her mum was from the islands. She knew it and scorned it. She had the rocks and the rivers and the air.

Only how do you know who you *are*? That was the worry that was gnawing at her. Is it your blood and your parents that govern the person you'll be? Or is it your longings and your loves that make the difference?

Or is it a mishmash of everything?

"You've got smoke coming out your ears," said Hapless.

"Sorry, Dad, I was thinking."

"You and your mum. Peas in a pod."

Jenny threw the rod at the wall. "Oh, boil your own clothes! I'm going to bed."

Life, I have learned, enjoys nothing more than a good joke. All Jenny wanted was to be alone and free from peas. And whom did she meet the next day on a bright Wednesday morning? Kam on his way toward the spot where her Cathedral tree stood.

"Hello, Jenny Girl."

"Hello, Kam." A fantail brushed past Jenny's cheek and perched on a branch overhanging the Arrow. She could feel her cheeks start to burn, and she did her best to make her voice sound breezy. "Where you bound?"

"I thought I'd drown myself in the river."

"Tough luck," said Jenny. "It's far too shallow."

She wished she were joking. The Arrow was now only five to six inches deep and still falling. Kam would have had trouble drowning his toenails.

"You skipping school today?"

"Yes," said Jenny. "You skipping work?"

Kam raised his eyes to the sharp blue sky. "Changing streams."

That did it. Whatever Jenny felt—or didn't feel—about Kam, she knew he was hurting something awful. A surge of human kindness swept through her, floating her hand toward his.

"Come and have lunch."

It felt strange to invite a boy into the Cathedral, a bit like the first time you go sliding on a frozen pond. Jenny was torn between explaining the merits of her volcano code, rearranging Pandora's ordered rocks, and fleeing for safety. She felt herself blushing again and tried not to smile.

Kam was ignorant of her troubles. On any given yesterday, he might have savored the rippled sand and the tangled threads that ran through the roots. Today he sat with his back against the riverbank and said nothing.

"I've got heaps of bread and jam," explained Jenny, reaching for her bag. "Dad says we should use it up before we—"

She stopped. She hadn't told Kam about leaving the valley.

"Before you have to go away," finished Kam wearily.

Jenny rocked on her heels. "When did you hear?" she asked.

"Mr. Polk told me at the bank. He said a lot of folks were moving on."

Jenny dropped down next to Kam and handed him a sandwich. "You went to the bank to ask Mr. Polk for a loan, didn't you?"

Kam nodded. "For the garden. To keep us going until the rains. He wouldn't give it to me. He said it was a matter of territory policy. We don't have any savings. So the bank has taken Little Eden away."

The strain of anguish in her friend's voice was almost past bearing. Jenny wanted the old Kam back, the one who gave her lectures on tubers and fertilizing. "What happens now?"

"We'll go looking for gold."

And that was the killer. After what Jenny had seen and heard of the Rush, she knew how hopeless things must be if the Lum brothers were thinking of taking up mining.

Kam threw down his sandwich. *"Gam Saan!"* he said bitterly.

"Pardon?"

"That's what my father called the peak by the Long-shank," said Kam. "Gam Saan, the gold mountain. It's where we are going, to the old Chinese settlement."

"You think it's worth the effort?"

"Many of the miners in the first years of the Rush were careless," said Kam. "It is possible we might find something that others missed."

Jenny had little hope for this. If any gold was lurking around the Longshank River, it would be more like flakes of dandruff than lumps of coal. She could see a time in the near future when Kam might be stuck on a ship bound for nowhere.

Or back to his roots.

"Kam"—Jenny hesitated—"do you remember anything about your country?"

"This is my country," retorted Kam.

Jenny drew a hasty breath. In her quest to understand whether it was her passions or her bloodline that dictated her fate, she had never thought to consider that Kam might be having the same feelings. He, too, had been made to feel like an outsider in his own home. He, too, was rooted by a deep love to Eden. There and then, Jenny vowed to listen hard before she made assumptions about people.

"Sorry, I meant your father's country."

Thankfully, her apology seemed to come as a relief rather than an affront. With a nod to the Arrow, Kam clasped his hands together and rested them on his knees.

"I remember a little. I was very young when we left, but I recall the voice of my mother and the way the mist slept in the hollows of the fields. My father was fatherless, but he owned land and two shops in the village. We weren't badly off."

Jenny sneaked a peek at Kam's face. She could imagine him, a serious little boy, crouched in the river sand, tracing the tracks of an ant.

"Why did you leave?"

"The rebellion came. My father said there was heavy fighting—soldiers camping on the floor and rotting corpses floating in the canals. Then the crops failed and my mother and her parents died and villagers took to eating grass."

Kam paused. Jenny was sure he was remembering something he didn't care to relate. A minute later, he began again.

"My father heard from his friend that ships were sailing men to the goldfields. 'They need strong arms,' his friend said. 'The land is cheap, and they like honest workers.' I guess my father could have left us with strangers, or tried to find another wife in the city, but he didn't. He spent his last money on a ship's passage and sailed for Gam Saan. Where he died by a mountain, broken and old."

Jenny had seldom heard Kam speak with such sorrow. They had chatted many a time about frightening things, about lightning strikes and losing your path in the night. But this was different. This was tragedy.

"Well, at least you'll still be near town," said Jenny, doing her best to find stars in a cloudy night. "That's something. I don't know where my dad and I are headed next."

Kam's smile could have broken the heart of the ocean.

"I had a lot of plans for Little Eden, Jenny Girl. You would hardly believe them."

Jenny had the uncomfortable sensation that Kam was talking about more than irrigation channels. "You mean your greenhouse?" she babbled. "And your tree nursery? Is that what you mean?"

"Yes, that's what I mean," said Kam, taking pity. "Plans for the nursery. I was hoping to try to grow maidenhair, the silver fruit. It has a very beautiful leaf—a fan." Kam drew the shape in the sand. "In the autumn, it turns to gold."

His eyes began to grow raw around the rims and Jenny searched for something to say.

"How about flowers?" she asked, a stubborn memory kicking at her head. "Weren't you going to grow flowers, too?"

"Ladies like flowers," conceded Kam.

"Especially roses," said Jenny. "Though I suppose we've got enough of those with all the briar growing wild."

Her diversion was having an effect. The color had returned to Kam's face, and he was assuming his customary role of tutor.

"You're wrong there, Jenny Girl. Briar roses aren't wild. They were brought here by miners—I harvest their fruit every year."

"Fruit from roses?" asked Jenny skeptically. "What can you make with that?"

"Tea, wine." Kam picked up his sandwich and dusted off the dirt. "Jam, jelly, marmalade. I'm surprised you didn't know that, seeing how much you roam around the mountains."

Jenny was starting to regret her strategy. Kam looked far too loving for her liking. "Yes, well, I'm no cook."

"Or doctor," said Kam.

Jenny's heart skipped. "Why did you say that?" she asked.

"What?"

"Doctor," said Jenny.

"Oh," said Kam, "I suppose I'm remembering the flower grove that Dr. Magee planted in the Crooked Man, up the Gorge on the road toward Troy. The syrup from rose hips is used for medicine to prevent colds, treat burns, improve digestion . . ."

Jenny was listening to Kam, but she was no longer hearing him. She was remembering the feel of a wooden chest in her hand and the scent of its petals and the triangular panels that crisscrossed to form a faint but unmistakable X.

"Kam, the place you're talking about in the Gorge—does it have a name?"

Kam rubbed the scar on his eyebrow.

"I believe . . ." He paused and smiled. "Yes, I remember now. Rosewood."

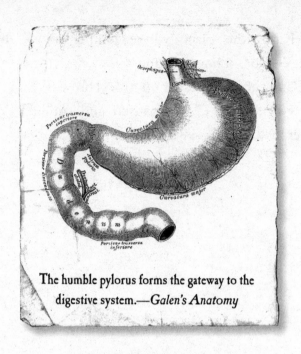

The humble pylorus forms the gateway to the
digestive system.—*Galen's Anatomy*

CHAPTER 13

"I don't understand. First you said the hunt was
over and you were giving up and yelling at me. Now
you want to go with Kam through the Gorge of the
Crooked Man because of a flower syrup that makes
it easier to eat your vittles? What do vittles have to do
with anything?"

Jenny bit her tongue. Explaining her theory to
Pandora was proving more fettlesome than expected.
She would have done it yesterday, but her father had
insisted on moving the flock down from Mount Lister.

By the time she had returned to town at eight, Pandora was away with her dreams.

The soonest she could get to Mrs. Quinn's flat was Thursday morning before school. Needs must when the devil drives, as they say. Jenny took a deep breath, choked a little on the mold from Pandora's blanket, and tried again.

"It's a hunch," said Jenny. "About the name of Magee's grove."

"What about it?" asked Pandora.

"Stick your face in this and tell me what you smell."

Jenny held the wooden chest close to Pandora's bony nose.

"I'm stuffed up," said Pandora.

"Try!"

Pandora took a tentative sniff. "Roses?"

"Do you understand?" asked Jenny.

Pandora shook her head and pulled on her plait.

"The chest wasn't a dead end," explained Jenny. "It's a clue! To the next stage of the hunt."

"There's no paper or letter with it," noted Pandora.

"I know!" said Jenny. "And that's the point! You said yourself that the paper clues were pretty easy. Maybe that's because Dr. Galen's letter was leading us down a false path. Maybe we'll find the nugget or another clue in the grove. And I'll bet you my best pair of knickers that the chest is made of rosewood—do you understand? It's a pun. Magee loved puns."

Using the leavings from her toast, Pandora began laying her crumbs in a grid. "Well, I hate them."

Stories of adventure always omit negotiations like this. Pandora was Jenny's best friend, and a smart one at that. It would be foolish to leave her brain behind. But Jenny did wonder why she had to spend three hours out of every day explaining things.

"So you'll come?" insisted Jenny. "To see if I'm right?"

"I think we should try to find Silent Jack instead," said Pandora. "He could tell us lots of things about Magee."

"Don't you see? If the nugget is buried in the rosewood, it won't matter anymore about Jack." Jenny threw a worried glance to the window. Light was already bleaching the tips of the buildings and Eden was yawning in protest. They couldn't wait much longer if they wanted to get through the Gorge and back in one day.

"What about your dad? Won't he expect you to work?" asked Pandora.

"I told him I had to help the Lums," retorted Jenny. "Besides, I gave him a hand yesterday. He can take care of himself today."

"But how does the rosewood tally with the skeleton

map? And why do we have to go now?" asked Pandora. "We have school."

"We'll find out about the map when we get there!" said Jenny, exasperated out of all reckoning. "And we have to go now because Kam said he would show us where the grove is before he heads over to the Longshank. It's my last chance, Pandora." She jumped off the bed to end the argument. "Otherwise I'm leaving forever."

Pandora placed the last crumb in the corner.

"So you'll come?"

Her best friend looked up. "Okay," she said. "But you can't tell the Lum brothers what we're looking for—I want that money for Mum." She added an afterthought. "And I get to do the packing."

The best resources for planning an expedition are money and time. Since our duo had neither, they were left to scrounge what they could from the kitchen. Unfortunately for them, the kitchen was also the dining room, living room, and sickroom. And though Mrs. Quinn was as sick as the dog that swallowed the cat, she had just enough energy left to be curious.

"What are you doing, Pandora?"

"Packing," her daughter said, stuffing socks, mittens, canteens, cheese, biscuits, extra bootlaces, and two pairs of oilskins into their satchels. Weather can turn on a penny in the mountains, so it's best to be prepared for searing heat and polar blasts. And, now and again, monsoons.

"You need all of that for school?"

"We're headed outside for class," fibbed Jenny. "A nature trip. With Mr. Grimsby."

It was tricky for Jenny to know where to look. In the past week, Mrs. Quinn had faded even further into the woodwork. Her eyeballs were about the only things detectable. In another month, she'd be no more than a wee tinny voice.

"Mr. Grimsby," sighed Mrs. Quinn, "is a very strange man. He came into the sweet shop yesterday asking me about baked beans and pork. Why would I have pork?"

Sod it! thought Jenny. The schoolmaster's curiosity was going to spoil the whole thing. She shrugged.

"Darned if I know. You finished, Pandora?"

"Yes," said Pandora, planting an oversize straw hat on her pate and heading for the door.

"We've got to be going," explained Jenny to Mrs. Quinn, "before we miss the bell." She buckled her satchel. "We might be a little late back, so I asked Dad to drop by at teatime and see if you need anything. You'll excuse us, won't you?"

The corner of Mrs. Quinn's mouth, barely visible

amid the dust motes, twitched. "Only if you'll excuse me."

Pinched by her instinct, Jenny paused on the threshold. She had a funny feeling she should remember what she saw.

There was nothing askew—the latch on the stove door was still missing, the plank in the floor was still cracked, pineapple knobs still graced the corners of Mrs. Quinn's bed—but time seemed suspended, like a raindrop caught on a bubble of glass. The faintest breath might make the whole room vanish.

"Have fun, girls."

Jenny caught up to her friend at the bottom of the squeaking stairs.

"Pandora, wait! Did you hear what your mum said about pork and beans? That means Mr. Grimsby was searching around the rocks near God's Army! He's been tracking us!"

"You have a very dramatic way of talking," said Pandora.

Jenny did her best to accommodate. "Sorry. All I meant was, we should be careful getting to the rosewood. He's teaching today, but if the schoolmaster hears that we've been walking toward the Gorge, he'll be even more suspicious."

"Mr. Grimsby doesn't know about the skeleton

map. But he probably noticed the earth where we dug up the key. And he was at the bank," said Pandora, bowed double by the weight of her satchel. "You're right. He will be suspicious. We'd better separate in case folks are watching."

"I'll take the river path," said Jenny, "and meet you by Blair's Gate in a quarter of an hour."

Jenny watched for a moment while her friend shuffled along Main Street. Then she ducked down the alley next to the Last Chance Saloon and headed for the river.

Weather was in the air; she could taste it. The sky above Eden had been a stew of gray since dawn, and clouds were sitting heavy on the peaks. Swallows fell like meteors from the treetops and skimmed across the Arrow. That meant insects were lying low. Rain was on its way.

She pushed the worry aside. Pandora was toting enough equipment to rival a donkey, and Kam would be with them. Of course, Kam might be crying. Or moping. Or giving her looks that rearranged her interior. But she would have to risk it. Straightening her shoulders, she set off for the gate that marked the start of the route to Troy. With each swing of her step, Jenny's temperature rose. Her fever had returned. She was on the hunt for gold once more.

You're not to blame if you haven't heard of Troy. It's one of those towns that came and went with the Rush, hardly begun before it was shuttered.

Besides, it's almost impossible to get to at the best of times. The shortest way to reach it is to walk or ride through the Gorge, wading across creeks and slogging up hillsides. On a day without hitches, the hike might take eight hours.

On top of that trial, the Gorge is part of the Crooked Man—the guts and bowels of an alpine range—and the Crooked Man is not an easy place to explore. It was formed when the ground was heaved up by the clashing of continents, tilted ninety degrees, and sliced through with water. The peaks of its mountains are sharp and the embankments are steep. Take a false step and you'll plunge to your doom.

That's why Jenny loved it, of course. It was a dangerous and daring place, far too risky for sheep. She had often wanted to explore the Gorge, push past the six-mile mark where she usually halted, and learn what lurked in the vitals. But Gentle Annie had warned her never to do it alone. The path was unstable and flash floods were common. If you were going to try to kill yourself, advised Annie, take someone with you.

Moreover, since Kam was always working and Pandora was never keen, this was the first time in Jenny's life that she had the prospect of seeing what lay beyond her imagination. She was rising with the happiness of this thought as she approached Blair's Gate—a folde-rol of iron put there by a farmer to stop his stock from wandering into the Gorge.

Three souls were waiting for her. Kam was gaz-ing at the Arrow, Lok was fidgeting, and Pandora was tracing the edges of leaves in the gate's metalwork.

"Hello, Jenny Girl," said Kam. "Ready to pick some roses?"

Jenny smiled awkward-like and shrugged. "I guess."

"I'd offer to carry your satchel," said Kam, hoisting a giant pack on his back, "but we must take what we have left to our father's hut."

Lok snorted.

"I am sorry, Lok—did you want to say something?" asked Kam. Apparently, Jenny wasn't the only one having difficulty with negotiations that day.

"No."

"Because I would like you to say something if you have something to say." Kam paused for a long second. "Good. Then I think we should move on."

"Lok is angry because we're making you trek up the wrong river," blurted out Pandora. "It's going to take you an extra half day to climb across the moun-tains and into the Longshank valley."

Kam scrutinized the gorse on the hillside, and

Jenny adjusted her satchel.

"I am right," insisted Pandora. "That's why you're mad, isn't it, Lok?"

"I've always thought," said Lok, "that older brothers don't appreciate how hard it is to be carrying eighty pounds of equipment."

"I've always found," retorted Kam, "that younger brothers don't worry enough about the safety of their private parts."

"Off we go," said Lok, hastily opening the gate.

In spite of some grumbles, the first few miles or so of the hike were remarkably civilized. The dry road was smooth, the gray sky was cool, and—thanks to the drought—the river crossings were but a hop and a skip to the other side.

After an hour of zigzagging along the bottom of the Gorge, they began a slow and steady jog toward higher ground. With their heights about equal, Jenny and Kam fell into an easy rhythm.

"What do you think you're going to find among the roses?" asked Kam.

"Dunno," said Jenny. "But I'm hopeful about staying in Eden."

"I would like that," said Kam.

"I'm hungry!" griped Pandora from the rear.

"I'm tired!" called Lok.

"Tough," said Kam. "We have miles to go before the grove."

Jenny was doing her best to ignore the prickles. Somehow, in the past twenty-four hours, her friendship with Kam had gone from a simple bond to a deeper grace. She knew it; Kam knew it. The whole thing made her feel slightly queasy. She paused.

"Are you going to hurl again?" asked Pandora.

"No," said Jenny. "Be quiet."

"She barfed on her father's shoes," said Pandora to Lok. "Spewed it six feet."

"Impressive," said Lok.

"Pandora, I told you to be quiet."

"You're not my foreman."

"Yes, you're not her foreman," repeated Lok.

"Everybody throws up now and again," said Kam sympathetically.

"Fine," said Jenny, putting on a burst of speed to get ahead of them all. "I'm fine."

For a few blissful moments, she was on her own, the road in front of her growing tighter and twistier and the clouds ever lower. High as she was with the peaks, she could still hear the water whispering to the trees.

God, how Jenny loved that river. Loved its youth and its anger and its truth. Whenever she had a question to answer or a trouble to face, she would stand at the edge of the Arrow and watch it flow over the rocks of creation. It told her that there was something bigger in the world than worries.

"Everything okay?" asked Kam, coming along beside her once more.

"I'm fine," repeated Jenny, meaning it. "I'm listening to the Arrow."

"It is beautiful," said Kam. He stopped and peered into the Gorge. "And it will look even better with the rain." He paused. "The water would have been good for my garden."

Jenny's initial instinct had been right. A fine mist of drizzle was beginning to tickle the shrub daisies. She swallowed.

"I don't like what you have to do, Kam."

"Me neither," said Kam, "but who else in the territory can I ask for help?"

"Mr. Grimsby!"

"I doubt he would be much use," scoffed Kam.

"No, Mr. Grimsby!" repeated Lok, yanking on his brother's pack and pointing. "There."

Jenny wheeled in her tracks. At the bottom of the Gorge, tucked in among the thistle and the broom, was the unmistakable form of the schoolmaster. From a distance, he bore a marked resemblance to a stick insect.

"Jenny Burns! I need to talk to you!"

"Oh, goobers and gum!" cried Jenny. "How did he find us?"

"He probably followed me from Main Street," said Pandora. "I'm pretty noticeable."

"But why isn't he teaching school?" asked Jenny.

"Dunno," said Lok.

"He's coming this way," said Pandora.

The stick insect was on the move, leaping over the very same stones that the hikers had hit only a half hour before. A lethal black string swung by his side.

"He's got his switch with him," noted Pandora.

"I can see that!" said Jenny. "Would you like to stand here and ask him what it's for?"

"That's a silly question. Why would I—"

"Oh, c'mon!" said Jenny. "Run!"

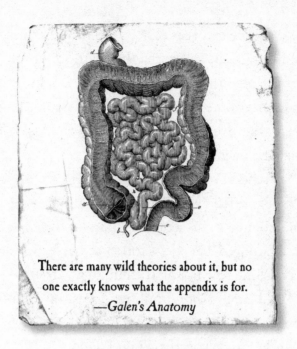

There are many wild theories about it, but no
one exactly knows what the appendix is for.
—*Galen's Anatomy*

CHAPTER 14

It was a stiffer chase than the one on the Sleeping Girl,
and rougher than rocks. Pandora was rusty, Jenny was
weary, and Kam and Lok were loaded for bear.

Plus, as luck would have it, the rain was picking up
steam. First it was a trickle, then a thrum, then a long,
steady beat. The hard road, which for nine months had
resembled cracked leather, began to soften and squish.
It took twice as much effort to lift one's feet as it had in
the step before.

"Are there any side routes?" panted Jenny. A curtain of murk had fallen between pursuer and pursued.

"Any place we can veer off?"

Kam nodded, splattering her with droplets. "One. There's a path that cuts across to the Longshank valley, a quarter mile ahead."

"He's sure to catch us before then," said Jenny. "What are we going to do?"

"Surrender," wheezed Pandora.

"No," puffed Lok, "hide."

He pointed to his left. Teetering on the edge of the road, a hundred feet above the roiling Arrow, was a fat mass of stone resembling the hub of a wheel.

"We'll stay there until he gives up and turns around," said Kam.

"Or fall to our deaths," said Pandora.

"Nobody is going to do that," said Jenny, losing her footing slightly as she made for the rock, "if we're very, very careful."

Clutching her satchel to her navel, Jenny edged herself around the lee of the stone. There were a scarce six inches between her and the side of the cliff. When she held her breath, she could hear the river churning with newfound rage. Even one of God's own angels would admit that the situation didn't allow much room for optimism.

Kam came after her, then Pandora, then Lok. It was past comprehension that Lok was standing upright—his pack was resting like a turtle shell on his stomach.

At any moment, he might somersault forward into the abyss.

"Can you hear him?" Jenny muttered to Kam. Her nose had begun to run with fear.

"Shhhh," whispered Kam.

"Double, double mud and trouble" came a familiar voice from the road. "Thunder sound and rivers bubble. Heaven take the hindmost, what a godforsaken country."

Jenny risked a swipe of her sleeve and an inch of remaining cliff tumbled into the Gorge. Fortunately for her flesh, the sounds of the downpour drowned the fall.

"Jenny Burns? Jenny Burns, do you heed me? I need to talk to you."

Jenny sniffed. She'd talked enough.

"Horn-backed toads and fustilarians," grumbled Mr. Grimsby. "My bunions do ache."

The schoolmaster's maledictions grew fainter and fainter until—finally—they faded altogether.

"Do you think it's safe?" whispered Jenny.

"Wait a tick," muttered Kam.

They waited. A few minutes later, Jenny heard sounds of the schoolmaster returning.

"Bull pizzle and prunes!" said Mr. Grimsby. "Where did they go?"

Gradual as the day, his voice grew softer, falling

back toward the road to Eden. When Jenny was sure she could hear him no more, she nudged Kam in the ribs. First Lok, then Pandora, then Kam shuffled their feet back to safety.

Jenny was on the verge of returning when she slipped. For a moment, she found herself flying, her arms outstretched and her body weightless. A hard yank on her satchel brought her sprawling back to earth.

"Wow," said Pandora wonderingly. "You almost died."

Jenny rolled off Kam's pack. "Are you okay?" she asked.

Kam opened his eyes. "Yes."

Oh, pepper and pots, thought Jenny, who found her cheeks flaming and her hairs rising. Not again.

She scrambled to her feet and smoothed the mud through her hair. "Then I guess we should split up now."

"Huh?" said Lok.

"Why?" asked Pandora.

"Because," babbled Jenny to Kam, "Mr. Grimsby is still out there, and we'll stand less of a chance of being spotted if we're not in such a large group. Besides, it will save you time if you take this path to the Long-shank. Pandora and I will head toward the rosewood, and you and Lok can make for your dad's hut."

"You want to keep walking?" asked Kam. "In this kind of weather?"

"Yes, I do." Jenny's pulse was pounding beneath the nape of her neck, but she ignored it. "Rain doesn't bother me any."

"It bothers me," said Pandora.

"You don't have to come," retorted Jenny. "You can head home."

"I'd meet Mr. Grimsby."

"Then go off with Lok!"

Jenny had reached the point in everyone's life when your head runs away from your heart. I've been in that race myself, and it's pointless to halt it.

"I'll go with Jenny," said Pandora. "I think she's busted her brain."

Kam was standing in the road, his eyes full of questions. "You want to leave me?"

"Yes," said Jenny. "It's for the best."

Rivulets of freezing rain were coursing down Kam's cheeks. He blinked. "Then we will wait here for a few minutes. You may walk ahead. The turnoff for the grove is at a blind corner, where the road widens and straightens. You will see it."

"Thanks," said Jenny, seizing hold of her friend. "Let's go, Pandora."

"Wait," said Lok. He held out his hand to Pandora. "Hand me your hat."

"Why?"

"Trust me."

Pandora took off her hat and gave it to Lok. "You speak when you have something to say. I like you."

After this astonishing admission, there was little left to discuss. Jenny and Pandora trudged for the hills, and Kam and Lok lingered a moment to rearrange their packs. For minutes, Jenny would not allow herself to look back. She would not admit there was anything worth looking back for.

The girls passed the rock. They passed the side route that led to the Longshank. They arrived at the highest point of the road. Only then did Jenny pause and glance behind her.

And as she did, the stone that they had hid behind lost its bearings and fell into the river.

❧

"Kam saved your life."

Jenny lowered her head and sloshed through six inches of churning soil that had once been a barren side stream. Water was gushing down her neck, through her sleeves, and out her fingertips. She was drenched from top to toe.

"I said," shouted Pandora from the depths of her oilskin, "KAM SAVED YOUR LIFE."

"I know that!" said Jenny, slipping on moss and

saving herself by bruising her knee. "I haven't lost my hearing."

"You didn't say thank you."

"Kam knows how I feel."

"That you like him," insisted Pandora.

"I don't like him!"

They *must* be close to the grove. It had been hours since they had started at the gate. Jenny strained her eyes to see in front of her, but the world around them was a watery slop of gray and brown.

"My chest hurts," said Pandora. "A lot."

"We're almost there," replied Jenny.

"You said that ages ago."

"Well, now it's true!" Jenny had a burst of irrational spite. This whole expedition would have been much easier without a truth-telling nag plodding beside her. She should have kept her trap shut and come by herself. After all, what law was there to say that she had to share the gold?

Luckily for Jenny's sanity, Pandora had begun wheezing too hard to issue any more complaints. They marched on into the afternoon, limbs freezing and nostrils numb.

Finally, at the hour when Jenny thought her skin might burst from saturation, they came to Kam's blind corner.

"Thank the bejitters!" cried Jenny, barreling toward the spot. Taking it at a soggy gallop, she skidded around the bend and hit the straightway. A few yards farther down the road, a wormy path wove its way up the embankment.

With visions of nuggets dancing in her head, Jenny wasn't going to wait for Pandora to catch up. She scrambled and clawed and cursed her way along the path, smashing leaves and branches as she went.

At the same time as she was scrambling, she was considering. What was she driving toward? Another box within a box? A fearsome code to crack? Or maybe—yes, maybe—a subtle trap. Thunder rolled through the canyon as the trees began to thin. Her heart thumped. She was almost there. But what, she whispered to herself, would she find?

～

She found a dead end. What had once been a grove of red roses, light with the joy of living, was now a patch of scorched wood clinging to the side of the mountain. You could have shot Jenny through with an arrow and I doubt she would have flinched. She was shocked out of reckoning.

A flash of lightning illuminated the sky as her best friend emerged from the bush.

"Bugger."

Pandora's oath loosened Jenny's jaw. "Oh, why don't you stow it, Pandora!"

Pandora threw her satchel over a stub of dead vines. "No, I will not stow it!" She pointed an accusing finger. "You've been doing silly things all week, and I'm tired of keeping my mouth shut."

"Like what?" challenged Jenny.

"Like being mean to Kam for no reason," retorted Pandora. "Like lying to Gentle Annie. Like not speaking out when Louis was insulting the Lum brothers. You didn't stick up for them once."

"Neither did you!" retorted Jenny.

"I don't like talking to people!"

Now, in the course of my long and eventful life, I have had spats with many a friend. I say something hasty; he says something pointed; we take a beat, remember our good fortune, and shake hands.

But Jenny and Pandora weren't having a spat. They were having a fight. And a fight with a best friend is the most dangerous kind in the world. Best friends are privy to your deepest fears and worries. They know your weaknesses inside out. They've seen you pee your pants or lose your mind or maybe even kill a man.

In times of trial, this kind of information is often a comfort. In a fight with your soulmate, it's ammunition.

"Really?" asked Jenny. "That's odd. Because you seemed to be quite chatty with my dad and your mum. You talk to people all right. You just talk to the ones who you think are dumb."

"That's not true!"

A second roll of thunder provided the bass to Jenny's insults.

"You always moan about being teased because you're different, but you *like* it, Pandora. You like being cold and strange and standing outside of the world. You say you're afraid to talk to other kids, but you don't even want to try. And now I know why!" cried Jenny, mistaking her anger for insight. "It's because you're scared! You're scared that trying to behave like a normal person will make you ordinary!"

Pandora was perilously close to having a fit. She was jerking with fury, rain spurting from her like a ruptured pipe.

"I want to be ordinary *every day*," yelled Pandora. "But I can't. I watch and I watch and I don't understand. I don't understand how people behave. It makes no sense!"

Jenny was merciless. "Then you're the stupid one!"

This was the limit for Pandora. She let out a bone-rending scream and stomped her foot. "You're horrible! You're horrible and you're mean and you lie to yourself!"

"I do not!"

"People talk about your mother behind your back!"

Jenny felt as if she had been punched in the heart.

"They say you're darker than your dad, and they call you awful names, and they laugh at your family. And you pretend not to hear!" Pandora was screeching now, her throat hoarse with rage. "You know what they're saying and you pretend that ignoring the words will make everything better. And it doesn't. This place will always hate us!"

Jenny was taking fright. Her best friend was seizing violently, her muscles galvanized with the storm's electric currents.

"You're the one who's scared!" raved Pandora. "You're scared of what people think of you. You're scared of liking Kam. You're scared of leaving Eden and finding out that the world doesn't care who you are!"

At Pandora's last word, a bolt of lightning cracked through the sky and sliced open the hull of a pine tree. Jenny shrieked and Pandora screamed as the entire hillside gave way beneath their feet.

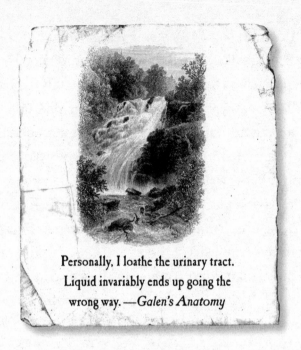

Personally, I loathe the urinary tract.
Liquid invariably ends up going the
wrong way. —*Galen's Anatomy*

CHAPTER 15

A mudslide is seldom something you want to be stuck in. Trust me—I've toured a city swallowed by one, and all that was left when the dirt had settled were tiles and teeth. Jenny was fortunate to be riding the slide on top of a snarl of roots. Otherwise, she might have been sucked into the center of the churn.

A few seconds later, she was shunted sideways by a tree trunk and chucked onto the flat of the road. She lay there, petrified, as half the mountain—and her satchel—cannoned toward the bottom of the Gorge.

"Pandora!"

There was no response except the pounding of rain.

"*Pandora!*"

A pause. Then . . .

"What?"

Jenny searched the high ground as best she could, but, for the life of her, she wasn't able to locate her best friend. "Where are you?"

"That's a stupid question—I'm in the Gorge!"

Apparently the mudslide hadn't dampened Pandora's energy for a fight.

"Are you hurt?" called Jenny.

"I've got a big bump on my head." Pandora's voice rose a decibel. "But I can still remember exactly what you said!"

Well, there's gratitude for you, thought Jenny. Here she was trying to make sure no one was punctured in eight places, and she was being roundly insulted for it.

"Pandora, we can kill each other some other time. But we need to get you out of there first. Can you see the road to Troy?"

Another pause.

"No."

This wasn't good. Night would be sweeping in behind the storm. Once that happened, things were liable to get dicey. And very, very dark.

"How about a waterfall at the head of the river? Can you see that?" From her vantage point, Jenny could spy the foam from the whitecaps near its top. "Kam said there's one that comes out of Lake Gaia near Troy."

"I think I see a waterfall."

That was a blessing, at any rate.

"Can you get to it from where you are?" asked Jenny.

"Probably. Unlike other people, I'm not stupid!"

Jenny was almost relieved Pandora wasn't standing next to her. She would have been tempted to toss her best friend right back over the edge. "Okay, you aim for the waterfall. I'll walk along the road and wait for you there. Have you still got your satchel?"

"Yes, but my cheese is in yours," said Pandora.

Jenny yanked a branch from her hair. "I lost my satchel in the mudslide."

"You didn't save my cheese?"

"Pandora!" yelled Jenny, plucking a web of thorns out of her backside. "Be quiet and get to the waterfall before it's dark!"

Though her best friend tried to be silent, Jenny could hear sounds of rocks being rolled and swears being sworn. Pandora was on the move—that much was clear.

Propping up her courage, Jenny examined the road. It was plain they were in a tight spot. The rain was ebbing, sure, but frost was already forming on her sinews. They were miles from civilization and heading for a ghost town. It was going to be a rough evening.

The best thing to do, reasoned Jenny, was to find a place to shelter in Troy. The settlement was deserted, but the buildings must be hardly more than fifteen years old. With a few sticks to start, she could light a fire most anyplace. Wiping an inch of slop from the bottoms of her boots, Jenny began walking.

∽

I've often found that the problem with solitary rambles is they give you time to think. On her way toward the waterfall, Jenny was slowly recovering from her shock and quickly remembering all the awful things Pandora had said.

She *wasn't* scared, she *wasn't* less than anybody, and she most definitely *was not* in love with Kam! How dare Pandora accuse her of being ignorant of what others said? Sure, over the years, she might have heard her schoolmates call her a vicious name or four. Or forty. But that was to be expected in a place like Eden.

Besides, what was she going to do about it? Round up the entire town and tell them how it feels to live on the skin of a bubble? Give adults a lecture on the importance of avoiding words like "degenerate"? Sure, she scoffed to herself—that was certain to work.

Going round and round like this, Jenny was beginning to appreciate what it's taken me sixty-odd years to fathom. Some people are plain ignorant.

Like it or lump it, the world is full of numbskull judgers and half-cocked judgments. Wherever you go, you're bound to find folks who will peg you by the cut of your cloth, the arch of your vowels, or the hue of your hide. You can argue with them until words have run out, and they'll refuse to see reason. You're lucky if you find one that will listen at all.

I've heard many a theory as to why bullies and bigots decide to persist, but none that seem to take. If I had to make a personal guess, I'd hazard they're frightened of change. They're cozy and content to believe in a system where they sit on top of the living ladder. But they'd best be careful. People who perch on ladders are liable to have the legs kicked out from under them.

Course, at the hour and place of which we were talking, Jenny wasn't thinking on ladders and bigotry. She was still in the stages of fuming about Pandora. Around halfway through another imaginary argument with her friend, she realized that, one: she was freezing. Two: she could barely see. And three: she must have gone far, far past the place where the road would have met the waterfall.

At that point, reality came crashing down with the cold and the night. Even if Jenny retraced her steps, there was no certainty she would be able to find the location. Kam had never actually said the road went straight past the waterfall. He had only said you could spot it from a height.

That meant Pandora might be standing there for years without help.

Worse than that, Jenny was having trouble maintaining her wits. In the past hour, her feet had grown numb and difficult to maneuver. Her breath had turned quick. She felt tired and dizzy and sick to her stomach, all at the same time. She knew in the back of her mind that there must be a way out of this pickle. But she was having trouble remembering the difference between pickles and plums. Though she wasn't to know it, the fact that she was soaking wet in the cold was giving her a touch of hypothermia.

Jenny's instinct told her to stumble forward. Every path, she reasoned in her confusion, must end at some point. Maybe there was a signpost. Or a turning. Or a way to stop this gosh-darn, lousy shivering.

It was darker than pitch that evening in the high country, black as the coal in a strip mine. The storm had sent every reptile and mammal scurrying for shelter, and Jenny was alone on the high road. On she trudged through the mire as the clouds above began to thin.

Sooner rather than later, she reached a rise in the

hill. Her shivers were easing off and the tip of a crescent moon was piercing the gloom. Weak as it was, it was light, and it snagged on a shape in the land.

The lake!

Instantly, Jenny's head became clear. With the moon and the stars to guide her, she could follow the shoreline of Lake Gaia toward the waterfall. From there, like her hero Still Hope, she would rescue Pandora and bring her friend to Troy. The weather was beatable. They were going to be fine.

Down the rise she went, groping toward the water's edge. With each quarter mile, her muscles grew weaker, but she was bound and determined to succeed. No matter what you might think of her temper, you can't beat a Burns for stubbornness.

She was almost at the water—she could hear the waves slopping—when she was yanked from her feet. A strong pair of arms encircled her back and her legs.

"Blet pea snow!" burbled Jenny, flailing with her fists, incoherent from exhaustion and the cold. "Blet pea snow!"

"Shut it!" barked her carrier.

After a full day of walking, this was the end. Whatever willpower she had left was gone. Jenny lay like a limp rag, head hurled back, watching the lake and the moon and the upside-down silhouettes of outbuildings trundle by.

It was only when they reached a door and a warm blast of heat hit her eyes that she finally remembered what she was there for. And whom she was missing.

"Manpora!" she gargled. "Manpora!"

"Stop fussing, Jenny. I told you I wasn't stupid."

It took the better part of two hours to bring Jenny's core temperature up to acceptable. She was set by a cast-iron woodstove, bundled in blankets, with one wrist tied to the leg of the bench she was lying upon. This, she realized groggily, was her punishment for elbowing her savior in the abdomen.

Pandora sat opposite, airing out her oilskin and chewing on jerky.

"Waterfall," mumbled Jenny after a lengthy interval.

"I waited for a bit," said Pandora. "Then I figured you'd left me for dead."

"I tried . . ."

"I walked here and found Silent Jack, and he told me that the road veers away from the waterfall. So we calculated you were probably roaming around the lake. Freezing to death."

Jenny wrenched her head sideways to catch a glimpse of the elusive hermit, but Doc Magee's partner was nowhere to be seen. What she got instead was a stone-cold room studded with panes of glass. They winked at her in the gloom.

"Where did he go?"

"He's out fetching fuel," said Pandora. "He said he wasn't expecting visitors."

"What is this place?"

"It's the old church at Troy. Silent Jack says he sleeps better in sacred spaces."

Jenny took a closer look at the interior. Ah, there they were, at the opposite end of the building—an altar and a stone basin. Silent Jack had left some of his washing up in the bowl. Though she wasn't much for pious buildings, it appeared a respectable enough place to live.

"He seems to be pretty chatty for a silent man. Maybe years of solitude have done him good," said Jenny.

"He talked because I asked," said Pandora. "You told me I can't speak to people. Well, I can. So there."

Jenny had hoped that hours of being nose-to-nose with death might have softened Pandora's feelings. Apparently not.

"Did you question him about Doc Magee?"

"Yes," said Pandora, swallowing the last of her jerky. "And he told me to shut my mouth."

"Wonderful. Then what are we doing here?"

Pandora stood up. "We're here because you started something and couldn't finish it."

Jenny made a move to counter and was yanked back

by the rope on her wrist. "You're the one who was raring to meet Silent Jack!" she said.

"You're the one who went searching for rose hips!" retorted Pandora.

"You're the one who found the skeleton map!"

"You're the one who wanted to look for gold in the first place!"

Picture a chained dog barking at an obstinate tree and you'd have some conception of the scene that met Silent Jack when he came through the door. As soon as they saw him, Jenny and Pandora fell silent.

Holy father of bovines, thought Jenny. He's a beast.

Beastly he was—that I'm bound to report. Many a man in the territory was fond of insulation, but Silent Jack had taken the cultivation of whiskers to the extreme. He was coated in hair, from the three feet of locks that trailed from his head to the curtain of brush that fell to his knees. The centers of his ears, the backs of his hands, the hollow tucked under his Adam's apple—everything was a mass of hoary fur.

After scraping the mud from his boots, Silent Jack lugged his box of cut scrub to the stove and refilled the interior. Then he clomped his way up the aisle, collected a mug from the basin, and filled it from a bottle on the floor. He sat down at the base of the altar and took a long pull. Finally, he opened his mouth.

"Murder," he growled.

"'Scuse me, sir," said Jenny. "Did you say something?"

"I said, murder."

"Well, that's helpful," muttered Jenny to Pandora. "And here I was thinking he was reciting the alphabet."

"What kind of murder?" inquired Pandora.

Silent Jack peered at her through the thicket of his brows. "Al-vays murders in the Rush."

Jenny was feeling close to uncomfortable. It suddenly struck her that an almost-empty church in an abandoned gold town with a man talking about murder might not be the best place for two twelve-year-old girls to spend the evening.

"Did you ever kill anyone?"

"Pandora!" hissed Jenny.

"I seen it done," said Silent Jack.

Jack cocked his head and tossed back a third of his bottle. Fragments of bark quivered in his beard.

"Tell us," challenged Pandora.

"The first vun vass a shooting," said Silent Jack. "Outside a hut. Vun man said his partner vass lazy, and the other man said he looked like a voman. So the vun who looked like a voman shot the lazy vun in the stomach. His insides fell out."

Sly and silent, Jenny began to pick at the knot on her wrist.

"You said the first one. What was the second?" asked Pandora.

"The second vun vass a stabbing in the post office. A drunken miner got a good-bye from his sveetheart. So he vent vild vith a letter opener."

The knot was too tight, Jenny realized. She would need a knife. Or a letter opener.

"Any more?" demanded Pandora.

Jenny wanted to take back everything she had said about Pandora being too afraid to talk to people. At this point and place, she would have cheerfully licked her best friend's feet if it stopped her from asking this extremely hairy man what he thought of murder.

"There vass alvays murders," repeated Silent Jack. "Men should not live in the mountains. It makes them mad."

As if to echo his point, Silent Jack hurled his mug against the wall, smashing it into scores of pieces. Then he began a slow walk down the aisle toward the girls.

"Pandora, we're toast!"

Silent Jack gave no response. Instead, he kept coming, walking right on up to Jenny's left side.

"Hold still," he commanded.

In the lick of a split, he had untied the knot on her wrist and dropped the loose twine on the floor.

"Enough talking," said Silent Jack, jerking a coat

from a peg near the door. "Sleep now." He shrugged his sleeves over his pelt and gave Pandora a long and searching stare. "And lock the door."

A frigid blast of alpine wind swept through the church. In the time it took for Jenny to draw a warmer breath, Doc Magee's partner was gone.

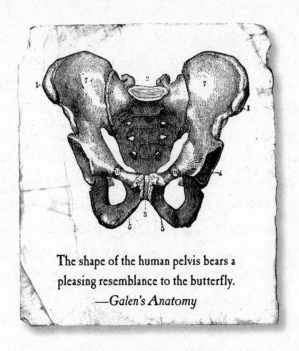

The shape of the human pelvis bears a
pleasing resemblance to the butterfly.
—*Galen's Anatomy*

CHAPTER 16

An autumn morning in the mountains, when the air
is still as glass and the peaks are brushed with snow, is
something you should experience at least once. It has a
way of clarifying priorities.

Nudged by the dawn, Jenny woke up feeling newborn. Who cared about nuggets and roses and useless
arguments? She was alive to the call of her senses: the
drought had been broken. The long rains had come.

Leaving Pandora asleep, Jenny nicked a piece of
jerky and headed for the great beyond. What she found
surpassed the boldest of her dreams.

Troy was fired in a riot of color. The blue of the sky was rimmed by the purple of sunlit rock. Caps of white crowned the mountains. In the hollow of the valley, the town was gray with wear, and green with turf, and yellow with aging oaks. Orange and red streaks, the scars of last night's polar blast, were fading from the east.

But that wasn't the best of the scenery—oh, by no means. The best of it lay in the water. Lake Gaia, that elusive stretch of dark that Jenny had tried so hard to find in the night, was now a giant mirror, reflecting every leaf and flake and speck in its surface. Up was down and down was up.

All of this was catnip to a high-country girl. Jenny wanted to run and run until thought and worry vanished. Down she dashed toward the lake, puddles splashing beneath her toes. When she was about six feet from the rim, she came to a halt. Nothing should be allowed to ruffle its surface.

Trouble being, something *was* disturbing it. A fly or a bug was making its way toward her, skimming so low that it made a trail of a snail in the water.

Closer it came, closer and closer, until Jenny was able to spy what it was. A stripe-breasted, sparrow-beaked bird with a new sheen of dew. It went whistling over her head and perched itself on a stump.

"Too late," came a familiar growl.

Jenny turned. The human tumbleweed known as Jack was emerging from a shed by the waterside.

"Pardon?" dared Jenny.

"The cuckoo should have left in summer. Now it vill die from the cold."

Silent Jack snapped his suspenders. The bird riffled its emerald feathers. Jenny had the courtesy to feel abashed.

"Thanks for letting us stay in your place last night," she said. "I appreciate it."

There was silence.

"Truly," she continued. "I know you're allergic to company."

Her host ignored her still. Curtly, he turned on his heels, stomped over to a distant tree, and—with his back turned—began peeing on its roots. The cuckoo giggled.

Jenny bit back a sigh of envy. There had been many a time when she'd wished she could pee standing up.

"I was meaning to ask," yelled Jenny. "Do you know if there was a forest fire near the head of the Gorge? There's this grove that got destroyed . . ."

She might have done better howling at time. His business through, Silent Jack buttoned his fly, brushed his hands on his trousers, and headed for the church. Her morning now spoiled, Jenny followed.

Inside the building, the ghost of last night's heat lingered around the woodstove, reluctant to return to the ashes. Pandora was busy divvying biscuits into equal portions. Jenny plonked down on the floor beside her.

"Morning," whispered Jenny. "I forgive you for what you said to me yesterday." Pandora's reply was a glare. "Fine," added Jenny. "Be like that."

"You must leave after breakfast," said Silent Jack, fishing out a box from behind the basin. "More bad vether coming."

"But the mudslide washed out the road to Eden," countered Jenny. "Nobody could go that way."

The furze refused to answer. Instead, he ripped off a hunk of cured trout from his stash and began to gnaw on the flesh.

"Why do they call you Silent Jack?" asked Pandora, following up on Jenny's comment from last night. "You speak to us."

Without skipping a bite, Silent Jack reached over his barrel of a chest and drew back the flap of his bushman's jacket. Tucked inside the lining, with its grip at a reachable height, was the end of a bone-handled revolver.

"But I let this do the talking ven the time is right."

"Were you a gunslinger? Did you use that in the Rush?" asked Pandora.

Their host responded by slamming his box on the

basin. "I hate the Rush! Men forget things."

"What things?" asked Pandora.

"They forget the land," said Silent Jack bitterly, "and the rivers that suckle them. They forget to be grateful for things they cannot see. They forget the cuckoo that stays too long."

Despite her advances in other areas of life, Pandora still had little use for poetry, in this week or the next. "What do cuckoos have to do with anything?"

"People shouldn't live in the mountains," rasped Silent Jack. "Or anyvere else. The vurld vuld be a much better place without the human race."

"Well, that makes no sense," said Pandora. "Because we're already here. Us and the rest of the animals and the plants and the seas. So we'd better find a way to muddle along together."

Jenny was grudgingly impressed. Before the mudslide, Pandora would have glued her lips to the floor to avoid conversing with someone like Jack. But here she was debating the concept of life itself.

Realizing he had been bested, Silent Jack gave Pandora a shrewd glance, picked up her satchel, and stuck out his thumb.

"Enough talk. Come vith me."

⤵

"Where are we going?" asked Jenny.

"Shut it," barked Jack.

Walking down the pitted road through town, Jenny had a fuddled notion that this might be her last day on earth. She wondered what Silent Jack was planning to do with them. Shoot them and toss them in the waterfall, perhaps? Somewhere deep and dank where their bodies would never be found? Maybe he had a nice cave in mind.

Pandora was unconcerned. Shrouded in her oilskin, she fell into lockstep with Jack. Doom be darned—the terror of Troy had met his match.

"Were you always best friends with Doc Magee?"

Jack paused beside a toothless fence. A leaf fell from a poplar above him and settled on his shoulder. "Vatt does that vurd mean to you—'friend'?"

Pandora considered the query. "I think it means someone who understands."

"Yes. Understands. That is good." He picked the leaf from his shoulder and crushed it in his palm. "But, you see, I did not understand Magee."

"Why not?" asked Jenny.

"Because he vass in love vith gold," growled Jack. "In love with a cold piece of stone? It is nonsense, no?"

This question was directed solely to one person.

"Gold can be useful," said Pandora. "My mum would find it very useful. She's dying."

Most folks would expect a civilized man to offer a few shreds of comfort to a girl who spoke these words.

Silent Jack, however, was unmoved. He tossed the shreds of leaf on the ground and resumed his march.

For a moment, Jenny was tempted to trip him for being so cold. Then she recalled her own wish to keep the nugget all for herself. Sad to say, she hadn't once thought of Mrs. Quinn or her condition since they had started up the Gorge.

"Did you fight with Magee?" asked Pandora, still nipping at his heels.

"Sometimes. Do you fight vith your friend?"

"Yes," said Pandora. "A lot, lately."

In the flash of a firefly, Jenny had a revelation. Maybe *Jack* had killed Doc Magee! He was tougher than oak, that was plain, and plenty used to violence. Maybe he had murdered his partner but missed out on the nugget. That would account for his wanderings. And his foul temper . . .

"So what did you do when Magee found the gold?" blurted out Jenny.

Silent Jack paused in front of the entrance to a forge. Startled by his presence, a long-legged spider skittered across the anvil and launched itself skyward on a line of silk.

"You know about the nugget?"

"Sure," countered Jenny. "Everybody in the territory knows."

Jack gave Jenny a look that went straight through

her marrow and lodged itself in her spine. She observed that his eyes were of a peculiar color, like the wet of a greenstone polished by rubbing.

"He vent a-vay," said Silent Jack. "And I never saw him again."

Think what you will about Jenny, she's got hold of something I wish more of us had. She can read the truth of people. Even when she was knee-high to a hare, she could tell that Pandora was a lost, loving girl and Mr. Polk was a right royal twit. These aren't things that you'd spot on the skin; they're embedded in the soul. And, to her surprise, in searching Jack's stare, she knew that he was being honest. She believed him—Magee had gone away. Jack had never seen him again.

Yet, at the exact same time, she was alive to the fact that he wasn't telling them the whole truth. Whether his partner was alive or dead, Jack knew more than he was speaking. She found herself smiling. The mystery of Mad Doc Magee was becoming very interesting.

Silent Jack didn't have a clue what to do with a girl who smiled. Flummoxed by Jenny's reaction, he tugged at his beard and scratched at his cheek and drew the wing of a fly from his eyelash. Then he shook his head.

"Come."

From the forge and the anvil, they trudged past a couple of saggy-lipped storefronts and a creaky hitching post. The wind had regained some of its breath and was muttering to a curtain that hung in one of the windows. I tell you true, it was a haunted place, that valley of Troy. Haunted and odd.

Finally, they reached the last building in town. To the south stretched Lake Gaia, sprinkled with the dust of the sun. In front of them ran a footpath that curved and cut into a tract of native beeches, leading west toward an unknown fate. And to their immediate north, at the scuffed end of their elbows, was a jail.

It was a small jail, to be sure—a crumbling cube of limestone and one lonely window with bars. But it was enough of an establishment to make Jenny's feet twitch. Then she noticed it was missing a key component. This made her feel better. It's hard to keep someone penned in without a front door.

"Why are we stopping here?" asked Pandora.

Silent Jack pointed a furred finger toward the path. "Take that and you vill cross a bridge near the head of the Longshank."

Jenny swallowed. The Longshank was where Kam and Lok had gone.

"Follow the riverbank down and you vill find a long route back to Eden."

"Wait? That's it?" asked Jenny.

"Yes," retorted Jack. "Go home."

This *can't* be how the story ends, thought Jenny. It was true: she had never held much faith in Pandora's plan to find Silent Jack. Still, now that she was here, she wanted to learn why Jack and Magee had fought. She needed to know more about the nugget and how Mad Doc had discovered it. She had to believe that she had been right to follow her instinct to the rosewood.

But the surly form of Silent Jack was already making its way past the forge. A few moments later, he was under the poplars. And then he was gone.

❧

Jenny remained stiller than stone.

"What are you doing?" asked Pandora.

"We didn't get any answers. Nothing!"

"We learned that Magee went away after he found the nugget."

"You can't believe him," said Jenny. "Jack was lying through his teeth."

"You don't lie through your—"

"Okay, fine!" shouted Jenny. "You lie with your brain. And he was lying with his."

Filled with a nameless fury, she slammed her fist on the side of the jail. The whitewash fractured, and a tiny cream butterfly, as delicate as paper, flew upward in panic.

"You almost killed it," said Pandora.

"I'm aware of that!"

The butterfly was flitting wildly above the X-shaped crack in the wall. Three times it zigged, and three times it zagged, and then, in a burst of panic, it darted sideways through the open doorway.

"Wow," said Pandora, stepping in behind it. "That's a lot of butterflies making babies."

With a show of annoyance, Jenny joined her friend. Though I give her credit for noticing the door, she had failed to realize that most of the roof was also gone. All that was left of the jail were four walls and one million butterflies.

You may think I'm joking, but I swear on my saddle it's true. Since the last days of Troy, the only things stuck in that prison were roots. Seeds had been blown in by the breezes or dropped by the birds.

With the hot sun to grow them and the thick walls to warm them, these flecks of life had blossomed into harebells and clover, bittercress and beebalm. There were about thirty-odd varieties of plants that Jenny could identify and a hundred or more she could not.

Above and around these flowers hovered the cream-colored butterflies. From the looks of it, they appeared to be courting. Many of them were joined together in pairs, circling round and round the room like dancers in a reel.

"It's a good place for a nursery," said Pandora.

Jenny was of the same opinion. Suddenly, her head felt clearer and her bones felt lighter. Her anger dissolved. Standing in this square of fragile life, she could just imagine what it was like to hold a baby or stroke its cheek. Nature was cruel and beautiful, that she knew. She hadn't realized it was motherly.

"I'd like to stay a few minutes," said Jenny. "If that's all right."

Miraculously, Pandora nodded. Maybe, thought Jenny, her best friend was remembering better days with Mrs. Quinn. Somehow it felt like the right time to be thinking of that.

Skirting the wall to the one spot where she might sit without crushing flower petals, Jenny rested her back on the stone and closed her eyes.

For a moment, she allowed herself to picture what it would be like to live on her mother's islands. Though she was without a compass to guide her, she reckoned there would be a lot of family activities. Swimming in the ocean and games with young cousins and sixteen hands reaching for the last of dinner.

And in the evening, when the fire was roaring, she imagined, there would be songs—songs about ancestors and curses and wild storms that blew wanderers to lands across the sea.

"I miss my cheese," said Pandora sadly.

Jenny nodded. "I miss my cheese, too."

"You don't have any cheese," countered Pandora.

Jenny nodded again. "I know."

The sun was so kind on her face that Jenny could

hardly bear to stir. She was almost tempted to lie down and become one with the soil. Skin to earth, heart to stone.

～

It was lucky for our story—if not for Jenny's soul—that the cuckoo spat on her hand. Muttering a few choice words under her breath, she wiped her palm on the dirt. Satisfied it had gained her attention, the cuckoo darted between the butterflies and alit on a ledge in the wall. From there, it began to peck at the stone.

"What's it doing?" asked Jenny,

"Probably trying to get insects to crawl out of the cracks."

Peck, peck, peck. Peck, peck, peck. After a spell of daydreaming, this kind of noise can be maddening as math.

"Oh, would you be quiet!" shouted Jenny. The cuckoo waved its tail feathers in her face and darted into the blue above.

"Can you read the writing?" asked Pandora.

"What writing?"

"On the wall," replied Pandora, pointing to a spot where the cuckoo had been investigating. "Right there."

Over to the opposite wall they shuffled. Between the stalks and the blooms lay a series of phrases scratched deep into the plaster:

SIC SEMPER TYRANNIS!
BRANDY IS DANDY, BUT STRYCHNINE IS QUICKER.
I SHOULDA BEEN A SAILOR.

"I reckon this must have been where the holding cell was," said Jenny. She ran her eyes down the messages. "I guess the drunks had some time on their hands."

ROARING SUE HAS LOST MY SHOE AND DOESN'T
    KNOW WHERE TO FIND IT.
DON'T READ THIS.
MUCH SUSPECTED BY ME, NOTHING PROVED CAN BE.

"They've got rubbishy handwriting," said Pandora.

"This one's not bad," said Jenny. "And there's a picture to go with it." She stuck her finger on a crude drawing of a rat with fangs. The nameless prisoner who had sketched it had also included a handy ditty:

I, A RAT, CAN BITE THE LEG.
I BITE THE LEG A RAT CAN.
A RAT CAN BITE I, THE LEG.

"He wrote it three times," said Pandora. Then she paused. And paused some more. With a surge of glee, Jenny waited for her best friend's refrain.

"Well," said Pandora, "that makes no sense at all."

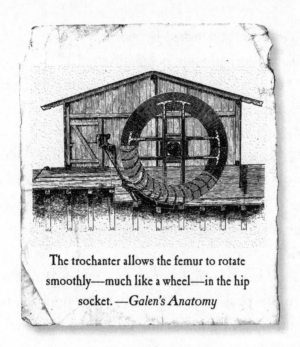

The trochanter allows the femur to rotate smoothly—much like a wheel—in the hip socket. —*Galen's Anatomy*

CHAPTER 17

"Do you think it's a clue?" asked Jenny, hopping like Hapless with glee. "It *must* be another clue on the skeleton map!"

"We don't know that," countered Pandora, "because we don't know if there was a clue in the rosewood. So we won't know what we might have known unless we find the next clue where we finally know what we didn't know doesn't matter."

"Come again?"

"It might be a clue," conceded Pandora.

"Because the drawing and the part about the leg is

suspicious, right?" asked Jenny.

"Rats normally bite people in the leg."

"They bite people everywhere. In the foot and the arm and hand . . . ," noted Jenny.

"That's true."

"So what do we do next?" asked Jenny, skipping over the columbines and vaulting through the door of the jail. "Do we go forward or backward? Over the bridge to the Longshank or around the road to Troy again?"

Jenny was chuffed to her toes to see Pandora was starting to pace. Sure, they might be fighting, but at least they were fighting with a common purpose.

"Say that again," said Pandora.

"Do we go forward . . ."

"The next bit," demanded Pandora.

"Over the bridge to the Longshank . . ."

"That's it," said Pandora, halting in her tracks. "Shank. It means leg, right?"

Jenny groaned. "Oh, lordy, lordy, Pandora! I'm a *farmer*. I raise livestock. How did I miss that one?"

"Because you've been worrying about Kam and his garden," said Pandora. "But now you're going to stop worrying and concentrate. We've already explored an arm and now we're going to follow a leg."

Caught in the whirl of her zeal, Jenny was willing to allow this mention of Kam to slide. Once. "Okay, then we'll head for the bridge and we'll think about rats while we walk. C'mon, we're wasting time."

See what I mean about gold fever? It's nigh on impossible to shake. Though she'd been almost frozen and frittered and swallowed by mud, Jenny was eager as ever to go after the treasure. It didn't matter what Silent Jack had said concerning madness and murder. Her luck was turning; she could feel it.

The day seemed to be conspiring with Jenny's belief. New grass was sprouting on the lip of the path and new moss was growing on the trunks of the beeches. Heavy rain had granted the earth a blessing. There was hope for beginnings.

After an hour or so, Jenny's good luck was telling her that they were close to where the Longshank River began. Sure enough, it wasn't long before they cleared the trees and came within sight of the bridge.

And a solid and substantial bridge it was, too. The citizens of Troy must have been a hardy crew, because they'd managed to fell nigh on fifty logs for the job. There were half logs for the base on the riverbank, whole logs for the length of the span, and saplings bound crosswise to create the road. There was even a strut or two to keep it from bowing in the middle.

It was also pretty clear to see why they had gone to so much care. The head of the Longshank was a rip-roaring torrent, bursting with mischief and malice.

You ever see a rabid animal foam at the mouth? Well, picture a pack of 'em crammed into a channel.

Jenny laughed at the sight. With her confidence full to bursting, she decided the bridge could take a team of six and a fully loaded wagon without so much as a squeak.

You may be bemused to hear she was right. As much as I enjoy the relating of hazardous falls and hair-raising escapes, that bridge was as solid as bedrock. The pair of them were safe on the other side in the time it takes to pound a nail.

"I'm guessing that's an old stamp mill," said Jenny as they wound their way along the overgrown embankment. She pointed to a rickety building with a lazy waterwheel below the bridge.

"See what someone did there? They've diverted the headwaters of the Longshank into a flume." She swung her finger around to a wooden channel. "The water charges down the flume, comes out the end, and pushes the wheel around. And the leftover water dribbles out the tailrace"—she gestured to another channel buried in the ground at the foot of the wheel—"back into the river."

"How do you know so much?" asked Pandora, blunt as blunt could be. Now that the sun was higher, Jenny's best friend was back to sweating and puffing and feeling aggrieved at losing her cheese.

"I asked up about mills. I was trying to interest Dad in running his own business."

"Your dad would be dead useless at running a business. He can't even subtract."

"True enough," said Jenny thoughtfully. "But I reckoned it was worth a go."

Pandora paused a moment to ponder this, then nodded. "Anything is worth a go with a dad like Hapless Burns."

It was a fair comment, and Jenny took it on the chin. Her temperature dropped a degree as she assessed her surroundings.

She had to pay heed—it would be like Doc Magee to plant a skeleton clue in an unlikely place. On the other hand, she was catching up with his tricks. All the markers so far had been found in places that weren't likely to go anywhere. The hut was sturdy; the stone pillars were stable; the jail walls were tall.

Only, what did he mean with respect to rodents?

"Pandora, does the skeleton map—the bone names, I mean—say anything about rats and legs?"

Pandora stopped, sat, pulled the damp diagram out of her shoe, examined it carefully, folded it, and stuck it back in her sole.

"Nope. 'Femur' means thigh bone."

Jenny grunted. "Maybe it's a pun."

"Rats are rats," noted Pandora.

"It's not a counting clue, right?" asked Jenny.

"Nope."

"Shoot."

Jenny fetched up a copper-colored pebble and sent it skimming across the water. Pandora had picked a good place for loitering. The headstream was widening and stretching as it came downhill, easing itself off into the bulk of the river.

"Three blind mice," hummed Jenny, sending a second stone after the first. "See how they run. They all ran after the farmer's wife, who cut off their tails with a carving knife—"

"*Tail!*"

"For the love of hearing, Pandora, you've got to work on making polite conversation."

"It was all mixed up in my head," said Pandora. "Then you said three and run and tails, and I realized it was all *mixed* up!"

"What are you going on about?"

"The letters," said Pandora, drawing a series in the dirt with a stick.

I A R A T C A N B I T E T H E L E G .

"So?"

"It's what Mr. Grimsby calls an anagram."

Under the first string, Pandora wrote another:

B E G I N A T T H E T A I L R A C E.

That darned stamp mill was just sitting there as they sprinted back toward the bridge. If you've been around the countryside, you will recognize the type of building I'm describing—a gummy old geezer with fragile boards and puckered skin, heeling to one side and sneering at passersby.

"We'll have to search the whole of the tailrace," said Jenny, running along the narrow channel and its wooden sides toward the waterwheel. "Magee's a crafty so-and-so. He's probably planted the next clue in a splinter."

"I like this part of the map," panted Pandora. "It's much better than a rosewood box."

"So now we know what we know?" drawled Jenny.

"Yes," replied Pandora firmly.

Since you may not be on speaking terms with stamping mills, Jenny asked me to explain that they're used for battering ore. They're simple enough arrangements. The wheel drives a rotating shaft that holds a series of rods with massive metal weights—much like the stamps you'd use to press paper. Rock goes in and crushed gray gravel comes out.

Course, the mill that the girls were exploring was well past its glory days, but by the size of it, Jenny was willing to bet there was a mine somewhere around the Longshank. Old Rush areas are full of hidden entrances to the underworld.

Jenny followed the logic of this thought as she rummaged around the base of the waterwheel. A mill meant a mine, a mine meant men, and men tended to get sick. It was likely that Magee had been up and down to Troy a number of times with his doctor's bag, treating the wounded and sobering the drunks. Those scratches on the wall of the jail were making more sense.

"Do you see anything?"

"No," said Pandora. "All I've got is a foundation stone."

Jenny examined the stone with a practiced eye. It was a plain piece of schist, with a simple shape carved into the top:

"I'm betting that's the symbol for the mill," said Jenny.

"Why?" asked Pandora.

"Dad told me that some of the men in the Rush

used a shape instead of the name when they were sign-
ing for credit."

"Why?" repeated Pandora.

"Because they couldn't read and write."

From the start at the foundation stone, their search
became more serious. On her hands and knees crawled
Jenny, scouring each burr and knothole in the wooden
walls of the tailrace. Pandora walked beside her, chewing
on the butt of her hair and gazing at the running water.

"Pandora, you're going to see squat from up there."

"I'm thinking."

"You don't have to be standing to think," replied
Jenny.

"It helps."

"Fine," said Jenny. "But you're going to be belly-
rubbing it when we start examining the other side."

"Mum says that lions like to have their bellies rubbed.
Something to do with being okay with getting licked."

"Not interested," said Jenny.

"I'm only making conversation," retorted Pandora.
"Like you said, I need to practice."

At the joint where the race met the river, Jenny sat
down and grimaced. She hadn't seen a word or letter
on the wall. "Nothing," she moaned.

"I noticed something while I was walking," said
Pandora.

"What?"

"The bottom of the tailrace has stones in it."

"We're in the *mountains*, Pandora. What were you hoping for? Coconuts?"

"No," said Pandora. "Coconut trees won't grow here. It's too cold." She sniffed. "Plus the stones are square. So I think someone put them there."

This caught the ear of her friend. "Is there anything scratched on them?"

"I can't tell," said Pandora. "They're covered in green gunk."

Isn't it always the way that the things you covet most are covered in green gunk? Shuffling her stomach over the edge, Jenny peered down into the water.

Pandora hadn't been kidding—planted in the center of the tailrace was a stone square covered in thick moss. Rolling up her sleeves, Jenny plunged her fists into the stream.

"Holy balms and alms, it's freezing!"

"Pull it up," suggested Pandora.

"It's stuck," panted Jenny, yanking her hands out of the glacier-fed trench and shaking them hard to bring the blood back to her fingertips.

"Then I guess we'll have to scrape it off."

"You do it!" said Jenny, shoving her fists under her armpits.

Pandora paused and examined her surroundings. Picking a few horsetails that were growing near the outflow, she ripped off their heads and retained the stems. Then down into the icy water they went, scouring the gunk off with a quick nip and a scrub of the surface. It took her fewer than five seconds.

"There," said Pandora. "What does it say?"

Jenny was befuddled. The following shape had been chiseled into the middle:

"Oh," said Pandora. "That's not what I was expecting."

"Maybe it's a cup?" suggested Jenny. "Or a diamond? Or an arrowhead?" She was clutching at the sharp end of a straw and she knew it. Still, at least the triangle looked vaguely clue-like.

"We need to start with the first stone that's next to the wheel," said Pandora. "The message told us to begin at the tailrace."

Back to the stamp mill they went. Alternating their hands between cleanings, they worked their way down the stream. By the time they had reached their original discovery, Jenny had forgotten what it was like to feel anything beyond her elbows.

But they certainly had a new puzzle. In seven paving stones, they had discovered the following pattern:

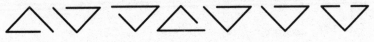

"I have decided," stated Pandora, "that I don't like people who make up treasure hunts. They should be doing better things with their time."

"Is it supposed to be some kind of map?" asked Jenny. "Or pictures of mountains and lakes?" She was fervently hoping to be wrong. Digging through the base of a mountain might take forever and a day.

Pandora was stumped. For a good long while she stared. Finally:

"It's probably a code, like the Decimus paper that we found at the pillars. The second, fifth, and sixth triangles are the same. But I don't know if it's letters or words or places or what."

"Maybe it's directions!" cried Jenny. "Maybe we begin at the tailrace, go north one pace, then south for two paces . . ."

"But what about the bits that are missing?" queried Pandora.

Jenny sighed and flung herself on the ground. "Oh, lordy, lordy, this nugget is more troublesome than a cat in a bath."

A rustle from the river prevented any more idle metaphors.

"Then, perchance, Miss Burns, you have need of another mind."

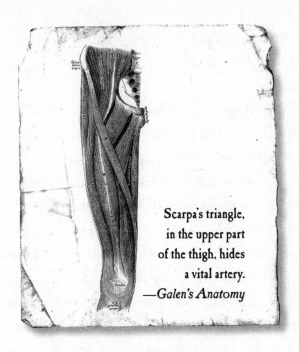

Scarpa's triangle,
in the upper part
of the thigh, hides
a vital artery.
—*Galen's Anatomy*

CHAPTER 18

The shadow of Mr. Grimsby was about twelve feet away from them, where the ripple of the river met the droop of the path.

Mr. Grimsby was looking fair to drooping himself. His suit was crusted with mud and the nap of his trousers was ripped from thigh to calf. Somewhere in the proceedings, he also appeared to have lost his switch and his spectacles.

"Before you come a whiff closer, Mr. Grimsby," said Jenny, "you should know that I've got Gentle Annie's revolver with me and I'm not afraid to use it!"

"You haven't got—"

"Quiet, Pandora," warned Jenny through gritted teeth.

Mr. Grimsby put his hands up. "I come not to wage war, fair ladies, but to make peace."

"What do you want?" demanded Jenny.

"I wish to speak," replied the schoolmaster.

"You can speak with us from there!"

Mr. Grimsby bowed his head, bent his right knee, and extended his left leg in the age-old manner of a courtier. "I am here to beg a mercy."

You're likely to encounter a variety of big surprises in your life—babies and bad news being high on the list—but it's not often you'll get the chance to see your enemy humbled. Jenny was taken aback by her schoolmaster's aspect. Even the veins in his forehead appeared contrite.

"What do you mean?"

"I know that you've been hunting the nugget of Mad Doc Magee."

Jenny was less than surprised. From what she had heard and observed, Mr. Grimsby had visited every point in their treasure hunt barring the rosewood and the jail at Troy. Denial was fruitless.

"And what if we have?" challenged Jenny.

"You are somehow in the weeds, am I correct? The visit to the bank was a disappointment, was it not?"

"Yes. But you're always in the weeds in a hunt."

"I understand that the gold will be yours by rights," acknowledged the schoolmaster, ignoring her reply, "but I would like to assist you in finding it."

"Why?"

"I need a job. I have no prospects of employment, Miss Burns." Mr. Grimsby's voice acquired a wobble. "On Wednesday, I was sacked by the school board for incompetency—Miss Quinn's speech about fathers and daughters was not to their taste. And you saw how Mr. Polk treated my appeal for clemency. I am broke."

"So you're willing to work with 'degenerates' now?" asked Jenny, eager to rub rock salt into Mr. Grimsby's wounds.

"Please, Miss Burns," yelled the schoolmaster, "I have been bruised and battered by the storms of fortune, and I am a foolish foundling of a man. All I wanted to do when I followed you through the Gorge was talk. Do not leave me here to die."

"Stay right where you are," bellowed Jenny. She turned to her best friend. "What do we do?"

"I don't like that man at *all*," said Pandora.

"I hate his guts," replied Jenny. "But it's not like we can force him to leave. And who knows? We may need his thinking to decipher these symbols. Unless you want to take them home and reason them out there."

"No, that won't work," said Pandora. "If we go home, he'll only follow us."

"He's got the letter from Dr. Galen, but he doesn't have the skeleton map," noted Jenny. "So he won't know about parts of the body being parts of the mountains. We've got that on our side."

"But it doesn't matter," insisted Pandora. "He's not going to leave us alone."

Truth may taste like sour lemons, but you'll end up eating it just the same. Pandora was right. Now that he had the gist of the matter, the schoolmaster was going to dog them down the line.

"How in a dammed creek did he find us?" asked Jenny.

"He probably followed my straw hat over the side trail," said Pandora, "before he realized Lok was the one wearing it. Once he was in the Longshank, he must have calculated we were heading for Troy."

Jenny returned her scrutiny to the schoolmaster. His crooks and corners remained frozen in the shape of an apology.

"Right then, rotgut, if you're serious, we need to talk terms."

"What are you doing?" whispered Pandora.

"I'm testing him," muttered Jenny. "Let's see if he takes it."

"What do you propose?" called Mr. Grimsby.

"First off, you've got to keep your swill of a cow's backside at a distance from us for the entire expedition. You agree?"

"Agreed."

"Second off, you'll take the job I give you when we've found the nugget. I won't be funding a tour of Shakespeare around the territory."

"Agreed."

"Third off, you're not to tell a single soul what we're doing unless I give you permission. You got that?"

"Agreed."

"So we have a deal. And stand up straight," ordered Jenny. "You look ridiculous."

Mr. Grimsby stumbled to attention and offered a crisp salute. Then, reaching around to his back, he swung a bundle clear over his shoulder.

"What are you doing?" asked Jenny, alarmed. "Remember what I said about Gentle Annie's revolver!"

"It's a gift!" yelled Mr. Grimsby. "A show of good-will and alliance. I will deposit it here for Pandora to fetch."

With the care of a beggar man laying out his best belongings, the schoolmaster rested the parcel on the ground and untied the cord. Off to the side he stepped again, the length of four men or more.

"Go see what it is," said Jenny.

While Pandora walked over to the package, Jenny kept the silhouette of the schoolmaster fixed on the horizon.

"What is it?" asked Jenny. "Somebody's head?"

Her best friend leaned over.

"No, it's a ham. Tied up with string."

"*Why* in the world are you carrying a ham?" asked Jenny.

"It was a farewell gift from the butcher," said Mr. Grimsby. "He seemed anxious to be rid of me."

"Well, that makes sense," said Pandora, returning to Jenny.

The schoolmaster looked as if he might say something cutting, then appeared to think better of it. "How can I help you?"

Jenny took Pandora by the arm and backed them both toward the stamp mill.

"We're stuck on some sort of code written on the rocks at the bottom of the tailrace," said Jenny. "We think it's to do with the placement of the nugget, but we're not sure."

"May I approach the tailrace?" he asked.

"Go ahead."

Hobbling a little on his left side, Mr. Grimsby limped around to the opposite bank of the water, dropped his knees to the ground, and squinted at the stone. In the family tree of nearsighted salamanders, I'm guessing the schoolmaster was a close relation.

"How can you see anything without your glasses?" asked Jenny.

"I am not entirely myopic," answered Mr. Grimsby testily. "There is a triangle with an area removed, no?"

"Yes," said Jenny.

Calm as can be, the schoolmaster edged his way along the border, squinting at every one of the seven rocks. Pandora and Jenny mirrored him on the other side. When he got to the foundation stone at the top, he let off a long, low whistle.

"Whewww. How very intriguing. But soft, they who sprint often stumble."

For a while he sat in a puddle of sun, hypnotized by the slap and tickle of the moving wheel. Just when Jenny was beginning to think he might have cracked his skull and drained his brains on that wild night of the storm, he rose and bowed.

"I believe I have your answer," said Mr. Grimsby.

Jenny was far too suspicious of the schoolmaster to be bouncing for joy. But a small part of her soul was secretly wishing for him to be right. "What is it?" she demanded.

"We will work it out together. Here"—the school-master pointed to the foundation stone—"where we begin our scene." Whereas you're free to loathe him for other reasons, you'll have to forgive Mr. Grimsby for his iambic pentameter. It's a common disease among stage players. "Now then, ladies, do you notice any-thing distinctive about the shapes in this square and the triangles down the tailrace?"

"No," said Jenny. Pandora shook her head.

"Every one is a right triangle," said the school-master.

"What's a right triangle?" asked Jenny.

"Miss Burns, this is the direct result of your tru-ancy. Industry and application to your studies—"

"Mr. Grimsby, you're fixing to be trimming dags if you start this way."

Though I'm guessing the schoolmaster had never once lopped off the matted end of a sheep's bottom, he appeared to know what Jenny was driving at.

"I am sorry; I do apologize," said Mr. Grimsby.

"Go on."

"The two legs—the shorter sides—of the triangle form a right angle: the corner of a square, if you will. The longest side is the hypotenuse."

"Then it's a mathematical code," said Jenny.

"Not quite," said the schoolmaster. "You observe

that the foundation stone is four right triangles put together?" He gestured to the piece of schist with the X on it.

"Yes," said Pandora.

"So we must marry the alphabet to geometry."

"Mr. Grimsby," griped Jenny, "only the juice of a stewed prune could understand what you're saying."

The schoolmaster tugged on his ear in bewilderment. "A stewed prune, Miss Burns?"

"Just explain it better!" cried Jenny.

Mr. Grimsby nodded and laid a dirty fingernail above the top left corner of the foundation stone. "Imagine an *a* above this."

"Okay," said Jenny.

He moved his fingernail along the line to the middle. "And a *b* here."

"Okay," said Jenny.

On went the finger toward the top right corner. "And a *c* above this."

"Oh!" cried Pandora.

"Very good, Miss Quinn. And the rest of the letters would be arranged in . . . ?"

"A circle."

"A spiral, to be precise," said Mr. Grimsby. "Round and round until we reach *y* and *z* in the middle."

As it may be a mite tricky for you to picture the

schoolmaster's motion without the benefit of being there, I'll give you an idea of what Pandora and Jenny were seeing in their mind's eyes:

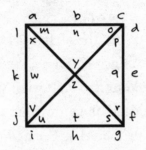

"That means the parts cut out of the triangles . . . ," said Pandora to herself.

"Correspond to letters on the square," finished the schoolmaster.

But Jenny was already racing down the line.

"Then this one's a *g*!" She stopped. "Or an *s*."

"It can't be an *s*," said Pandora, "because an *s* would be cut out of the right leg going up toward the middle."

"The next is *a*,'" noted Mr. Grimsby, tottering to the stone in front of them. He paused. "But this surely cannot be true. For that would imply that the fifth and sixth letters are also both *a*."

"*G*," repeated Jenny. "*A*."

"*M*," called Pandora.

Though the schoolmaster and her best friend were barreling toward the end, Jenny stayed where she was. Thanks to a talent for talking and a habit of wandering, she knew exactly what the rest of the stones read.

GAM SAAN.

You'd be surprised at the number of feelings your body can hold in a moment. Jenny was ruffled and raring and frightened and fierce. She was going to see Kam again. This ought to have made her happy.

The thing was, she was going to see Kam again.

"Why would a nugget be buried in the Chinese settlement?" asked the schoolmaster.

Jenny could have told him about the name of Gold Mountain, and her theory of Doc Magee making medical visits to the Longshank valley, and the fact that she'd once heard King Louis refer to Gentle Annie's legs as "great-looking gams." But she wasn't feeling the urge to enlighten anyone.

"Dunno," said Jenny.

"It's going to rain again," said Pandora, cricking her neck to look at an onrush of clouds. "Probably a lot."

"There will be huts at Gam Saan," said Jenny. "And we've got ham for lunch." It was up to her, she had decided, to see this dangerous trip through. Great leaders answer when the call is given. "We should be moving. Mr. Grimsby, you're going to walk ahead of us. I don't want any more surprises."

"Very well," said the schoolmaster.

"You even think of running and you know what will happen," said Jenny, sticking her hand in her coat and pointing her finger.

"I do indeed," replied Mr. Grimsby.

"Right then, time to get your blood flowing."

The schoolmaster nodded and turned on his heel. Quiet and steady, he began his patrol. Jenny waited for a minute before she grabbed Pandora by the elbow, caught up the ham by its string, and started the journey down the Longshank.

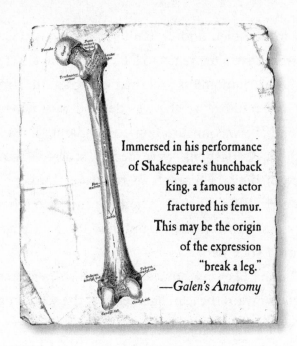

Immersed in his performance
of Shakespeare's hunchback
king, a famous actor
fractured his femur.
This may be the origin
of the expression
"break a leg."
—*Galen's Anatomy*

CHAPTER 19

Spend any time in the mountains and you're likely to find that rivers have their own way of speaking. Jenny had passed many a morning with the Arrow, laughing and shouting and shooting the proverbial.

But the Longshank was a glacier-fed river, and glacier-fed rivers tend to keep to themselves. Their valleys were formed in the age of ice, plowed straight and plowed long by the slow creep of cold. They have wide-open spaces, deep as the bend of a cauldron, and they're littered with boulders and till. You can't joke or jostle a river like this; you have to respect it. You must learn to be quiet, and careful, and cautious. Glacier-fed rivers have a tendency to look pretty staid. Yet their motives are fathomless and their currents run strong.

Jenny could sense she was dealing with new territory and she was unsure how to handle it. The ridges along the Longshank were deeply scarred from the scrape of bergs. Cataracts of rainwater cannoned off the steep of the far side. The path ran through acres of scree shed from the mountains. It was a place for watching your step.

"I don't like this," muttered Pandora, her attention directed toward the lean ligaments of the schoolmaster. "He's only after the gold."

"So are we," countered Jenny. "But I know what you mean." She watched Mr. Grimsby pick and toe his way over a pile of rocks. "The trick is keeping him ahead of us. Once we get to Gam Saan, we'll meet back up with Kam and Lok. He'll have trouble taking four of us all at once."

And if worse comes to worst, thought Jenny, I can ask Lok to sit on him.

Pandora had something else nagging at her pate. "Do you think Silent Jack was involved in laying the stones at the tailrace?"

"How do you mean?"

"He was Doc Magee's partner," said Pandora. "He might have helped with creating the skeleton map."

"I don't think he and Magee were on speaking terms," replied Jenny.

"That's a fair point," mused Pandora.

"Did Jack tell you how long he had been living in Troy?"

"A couple of years," answered Pandora. "He came back from working on the coast."

"Well, then, that's another thing," said Jenny. "Whoever planned this malarkey must have done it ages ago, when the skeleton first arrived in Magee's office. You can't plant a clue after the fact."

"Jack could have been lying," retorted her friend. "Maybe he was in Troy before he left for the coast, chiseling out the triangles."

"I suppose," said Jenny. "Still, it would be a strange thing for a man who spits on the Rush to do. He said he hated greedy men."

"Are you speaking about Silent Jack?" called the schoolmaster.

"Pea shoots," sputtered Jenny. The two girls had spent so long amongst themselves that they had forgotten how to keep their voices low.

"I knew him, Miss Burns," said the schoolmaster. "A fellow of infinite gripes. He was not someone I would care to meet in a darkened theater."

"You were here during the Rush?" asked Jenny.

"Yes."

Mr. Grimsby had been moseying around with the toughs and the roughs? Counting cards at the Last Chance Saloon? Squiring the likes of Gentle Annie through the streets of Eden? No, thought Jenny, he couldn't be telling the truth. A man like him would have been eaten alive.

"I see you don't believe me, Miss Burns."

"You bet your best horse I don't," said Jenny.

Mr. Grimsby rubbed his left leg and sighed. "Would you permit me to sit for a few minutes? I can tell you of my experiences."

As the rain had yet to begin, Jenny was willing to allow this liberty. The schoolmaster sitting was a safer prospect than he was walking. Besides, she was aching for a taste of ham.

Light as new down, Mr. Grimsby alit on a piece of glacial scrap and studied his scratches. Scenting dried blood, a swarm of sandflies darted in for the kill. Jenny and Pandora found seats a good way away from the river—and the flies—and waited.

"Well?" demanded Jenny.

"My apologies," said the schoolmaster, brushing the grit from his fingers and raising his square lump of a skull. "What would you like to know?"

"How did you get here?" asked Jenny.

"No doubt Eden's gossips have informed you that I was part of a troupe of jobbing actors," answered Mr.

Grimsby. "When the bottom fell out of business in the old country, we decided to tour the ports of the new world."

"But not Eden?"

"No," said the schoolmaster. "Eden was too small. We mainly hugged the shore."

"Then how did you get here?" repeated Jenny.

"I know," said Pandora. "He followed the Rush."

Mr. Grimsby nodded sadly.

"As you say, Miss Quinn, I followed the Rush. The troupe made little money. I thought I might have better financial luck elsewhere."

"Mr. Grimsby! The big miner in town!" teased Jenny. "I reckon you panned yourself some gold, bought a pair of hand-tooled boots, and took to wooing the women."

"No," said the schoolmaster. "I failed at my mining ventures. But I am sure you were already aware of that fact."

Jenny had a twinge of shame. She doubted it was easy being a small bloke in a large territory. And Mr. Grimsby's presence had a way of irritating one's nerve endings. It wouldn't have been easy for him to defend a claim.

"So what did you do after?" asked Jenny. "There wasn't a school in the Rush."

"I washed dishes," said the schoolmaster. "I swept

floors. I ferried messages. I've probably journeyed through this valley a full score or more."

Mr. Grimsby twisted his gooseneck toward the river. There was a rueful tilt to his jaw and a faraway gleam in his eye. Perhaps he was remembering a rare day when life wasn't a trial, and a thin-chested man could enjoy the feel of the sun on his back.

"You must have been glad when the schoolhouse opened," said Jenny, taken aback by her own tact.

"Yes," said Mr. Grimsby. "I was able to read books again."

"Is that what you would do with the money from the nugget?" demanded Pandora. "Buy lots of books?"

Apart from her exclamations over the triangle code, Jenny's friend had been doing her best to avoid speaking. It's a commendable action—when you've got nothing good to say to a man, you're wise to ignore him.

But Pandora was also a practical girl with practical suspicions. In her mind, Mr. Grimsby was up to something. And the only way she knew how to fathom his true intentions was to ask him point-blank.

"I won't have any money from the nugget," corrected the schoolmaster. "You and Miss Burns will. However, if you are inquiring what I would do with a fortune, I would probably answer: Sail the seas. Fly to worlds I know not of."

This was so close in poesy to Jenny's fevered dreams that she was tempted to tell him just that. Pandora's bristling decided her against it.

"We'd better not linger," said Jenny. "The weather won't wait."

"I want my lunch," said Pandora.

"Sure, sure," said Jenny. She picked up a sliver of stone and hacked off a piece of ham for Pandora. Then she did the same for herself.

And then—for no other reason than instinct—she cut off a third piece and laid it on a rock halfway between Pandora and the schoolmaster.

"There," called Jenny. "You get some, too."

She retreated toward safety and watched. Stiff as a corpse in his coffin, Mr. Grimsby rose to his feet.

"Miss Burns."

"Yes?"

"I would like to apologize for my behavior in the schoolroom."

"You called her horrible names," reminded Pandora.

"Yes," said the schoolmaster. "I called Miss Burns names. It may have taken me a reversal of fortune to learn it, but I now know I was wrong. You must judge a man by the truth of his actions or not at all."

"And?" demanded Pandora.

"I behaved shabbily toward you and your friend, and I am ashamed."

Jenny tasted the sugar of justice on her tongue and smiled. Sure, it was still possible that Mr. Grimsby was conniving at some sort of ruse. But it was equal odds that he was in earnest. And as far as Jenny was concerned, those were good enough chances these days. "Well, Mr. Grimsby, I'm right glad to hear that."

Now, then, in the course of this tale, you may have noticed a fair amount of prose on poppies and butterflies. Well, here's where the valentine ends. Because if you've never seen a valley that's been ruined by gold mining, you've got a hard shock in store.

Wide and flat are the banks of the Longshank, and many were the men who squatted on it. All the way down the river, Jenny spied dozens of worn-out wooden contraptions resembling hollow shoes. These were the rocker boxes, where a sieve at the top of the heel and a series of ridges running toward the toe allowed a miner to separate the gold flakes from dirt.

From these cradles grew the Long Toms—troughs of ten, twenty, thirty feet or more. And from the Long Toms grew the greed. Gallons of pure stream were forced into ditches, punched into rocks, and ferried toward sluice boxes. By the time the water reached the river, it was brown with silt and crud.

As the trio progressed through the valley, Jenny was also appalled to see that miners had tried hosing the cliffs. Whole sections of hillside had been stripped clean of their skins, exposing raw vein and muscle to the cold, bitter winds. Every which way, the mountains had been tortured.

"Depressing, is it not?" commented Mr. Grimsby.

"It ought to be against the law!"

"That's an interesting judgment coming from someone who seeks a gold nugget."

A challenge given is a challenge taken with a girl like Jenny Burns. "I wasn't the one who went fossicking for it. I'm simply searching for the leftovers."

"But you wouldn't be able to search for leftovers if you lived somewhere else," noted Mr. Grimsby. "Didn't your father come to Eden to mine gold?"

"And what if he did?" challenged Jenny. "You think kids are to blame for the choices their parents make? That's like saying trees are to blame for the soil they grow in."

The schoolmaster paused and twirled. "But that is quite brilliant, Miss Burns. Why didn't you display this attention to logic when you were skulking at the back of my classroom?"

Jenny scowled. "Mr. Grimsby, I've decided against you trimming dags. I going to put you on gutting carcasses."

The schoolmaster took a hasty step back. "Of course. I apologize for my reprimand." Grasping for a change of subject, he found one in the sight of an abandoned hut. "And I will grant you that the Rush had its positive points. A great many fair and wayward characters peopled the scene."

"Like who?" challenged Pandora.

"Like whom," said Mr. Grimsby, unable to help himself. "Like the man who lived in that abode." In the split of a second, his shoulders dropped and his knees bent. His jowls softened and sagged. He wrapped his left arm around a circle of nothing. "Name is Potbelly Pat, how do ye do?" The schoolmaster wallowed to one side and wobbled to another. "I'm the youngest son of the youngest son of the King of Poltree, and the fifteenth child of a fairy queen." He threw open his interior and belched.

"He's gone off his chump," whispered Pandora.

"I think he's exercising his dramatic muscles," replied Jenny.

"Go on with you then, ask me a question," said Mr. Grimsby, still with the lilt.

"Okay," said Jenny, willing to humor him for a moment. "Why did you decide to be a miner, Pat?"

"Well, I was nibbling my way through a four-poster bed when I said to myself, 'Pat,' said I, 'you'll eat your-self out of house and home.' So over I came to Eden, where food was plentiful. That's how I lost my roof. I ate it one morning for breakfast." The schoolmaster belched again, loud enough to startle the swifts.

"You know, Pandora," muttered Jenny, "maybe I spoke too soon. . . ."

With a brisk twitch of his sartorius and a switch of his stance, Mr. Grimsby became a fiddly young man. He adjusted the position of an invisible chair, brushed a crumb off its surface, and took a seat in midair. His left ankle came to rest on his right knee and his hands flew up to grasp a needle and thread. Deftly he stabbed at the cloth that lay in his lap.

"I do not know, do not know, do not know what to do," said the schoolmaster, stitching a line through the sky. "I am Tailor Tip, oh poor Tailor Tip, how little I see and how little I find."

"And why are you here, Tip?" asked Jenny. Ignoring the question of his sanity, Mr. Grimsby was pretty good at impressions. She was beginning to enjoy herself.

"Oh, Tip, poor Tip," said the schoolmaster. "I was sent by my father. Too simple for home, too frightened of speech. My mother cried and told me to remember my handkerchief." Quick flashed the needle through the cloth. "But I lost it in the rain . . ."

A drop of water—a real one, this time—landed on Mr. Grimsby's nose.

". . . and know not where to find it," wept the schoolmaster.

"There, there," said Jenny. "No need to cry."

Faster than a slip in the hay, the schoolmaster's foot came crashing to the ground. Needle and thread were thrown to the wind. Mr. Grimsby drew a deep breath and rammed his fists on his hips. "I don't cry. I am a man known as Ox!"

"No first name?" joked Jenny.

"Ox," bellowed Mr. Grimsby. "You see this hide?" He banged the flat of his fists together and began to pull his hands, slower than slow, away from each other. "I stretch this hide," gasped the schoolmaster, "until it is very, very, very wiiiiidddde." Red in the cheeks and breathless to boot, he continued to pull until his arms were horizontal with the ground. "And. Now. I. Die." The schoolmaster released the imaginary band and fell to the ground.

There was nothing for it but to applaud, which is what Jenny did. She was amazed that her former teacher—that weak-spirited man who sneered at children and punished thought—could hold such reservoirs of silliness. What did it mean when a person contradicted his past?

Jenny was dazed, but Pandora was not. She promptly stuck out her tongue.

"Our play is done," said the schoolmaster, getting

to his feet. "And it appears the rain has returned."

Jenny shook herself three times to resettle her wits and nodded.

"How far do you think it is to Gam Saan?"

"Less than half a mile," said Mr. Grimsby, flicking lumps of clay off his trousers. "You'll spy shelter by the red roofs. The color is the result of the iron in the metal."

Incredible, thought Jenny. Without so much as the flick of an eyelid, he was back to being the same dull bloke as before.

"I think you're completely nutty," said Pandora.

The schoolmaster repeated his courtier's bow. "Thank you, Miss Quinn. I take that as a compliment." He turned up what remained of the collar on his coat. "We should hurry. It will be chilly at Gold Mountain, and we'll be without the comfort of bed and company."

"Yes, well," said Jenny, shifting uneasily in her boots, "you might be surprised."

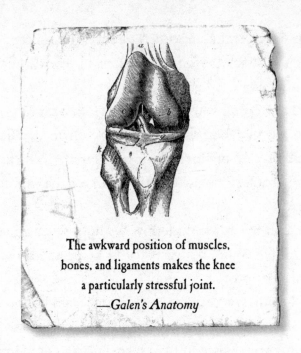

The awkward position of muscles,
bones, and ligaments makes the knee
a particularly stressful joint.
—*Galen's Anatomy*

CHAPTER 20

Gam Saan was always going to have a fair amount of trouble living up to its name. To echo the residents of Eden, a hill is a hill, and a hut is a hut. It's rare that you'll find anything rich or gleaming in a Rush settlement.

On the other hand, the small cluster of buildings on the riverbank was far neater and tidier than any Jenny had seen up the valley. Most of the walls were mortared with river stone and almost all the huts had roofs. A few were scarcely long enough to hold a man. But the one in the middle of the group was large and square and sturdy. It was also wreathed in smoke.

"Oh," said the schoolmaster, as they came down off a rise and through the dusky drizzle. "Enlightenment. This must be where the straw hat of Miss Quinn finally came to roost. I did wonder why I was heading toward the Longshank."

"You didn't know the hat was on Lok?" asked Jenny.

"No," said Mr. Grimsby. "I lost sight of the hat near the junction where the pass meets the valley."

They drew closer to the hut—and to Kam. Jenny swallowed. Fate was arranging for her to face the consequences of her actions in the Gorge when her knee-jerk reaction was to run for the hills.

"Miss Burns?" queried the schoolmaster.

"What?"

"Would you like me to . . ." He gestured to the middle hut.

"No, it's okay. I'll do it."

Without giving herself the option to retreat, Jenny pounded on the door.

There was a minute or two of silence, then a splash of light.

"Hi, Kam. I've been out leaping mountains."

Jenny had been fretting that her meeting with Kam would be embarrassing. She was wrong in that. It was mortifying.

"Hello, Jenny Girl."

"We had some trouble after we left you in the Gorge," said Jenny, trying to determine how much she could say about their travels with the schoolmaster listening. "And then we found Mr. Grimsby wandering lost. We'd be very grateful . . ." She stopped and swallowed again. "If we could all stay for the night."

Kam's hand remained right where it was on the doorjamb. "That depends."

"On what?"

Kam held her gaze to his own. "Tell me what's in the rosewood."

Oh, to heck with it, thought Jenny, what was the point of fibbing anymore? She was homeless and hungry with a grown captive in tow. They would have a ticklish time hiding their search for clues, and Jenny was tired of watching her words. Pandora would have to trust that there would be plenty of the nugget to share.

"We're on a hunt for the treasure of Mad Doc Magee."

Against his best efforts, her inquisitor began to laugh.

"It's not funny, Kam!"

Kam squelched his chortle. "It is a little, Jenny Girl."

"Can we come in?" pleaded Jenny. "I've been bathed enough this week."

Kam peered over her shoulder at the meek outline of Mr. Grimsby, who was shrinking rapidly in the rain.

"I guess you should. Do you want me to invite your schoolteacher as well?"

Jenny leaned toward Kam and did her best to ignore the jolt of excitement that passed through her. "Yes, but we need to watch him. He's shifty."

Kam nodded. "That's fine. I am used to dealing with shifty people."

This was a dig at her behavior, and Jenny knew it. But she wasn't going to argue with hot soup and a warm hearth and the chance for someone else to play guard. Whatever the cost, it would be a relief to have a change of view from Mr. Grimsby's backside.

"Come in, please," said Kam, ushering the trio into the room and closing the door. "Welcome to my father's house."

In most respects, the house of Ah Lum was more honeycomb than home. The main room, where the fire was lit, was stuffed with a variety of rickety chairs and a table. Between the walls were four low doorways. Beyond those doors were rooms with bunks. In the old days, the place must have buzzed with voices.

Jenny sat down in the chair that Kam offered. To come from a land ripe with green to this vista of brown would have been a melancholy prospect for any man. And Kam's father had brought a small boy and baby along. He must have been very determined to keep his family together.

She looked to Kam's brother. He was slurping his soup and grinning at her over the rim.

"How's the grub, Lok?"

"No peas."

Jenny grinned back. "Fair enough."

As Kam handed her a bowl, a tangy blast of steam made her eyes glisten. Ginger root, she was guessing. And dried mushrooms.

"Would you like some, Mr. Grimsby?" offered Kam. "I seem to recall you stopped here once or twice."

The schoolmaster smiled a shy smile. In the soft of the evening, he appeared almost normal. "I was wondering if you would remember that time, Kam."

"Yes, sir, I remember."

Jenny stared at Kam in bewilderment.

"The little boy interpreter," said the schoolmaster, "darting this way and that. Chatting to your father's men and bartering with storekeepers. How you kept all those dialects in your head I will never know."

"You learn quickly when you are young," said Kam.

"That is very true," acknowledged Mr. Grimsby.

"Is that how you learned English?" asked Pandora. "You were practicing with the miners?"

"For a few years," said Kam to Pandora. "After my

father died, I moved to town and practiced with my customers."

"I remember your father," said Mr. Grimsby. "Grave, stately. He seemed to be thinking of forgotten things."

"He was," said Kam.

Mr. Grimsby nodded. "It was a difficult time to start anew."

Once again, the schoolmaster was confusing the bats out of Jenny's belfry. How could he speak so gently to a boy he might have switched only one month before? She trusted her instinct—there was kindness in Mr. Grimsby's tone—but what in the world were grown folk coming to?

"I am sorry to be a poor guest, but my head is fair aching," said the schoolmaster, pinching the bridge of his nose in pain. "If you will permit me, I think I should retire."

Kam glanced at Jenny. Jenny glanced inside the room next door. Nothing but bare bunks and an earth floor. She hesitated.

"The Lums will be at liberty to search me," added the schoolmaster, "when I emerge in the morning."

"Okay," said Jenny.

Weary and worn, Mr. Grimsby limped into the bunkroom and closed the door.

"I'll block it!" whispered Pandora, bolting from her seat.

Spooked by her movement and awed by her speed, Jenny needed a second to understand why her best friend was hurling herself against walls.

"Pandora, he's not going to find a lump of gold in the floor. Anyway, we would see the marks in the dirt if he did."

"I don't trust him," retorted Pandora. "I don't like him. And I don't want to be around a man who hates us."

Valid concerns all three, but Jenny was beginning to feel ornery. She had kept her temper for so long that day that she'd almost forgotten she had one. Who was Pandora to be giving orders? A lickety split of anger was spreading through her limbs, adding warmth to her cheeks and fire to her belly.

"You don't know that he hates us. You heard what he said about being sorry for calling us names."

"And you think saying sorry makes everything all right?"

"That's not what I think."

"I—" began Pandora.

"Oh, for the love of reason, Pandora! Stop talking about—"

"Excuse me," said Kam, escorting Jenny to the entrance. "I'd like to show Jenny something outside.

Lok, please sit by the door and make sure Mr. Grimsby stays in his bunk."

"Sure," said Lok, "Pandora and I can play *Chák T'in Kau*." He thumped himself down on the floor next to the bunkroom and pulled two oversize dice from his pocket. "I'll go first."

Even if Jenny had wanted to learn how to play Throwing Heaven and Nine, she wasn't going to get the chance. Kam had her out in the night before the cubes of white hit the wood.

〜

"What gives?" demanded Jenny, wresting herself away from his grip. "It's freezing out here!"

"You were about to yell at your friend."

"Pandora doesn't care. We've been yelling at each other all week."

"I think that's wrong," said Kam.

"Like I care what you think," said Jenny, and immediately bit her lip.

As usual, Kam waited his customary century or so before giving his answer. "You do care, Jenny Girl."

Above in the dark, the easterly was driving hard, herding the clouds between the peaks toward the sea. For the most part, the sky was obscured by the dust of the rain. But occasionally, just occasionally, the dust would settle to reveal a wide field of stars. It did so now.

Jenny was too nettled to pay it much heed.

"Darn it, Kam, don't you ever get angry?" Jenny stomped ahead into the night. "Look at where you are! Stuck on this godforsaken river with your little pan, grubbing in the mud, searching for scraps . . ." She whirled on her follower. "The world crushed your dreams and ground your face in it. Why aren't you burning the bloody territory down?"

The whites of Kam's eyes were silver in the light. "I'm always angry."

"Yeah, right," said Jenny.

Up in the stampede, a cloud broke free from the pack and began to pummel their section of the riverbank with a downpour. Jenny stamped her foot. "God, how I *hate* rain!"

"Follow me!" shouted Kam above the din of the weather.

"Why?"

"I want you to see something."

He dashed toward one of the smaller huts, with Jenny close behind. A gust rose up and blew them into a small room.

Beset by the dank smell of loneliness, Jenny looked for a warm place to sit. There was none. The lone piece of furniture was a slab at the far end of the wall. Kam knelt by its side and lit a couple of candles. A tall wooden tablet rose like a flame. Columns of characters sprang to life.

"I come here," said Kam, "when I am angry and confused. When the feelings inside me eat through my skin and I want to . . ." He paused. "'Burn the bloody territory down.'"

She raised an eyebrow. "To stare at a plaque?"

"To remind me I'm a dot in the dust of the universe," retorted Kam. "This is my ancestor table. It honors the memory of my father and contains the earthly part of his soul."

"Oh," said Jenny, ruing her tone. "That's nice." She groped for an appropriate question and knelt down beside him. "So . . . then . . . what does the writing say?"

"His name, his birthday, the day he died," said Kam, reading the inscription. "His place of burial, his ancestors, and the name of the son who honors him."

"And that's you?" asked Jenny.

"That's me," said Kam. "When he died, I made two tablets. His spirit was given to the wooden one, and a paper one was buried with him."

Kam's recital was accompanied by the sound of rain pounding on the corrugated iron. Jenny thought of her mum and a cross on a hill.

"Is he buried round here?"

Kam shook his head. "He was. But last year, to fulfill a promise, I took the money I had saved from the stall and sent his bones back on a ship. His best friend buried him near his home."

The crush of this fact took Jenny's breath away. *This* was the reason why Kam couldn't pay back the bank. He had lost Little Eden to keep his word to his father.

"Lordy, lordy, Kam, I'm awfully sorry."

The words had good effect. Kam smiled slightly.

"Can you imagine, Jenny Girl? If I had never come here? I might have been in the imperial government. My mother wanted me to become an important man like her great-grandfather. Most of our land was gone, but my father said it didn't matter. The son would make the family rise again." The candle sputtered. Kam reached out to touch the line of his ancestors, stopped, and held his hand. "I failed them."

"But your mum didn't know all those other horrible things were going to happen to you," countered Jenny. "You can't be responsible for that."

"No," said Kam, bitter as gall, "that is not what I mean." He was silent for a minute, and Jenny squashed her impatience. "I had a different dream, Jenny Girl. I didn't want to go back. I wanted my own country. To grow my own life."

"But you can still do that!" said Jenny eagerly. "We'll find Doc Magee's gold and you can buy back Little Eden and start again."

Kam shook his head and laid his hands in his lap. "No. There is too much history in this earth already.

Our fathers brought the weeds of the old world into the new, and they ruined it."

Jenny understood far more than others what Kam was driving at; she knew how he felt about the sneers about his race, and the slog, and the hardship. But this was their land, hers and Kam's, not their fathers'.

"I think you're talking rubbish."

Kam got up from his knees.

"You're not angry at your friend, Jenny Girl; you're frightened of yourself. You must face up to the truth of things."

Sound familiar? You may remember Pandora giving Jenny some of the exact same advice in their grand set-to in the Gorge. And Jenny was just as pleased on hearing it again—which meant she was madder than a cricket in a can.

"I'm not scared of anything!" shouted Jenny, snatching at the coattails of Kam as he blew out the candles and opened the door. "Do you hear me, Kam? I'm never scared!"

But Kam was walking over a path of stars to the river. Jenny paused on the threshold. The sky was clear. The rain had gone.

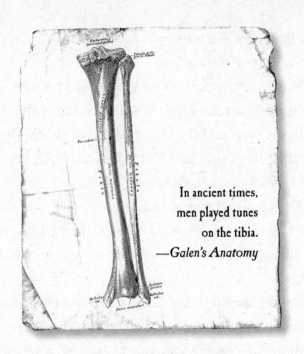

In ancient times,
men played tunes
on the tibia.
—*Galen's Anatomy*

CHAPTER 21

"Double fives," said Lok. "Plum flower."

Pandora threw two ones.

"Earth. I win."

It may have been a sunny morning in the hut of Ah Lum, but Jenny was grumpy as grief. Thanks to Pandora's worrying, she had spent most of the night on the floor, squashed beside her best friend and the door to the schoolmaster's bunkroom. She had bruises in places where light seldom shone.

"Would you two stop fooling around?" griped Jenny. "We're supposed to be looking for a nugget.

See? Mr. Grimsby's already got his boots laced."

The schoolmaster clicked his heels in a modest reply. Jenny sighed. She had spent most of breakfast trying to persuade Kam to help with the search, and he still hadn't agreed. Mr. Grimsby—clean as a proverbial whistle and very well rested—was the only one who seemed keen to start.

"I don't want to look for a nugget now," said Pandora. "I want to play the game."

"Pandora! We've got the whole of Gam Saan to comb."

"Don't care," said Pandora. Lok sniggered.

"What are you laughing at? You're doing a fat lot of good sitting on your duff," scolded Jenny.

"In my opinion," said Lok, shaking his hands, "girls from Eden spend too much time chasing after dreams."

He let the cubes of ivory fly. Perhaps it was the angle of a sunbeam, or a trick of the whirl, but as Lok released the dice, Jenny caught a prism of colors. Curious, she reached over and picked up a playing piece.

"Hey!" said Lok. "That was a six!"

Jenny rolled the large die in her palm. "Lok, did you bring these with you from Little Eden?"

"No. I found them here," said Lok.

"Found them where?" demanded Jenny. Everyone in the room heard the extra thump of her heart.

"What is it?" asked Pandora.

"It's been glued," said Jenny, showing Pandora the clear layer of paste on the bone-white object. "Now does that make any sense to you?"

"No." Pandora took the die and paused. Then she began to pace. Back and forth, back and forth. Then she stopped. Then she stared. "Because we forgot the finish." Pandora lifted her foot.

"The talus on the skeleton map!" cried Jenny.

"What's a talus?" asked Lok.

"It's the heel bone," said the schoolmaster, smooth as corn silk. "In Latin, it means a playing piece." He lifted the second die and rolled it in his palm. "So you two have a skeleton map? How very interesting."

"If they have a map, it is theirs to keep," warned Kam, standing tall behind the schoolmaster's shoulder.

"Naturally, naturally," said Mr. Grimsby, handing Pandora the die.

Lok was watching this tableau with amusement. When he felt the fun was done, he stepped to the mantel of the fireplace, which was carved with a series of crescent moons, and took down a convex object from a hook above it.

"I found them in this."

He placed a weather-beaten pan on the table. Glued to the interior, in the curve of a semicircle, were six more dice.

"It's a number code—it's got to be!" said Jenny, grabbing the two dice off Pandora and trying to shove them back in their spaces.

"But which one came first?" asked the schoolmaster.

"Four," said Lok. "Four for friends."

"An unlucky number," said Kam.

"Forget luck," said Jenny, matching the sheen of glue to the bottom of the dish. "We have brains. Here. This is what we've got."

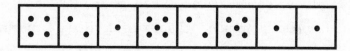

"Four, two, one, five, two, five, one, one," said Mr. Grimsby. "Well, the numbers cannot correspond to letters in the alphabet, because four would be *d*, two would be *b* . . ."

"Dice come in pairs," pointed out Pandora. "Maybe two numbers go together."

"Forty-two, fifteen, twenty-five, eleven," said Jenny.

"But there are twenty-six letters in the alphabet," said the schoolmaster. "What would be the meaning of forty-two?"

"Only four," countered Lok.

"What?"

"One, two, four, and five," said Lok, touching each of the dice in turn. "I don't see the numbers three or six."

"He's right," said Jenny.

"Oh my heavens, oh my spheres," exclaimed the schoolmaster, dancing on his toes. "Not forty-two, not forty-two at all!" He pirouetted. "Twenty-five!"

"You look really silly doing that," said Pandora.

"Is this another one of your impressions, Mr. Grimsby?" asked Jenny.

"I used to peruse a variety of private detective stories," said the schoolmaster, dropping to the ground, "on my sea voyages. And there was one tale about a mathematically minded villain who devised a fiendish code."

He sketched out a grid in the dirt:

1	2	3	4	5	
A	B	C	D	E	1
F	G	H	I	J	2
K	L	M	N	O	3
P	Q	R	S	T	4
U	V	W	X	Y/z	5

"You see? You marry the *y* and the *z* to create an alphabet of twenty-five. Then you take the square root to create the rows and columns."

"Two fives," said Lok. "Plum flower."

"So to solve the code . . . ," said Jenny.

"You go along the row and down the column,"

chirped the schoolmaster, examining the dice. "Forty-two equals *i*, fifteen equals *u*, twenty-five equals *v*, and eleven equals *a*."

"IUVA?" asked Jenny.

"Latin again?" queried the schoolmaster. "A conjugation of *juvare*, to help?"

"I think you are wrong," said Kam. It was his first comment in the debate, and his words held the ring of authority.

"How do you mean?" asked the schoolmaster.

"We are not in a country with Latin, we are in Gam Saan," said Kam. "And in my father's language, words are read top to bottom, and right to left. You must marry two hemispheres: a Western alphabet and an Eastern practice."

Kam knelt down beside Mr. Grimsby and redrew the numbers:

5	4	3	2	1	
A	B	C	D	E	1
F	G	H	I	J	2
K	L	M	N	O	3
P	Q	R	S	T	4
U	V	W	X	Y/z	5

"Then forty-two, fifteen, twenty-five, eleven would mean . . ."

"SAFE," said Lok.

"Pandora!" cried Jenny, leapfrogging off the floor and sending man and boys sprawling. "Remember the christening of King Louis? Remember what he said about being friends with Doc Magee? He said they liked to hang out . . ."

". . . in his back room at the saloon," finished Pandora.

"Where would you find a place that has a safe and chalk and men playing games with dice?"

"A gambling den," said Pandora. She nodded. "I like that. It's clever."

"The nugget is in the Last Chance Saloon!" yelled Jenny. "That ruddy map is leading us right back to where we started. And you know what else?" She pounded her fist on the table. "I bet King Louis isn't a murderer. He's an *accomplice!*"

"Louis is the one who planted the clues and put together the skeleton that Magee sent from overseas," continued Jenny. "That's why he was hanging around the office! No wonder he didn't care about us keeping hold of the rosewood box. He always knew we would end up back at his door!"

"Why would Louis agree to plant the clues?" asked Pandora.

"Because he and Magee loved playing practical

jokes. Can you imagine? He's been laughing at us since the beginning."

Pandora frowned. "I don't like people laughing at me."

"But if he hasn't already sold the nugget . . . ," began the schoolmaster.

"I'm sure he hasn't," said Jenny, spurred by the spike of her fever into overconfidence. "That would spoil the punch line to Magee's joke. Besides, everyone in the territory knows who King Louis is. He's bound to be recognized if he tried to exchange a rock like that at a bank, and he sure wouldn't trust anyone else to sell it for him. I bet he's sitting on it until he receives instructions."

". . . how are you going to get it off him?" finished Mr. Grimsby.

"Oh, I've got ways," said Jenny, remembering her snake-charming efforts with King Louis on Poplar Street. In her mind, she was already devising a cunning way to play on his one major weakness. All it would take was a sentence or two.

"If he's still alive, Magee might want his property back," Pandora pointed out.

"Stuff Magee. As far as I'm concerned," said Jenny, "the nugget now belongs to the person who wants it most."

Perhaps it was the ruthless curl in Jenny's voice. Perhaps it was the line of the schoolmaster's shadow on her cheek. Whatever it was, her old friend wasn't happy about it.

"You cannot be alone. We will go with you," said Kam, hauling his brother to his feet.

"I'm perfectly happy here," said Lok, trying to wriggle out of his brother's grasp.

"Ask me if I give a toss," answered Kam.

"Oh, fine," said Lok, shaking himself free.

"When do you think we'll get to Eden?" asked Jenny, cramming herself into her coat. Pandora was busy ushering carrots into her satchel.

"Under clear and sunny climes?" asked the schoolmaster, craning his head past the door.

"Nightfall," completed Kam.

It's a well-known saying in Eden that the last leg of a journey takes a hundred percent of the grunt. It had been a long week of hiking for the girls, and they still had a little left to go. Jenny was willing to run the river that Saturday—she could have covered a continent with her tracks—but she had to obey the law of averages. The pace of the group was stuck at a slog.

Rather than fight the inevitable, she chose to lead the pack. Kam had a watch on the schoolmaster, and Lok had a companion in Pandora. No one was clamoring for her company. She was free to concentrate on things of importance.

You might imagine that would be her entrance to the saloon. And, to be sure, that was true for the first quarter of an hour or so. But there's only so much you can ponder a challenge before you encounter it. After shaping and perfecting her opening line, Jenny found her mind moving toward the Longshank and its inhabitants.

As she figured it, most adults in the world made the mistake of behaving like fish. Take Mrs. Quinn. Instead of sticking to her goals of becoming an animal doctor, instead of looking forward and not sideways, she had let the current drag her into whirlpools and rocks. She was doomed before she began.

This wasn't going to be Jenny's fate. No, the trick in life was to act like the river itself—strong and fast and rough. That was the way you got ahead in this world. After she had wrested the nugget away from Louis, Jenny was determined to keep charging ahead. Nothing and nobody would slow her down.

"Wait!" called Lok, running to catch up. "We should stop for the pipe."

"You want a smoke?"

"No," said Lok, veering off the path and pushing back the brush. "The pipe."

He stood aside. Under his hand was the trunk of a

large, hollow tree. Around and about the wood, someone had bored scores of holes into the surface. Picture
a flute dropped from a pocket of a giant and you'll have
an idea of the sight Jenny was seeing.

"What is it?" asked Jenny, her curiosity getting the
better of her drive.

"It's a carving," said Kam, "like an organ. To make
music."

"How does it work?" asked Pandora.

Lok stepped up to the nearest hole and puffed. A
mournful note, like the low of a calf, rose from the
center.

"Let me have a go," said Jenny, kissing her lips to
the wood. A higher note, like the call of a bellbird, created a counterpoint.

Pandora had a try, and the peel of a diving hawk
provided the harmony.

"Your turn, Mr. Grimsby!" said Jenny, forgetting
herself.

"No, thank you," said the schoolmaster. "I'd much
rather listen." As Mr. Grimsby stepped back, so too
did Kam.

"It's been worked on a lot," said Pandora, shoving
her forefinger into one of the holes. "This one slants up."

"And this one slants down," said Jenny.

"I like it. Who made it?" asked Pandora, craning
her head to examine the whole.

"Still Hope," said Kam. "He used to reside in these parts."

"I thought he had a job near Lake Snow," countered Jenny.

"He did in the few years before he died," explained Kam. "But my father said that the Longshank was his favorite river. It's where he discovered gold."

Once again, Jenny felt an eerie sense of kinship with Eden's most famous inhabitant. Still Hope was the first of the finders, and she would be the last.

"Hope of the Longshank," said Jenny, thinking of how her own epitaph might read. "Brave and mighty and wise."

"Hope of the Longshank," repeated Mr. Grimsby. "A sot and a rube and a waste." Jenny wheeled on him. The schoolmaster presented his palms. "I'm sorry, Miss Burns, I know I have vowed to be a more tolerant being, but Still Hope was no hero."

Jenny turned to Kam. "Is that true?"

Kam shrugged. "My father said Hope could get pretty fired up."

"Fired up? The first day I met him, he was three sheets to the wind and cursing me!" said the schoolmaster, enraged by the memory. "He said I was doomed to become a fleshless spirit, ever thirsty, ever cold, tormented by animals without eyes, haunted by the dead of caves."

"He said it like that?" asked Pandora skeptically.

"Well, near enough," conceded the schoolmaster.

"What did you do to deserve that kind of scolding?" Jenny waited for an account of a switching or a dark deed in the night.

"I criticized his art," said Mr. Grimsby.

Jenny waited for the rest, but there was none. "That's it?"

"He said he didn't fancy my tone," huffed the schoolmaster. "He said I could not see the beauty in growth or the grace in nature. He said men like me were the reason that beautiful countries were going to the dogs. Then he nicked my bottle."

Here was a reversal! All of Jenny's life, the people of Eden had spun her a story of Hope's unspoiled virtue and patience in trial. Now she was learning he was a cuss and a boozer? Jenny was pleased that her hero had possessed an artistic temper, but becoming a bitter drunk? She could do without that part of the story.

"Can we depart now?" pleaded the schoolmaster, grabbing feebly at his torn trousers. "My shins are shivering."

"In a minute," said Jenny, giving the pipe another long look. Pausing midstream and hearing about Hope's personality was causing her to think deeper about humanity than she was accustomed to.

All in all, Jenny reckoned, Pandora had a point about men being idiots. Wherever they planted their feet, folks dug and they mucked and they ruined. Even blokes who believed in emptiness and silence felt the need to make noise.

But how can anyone exist without contradictions? Jenny asked herself. Survival is cruel by design. The fish eat the flies, the flesh eat the fish, and the flies eat the flesh. We're always going where we shouldn't and arriving where we're not welcome. You can't help but intrude on the earth.

So if you're born to trouble, what choice do you make about living? Do you stay and cheat and connive? Or do you run and hide and fossilize? In a cold and forbidding land, should you choose the life of Louis or the life of Jack?

These are critical questions for any breathing soul. Yet as much as I'd like to tell you that Jenny was blessed with enlightenment that day, I can't. With no immediate answers to the problem, these interesting ideas didn't have a chance to linger long. Tweaked by her fever, our heroine gave up on being a philosopher and decided to be a millionaire instead.

Truth be told, Jenny was off down the path before she had finished her thoughts. A trail of gold was streaking across the sky, the river was veering left, and she had a hunch that the turn for Eden was close.

"My poor, poor trousers," lamented the schoolmaster, trying to keep pace.

"Annie has some safety pins," puffed Pandora. "If you promise to be quiet, I'll ask her for one."

"You can do that later," retorted Jenny. "I've got a bone to pick with King Louis first."

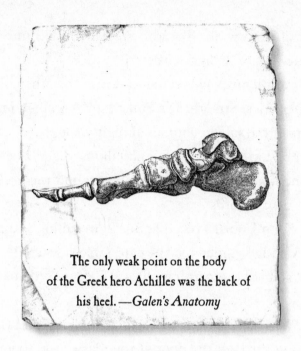

The only weak point on the body
of the Greek hero Achilles was the back of
his heel. —*Galen's Anatomy*

CHAPTER 22

The sun was setting over the hills as the five members of Jenny's band strode into town. Sullen waves of warmth rolled down from the rocks. Shutters slammed fearfully in the gusts, and puddles in the street grew a thick skin of dirt. A dog barked twice.

Thanks to the dying of the easterly, and a surge of unexpected hot weather in the low-lying valley, the Last Chance Saloon was having a good Saturday night. A circle of lamplight formed a welcome mat under the swinging doors. The sound of pool balls striking, the clink of glasses, and the roar of men's laughter rose and fell with the wind. Tobacco smoke whirled in eddies before scattering like skittles.

It was Jenny who led the way, with the others flanking her sides. Straight as a bullet they shot, piercing the doors of the saloon with an almighty *bang!*

The bartender froze. The talking died. The balls on the pool table went careening around the green of their own accord.

"King Louis!" yelled Jenny. "I'm calling you out!"

A pudgy gambler at the card table snickered.

"You say something, Dean Griggs?" demanded Jenny.

"What in the darn fool is all this . . . ?" said Louis, barging through the door at the rear of the room. He halted when he saw the cast of characters ranged in front of him. "Jenny Burns."

"You've got something that doesn't belong to you, Louis."

Louis flashed a canine. A ray of pure bright ricocheted off the white of his lapel and partly blinded the bartender.

"Are you referring to the object you were seeking at Gentle Annie's?"

"You're darn right I am," barked Jenny.

"Well, now," said King Louis. "That's very interesting."

Jenny frowned. There was something off about the whole business. Louis didn't look like a man who was guarding a gold nugget. He looked like a man who had spiked the mug of his best friend's beer with salt.

"Take me to see it," demanded Jenny.

"And why should I?" asked Louis, the words oozing with warm treacle.

"Because if you don't, I'm going to tell every mean and hungry man who comes into town what you're sitting on," said Jenny, leaning forward with a smile. "You may be the king around here, Louis, but I reckon I can find plenty of twitchy gamblers who aren't—how did you put it?—'bosom companions with the law.'"

King Louis nodded. "Touché, Miss Burns."

The air was so ripe with intrigue that you could smell the sweat on the palms of a man's hands. Jenny held her breath—would Louis be willing to compromise on the nugget in order to protect his hide? If she could just get into the back room and see it!

"I'll tell you what I'll do," he said finally. "I'll play you for the privilege."

"What?" asked Jenny.

"One hand of poker. You win—I give you what's in the back room. I win—you're on your own in this saloon."

"And why would I agree to that?" demanded Jenny,

puzzled by Louis's daring offer. She wasn't expecting him to give up the nugget so easily. "It's only a fifty-fifty chance."

"Because I don't know if you've noticed." Louis smiled, tilting his head toward the tables. "But you're not the one holding the cards."

Alerted by a second snicker, Jenny suddenly became aware of the hostile faces encircling her posse. Whatever else he lacked, Louis still had the loyalty of his barflies. Without their ken or approval, Jenny's mates had somehow been herded into the middle of the saloon. It was the same trick knackers used to lead horses to the slaughter.

"Okay," said Jenny slowly. "One hand."

"You'd better keep those Lums away from the table," shouted a bloke with a voice like cold porridge. "Ain't no room for Chinese boys."

Jenny swung around to pound him. Pandora stepped in before her best friend could complete the turn.

"We'll be dead if you fight him now."

Louis laughed. "She's right there, Miss Burns. Anyway, you simply need to win a card game."

Jenny looked to Kam. The silver had appeared in his eyes. He nodded.

"Fine," said Jenny. "Deal."

⌣

The true art of poker lies in the reading of a man. Good cards are a blessing, but the trick is in the watch. Most players give themselves away within the first minute of a game. They tug on their hair, or gnaw on their gum, or tap their foot three times on the floor. I've known gamblers who could spot a bluff by watching a pupil widen. King Louis had been a long time at this sport, and he wasn't about to lose.

So it's probably a good thing Jenny didn't know what she was up against when she collected her cards.

She had the king of diamonds, two black eights, the five of clubs, and the two of hearts. Not much to play with beyond the eights, though the king was a boon.

"Make a bet, Miss Burns. It will feel more suspenseful for our audience."

"I don't have any money," countered Jenny.

"Here," said Louis, setting ten silver dollars on their ends and flicking them toward her. "This is what your dad gave me to pay the debt on his drinks. Knock yourself out."

Cool as a winter cucumber, Jenny snagged each of the coins in turn and laid them down in front of her. Then she pushed the last one to the middle.

"That's my bet."

"I call," said Louis.

"Hey, Hiram, remember when Lottie Quinn did her dance of the seven veils in here? Phewwheee!"

Jenny dug her nails into the wood. She knew why Roger Boone was insulting Pandora's mother. The drinkers were spoiling for a fight as much as she was. And there wouldn't be one unless she became distracted and lost.

"I want three," said Jenny, putting the king, the five, and the two of hearts facedown on the table. "From the top of the deck, Louis."

"For. The. Lady," said a smiling Louis, laying down each of the new cards in a slow and studied motion. "And I'll take one."

In the lore of poker, one card meant Louis probably had two pair or better. Jenny scrutinized the lines in his face with the care of a surveyor. His countenance was amused and becalmed. As usual.

"Hey, Chewy," slurred one of the gamblers, "who you think they're gonna hire for the new schoolmaster?"

"Dunno," said Chewy, picking at the wart on his neck. "But I hope he'll be better than the last one. That man couldn't drive a nail in butter."

"I think I met him once on the Longshank," shouted his companion. "Uglier than a new-shorn lamb."

"And studying to be the village dolt."

Mr. Grimsby sniffed. Lok scowled.

"Gentlemen, gentlemen," said Louis. "The game is not yet finished."

"He means he wants you to shut up," Pandora instructed Chewy. Jenny grinned. Hiram made a feint to his left and Kam neatly cut him off.

"You haven't looked at your cards, Miss Burns," said Louis. "Care to make a bet before you do?"

Jenny gave him a look. With the cards Louis was likely to be holding, she had a thousand-to-one chance of besting him. Her dad would be terrified at losing his money, and the men around her were breathing hate. But she was feeling full of vim and vinegar, and when Jenny Burns is feeling full of vinegar, you'd be wise to step aside.

"Sure," said Jenny, chucking two more coins in the middle.

"I'll see your two," said Louis, "and I'll raise you two."

Six dollars in total on the table. Louis must have a hand full of royalty.

"Why not?" asked Jenny, chucking two more coins in the pot.

The gamblers in the room were getting antsy now. They weren't used to this kind of fearless betting.

"Hey, girl, aren't you gonna look at your cards?"

"Her name is Jenny," said Kam.

"Oh, look, boys, the Oriental can talk. But he's happy to let a girl do his fighting for him."

The words pierced Jenny to the core. To talk of

Kam's heritage like that, to imply the boy who'd saved her life was a coward, was more than her gut could bear. She wanted to stuff the slur down the speaker's throat.

Kam must have been feeling the same way, because he clenched his fist around a glass and raised it in the air. Jenny's chair let out a fearful screech as she pushed it back. Hiram grabbed hold of his pool cue with two hands. Lok picked up a ball. Chewy and his mate moved to block the door.

"Sit down, everyone!" commanded Louis, a cloud of chalk dust crowning his immaculate curls. "You too, Miss Burns. We will finish this game."

Jenny could feel the fire churning in her stomach, but she was strong enough to keep it from rising to her throat. She picked up her new cards. Two black aces and the jack of diamonds. Two pair and a jack. Maybe, just maybe, enough to win.

"Well, Miss Burns?" asked Louis.

Jenny thought of her mother's cross on the hill, Kam's father's tablet in the hut, and Mrs. Quinn, sick in bed. She took her remaining silver dollars and hurled them on the pile.

"All in."

Louis smiled his regal smile. "I admire your boldness, Miss Burns. All right then." He threw his money on top of hers. "Let's see what you got."

"Two pair," said Jenny, chucking her cards in wild abandon and clenching her fists.

"Possible straight flush," said Louis, laying down the ace, two, three, and four of diamonds.

"Possible?" asked Jenny, her color deepening. "You mean?"

"I took a chance," said Louis, laying down the six of diamonds. "And I lost."

❧

Jenny inhaled. A strong noose of beer breath and muscle tightened around her.

"Stop!" said King Louis, raising his hand. "A deal is a deal. The lady and her posse get ten silver dollars and anything that's in my back room." He smoothed a kink in his cravat. "The thing is, Miss Burns"—Louis grinned—"I don't know if you're going to be pleased with what you find in my wee metal safe. That was what you were after, wasn't it?"

Jenny had lost the order of her words.

"You see," said King Louis, "I've looked in that money box many a time in the past decade, and there's absolutely nothing in it. I'd be the king's own fool if I kept valuables around in this kind of company."

Hiram snorted.

"If you don't believe me," added Louis, "anyone in the room is welcome to inspect it."

"You are such a liar!" blurted Pandora.

"Yes, I am," admitted Louis. "But not about this."

"Why?" croaked Jenny.

"You mean why did I tease you along tonight about having the nugget?" asked Louis. "Oh, maybe because I favor your grit. Despite your dubious choice of company, I reckon you'll grow into me soon enough."

After the events of the week, and the words of the drunks, this was the last sentence on earth that Jenny was willing to tolerate. King Louis was wrong. She wasn't his pet or his toy or the heir to his creed. She was the daughter of Hapless Burns, and she was finally ready to stand up and be counted.

"Well, nuts to you, Louis." Jenny rose to her feet. "Because I'm nothing like your kind. I have a mother from the islands and a father from the prairies and a life in the mountains."

"I'm not eyeless, Jenny Burns," said Louis. "Anyone can see where your mother was from. Sure, I like you well enough, but you'll never really belong here."

That did it. Twelve years of avoiding the truth of her feelings ended with a holler. Jenny ripped open her chest and let all her rage and regret and punishment and passion erupt. She jumped on her chair, lunged over the table, and whacked King Louis square in the jaw.

The Last Chance Saloon erupted in chaos. Cues were shattered. Private parts were twisted. Chairs went hurtling toward the ceiling. I've been in one or two bar fights myself, and it doesn't matter who's knocking whom in this kind of situation. It's pleasure enough to be caught in the middle.

"Yeaaaooowww!" cried Chewy as his hair was yanked through the banister.

"Withers and wit!" yelled Jenny as she vaulted onto the back of Dean Griggs.

"Duck!" shrieked Pandora as a bottle of gin went cartwheeling over Kam's head and smashed into the mirror behind the bar. The reflections of thirty blood-thirsty men shattered into a hundred pieces.

You may be wondering how Mr. Grimsby was faring in this skirmish. After all, he was neither a noble nor a hardy man. When Jenny had a chance to raise her head above the fray, she thought she saw him cowering under the pool table. But it was hard to tell which bottom was whose.

"Jenny Burns!" came the shout of King Louis, locked in the arms of a digger named Olaf Turpin. "What have you done to my saloon?"

"It's a new world, Louis," bellowed Jenny. "You'd better get used to it!"

"Jenny!" yelped Pandora.

Jenny scrambled onto the bar for a better view. From there, she spied her friend in the grip of a burly bloke near the door. He was slowly twisting Pandora's arm into a spiral while she kicked at the air in agony.

"Hell and high water!" screeched Jenny, flying out over the crowd. Her left foot came down on Hiram's clavicle and her right foot on Dean's hat. Skipping from man to man, she charged across the room in six seconds flat.

"Lord almighty . . . ," began Pandora's torturer as he saw the great bird of fury diving toward him. The rest of his thoughts were splattered as Jenny pinned him to the floor.

"Oh no, oh no, oh no," moaned Pandora, rolling on the ground.

"It's okay," panted Jenny, wiping the blood from her streaming nose, "I got him licked."

"I don't care about that," said Pandora, scrambling about the floor on all fours. "My boot came off. I've lost it. I've lost my boot!"

"So what?" shouted Jenny, crouching to avoid a careless backswing. Pandora sure knew how to pick her moments.

"The map was in that boot!"

"I don't think it matters right now. Owww!" cried Jenny as the man beneath her pinched her ankle. She shackled his wrist. "Lay off it, you lumbering lug."

"But it was very important!" wept Pandora, ignoring the splinters of wood exploding around her. "I wanted to read it again!" She threw her arms around herself and moaned. "Lemonade and cherry pie and zebras. What else could go wrong?"

You ever find that the universe likes to lay it on thick? Pandora was finishing up the last of her question when the doors of the saloon swung open and Hapless appeared in the lamplight.

"Jenny? Where in the world have you—" He caught sight of Pandora rocking in the corner and rubbed his nose. "Oh, so you've heard."

Pandora dropped her arms. That remark had been directed toward her.

"What?" asked Pandora.

"I'm very, very sorry. But your mum is dead."

Unlike some, I have always found
cemeteries to be restful places.
—*Galen's Anatomy*

CHAPTER 23

"Therefore we commit her body to its resting place, ashes to ashes, dust to dust, with the fervent hope that we shall meet in the hereafter."

There are many men suited to giving a funeral service; a banker with aches in his wisdom teeth is not one of them. In the past three days, Mr. Polk's gums had swollen to the size of berries. Jenny could have cheerfully punctured them.

It had been a ghastly interval between the bar fight and the burial ground. Her father had been slow to forget his worry over their time away, and Pandora had gone into a frozen trance where Jenny was unable to reach her. Our heroine had spent most of the hours apologizing to Hapless for her thoughtlessness and cleaning out Mrs. Quinn's flat.

Even worse, Jenny felt no better for her bruises. Sure, the brawl at the saloon had given her a chance to air her grievances, but it didn't change her circumstances. Men were still narrow, life was still cruel, and death was a given. Nothing had been resolved by barbarity.

"Your turn, Miss Quinn," prodded the banker.

Pandora stepped up to the grave with a clod of dirt clenched tight in her fist. Jenny raised her head to the hills. Eden's cemetery was filled with memories like this. Raw wood crosses and black wool dresses and the thud of the world on an eternity box.

"Now what?" asked Pandora, brushing the earth from her hands.

"Now we will bury her," mumbled Mr. Polk, shoving his handkerchief in his mouth.

The "we" in this instance was the Lum brothers. Kam had volunteered for the duty, and Lok had agreed without protest.

"Would you like to sit down, Pandora?" asked Gentle Annie. Her penciled eyebrows were sketched in two peaks of sorrow. "There's a bench under the firs for the purpose."

"Sure," said Pandora. "These shoes pinch awful."

Quiet as a clock that has stopped, the three sat down in the shade of the Sleeping Girl. The cold of the morning had left a spatter of frost on the curled iron armrest. Jenny brushed it off with her sleeve.

Death is seldom easy to put into words. You grieve for the body, and ache for the heart, and find yourself saying silly things like: "It's a darn shame."

Jenny wanted to tell Pandora that you don't really lose someone, that life was bound to get better, but she worried her speech would sound hollow as tin. Pandora was alone, and Mrs. Quinn had been a phantom long before she died. It would be a lie to pretend otherwise.

"Dad says he's sorry not to be here today," Jenny said instead. "He had to load some goods to take toward the coast. He won't be back for a while."

"He's earning extra money for your move," said Pandora.

"Yes."

When you have lost the hope of your life, the future is seldom a prospect worth contemplating. Jenny knew she was going to a place without mountains, and Pandora was headed for an orphanage. No one had the money to stop it. They were being stripped of everything that made them who they were.

Gentle Annie took her hat off and patted her crimson hair.

"Oh, Lottie, how I'll miss you."

Pandora looked up. "What will you miss?"

"Pardon?" asked Annie.

"People always say that when someone dies," insisted Pandora. "But what part in particular will you miss about Mum?"

The slick of Annie's lipstick fissured into a smile. "You know, I think I'm going to miss the way she knotted a line."

"Come again?" asked Jenny.

"When she first arrived, Lottie was so particular about her professional skills. She wanted to stitch up animals without leaving a scar, so Doc Magee taught her a few tricks. See this?" Gentle Annie peeled off a glove and held out her palm. "Sewed together my knife gash like it was nothing. And she did it quick."

Jenny examined the skin on Gentle Annie's hand. The braids of her folds ran in rivers and streams, but there was no trace of a wound.

"She was pretty good."

"That she was. But life got the better of her," sighed Annie, tracing the line around her thumb, "as it gets the better of most of us."

"I don't think that's fair," countered Pandora. "My mum wasn't fighting against life. She fought for it every day. If she hadn't gotten poor and sick, she'd be pulling foals out of mares right now."

"I'm sorry, Pandora, you're quite right," said Annie, shaking the sentiment from her shoulders. "And as you say, she was particularly skilled at birthing."

Gentle Annie's glance toward the wooden cross on the hill was lightning-fast, but Jenny caught it.

"Did you and Mrs. Quinn know my mum?"

"For a brief time," answered Annie. "Didn't your dad tell you?"

Jenny shook her head. According to her understanding, her mum had lived in hiding with Hapless.

"Lottie helped with your delivery." Annie smiled again. "Lord, Jenny, your mother was one tough lady. She came across the mountains with eight months of belly and a child pointed feet-first toward the world. You were roaming the hills long before you were born."

This was news to Jenny. Hapless had always said she had been born on a ship. She tried to conjure up the scene of her mother's arrival. New snow, hard ground, and a scant welcome at the door.

"We sent a message to your dad, but Hapless was up a river and couldn't be reached. The trip from the coast must have been a trial, because she went into labor a couple of days after."

"Did she say anything about her family?" demanded Jenny. "Or the place where she was born? Or her home?"

"No. I reckon she was in a lot of pain. If it's any

consolation, I know she was anxious to get your dad away from the Rush," added Annie. "She said she had come to save him from himself."

"Dad lied to me. He said she holed up with him in the mountains. He said she died in his arms after catching influenza."

"He was probably trying to spare his own feelings," said Annie. "He got back from the goldfields a week after she died and found you screaming and scrawling and punching the sides of your cradle. One look and Hapless gave up on gold right there and then."

In tales about family, I've found that writers like to tie the final chapter in a tight little bow. But Jenny was discovering what the oldest of us know—most of life is spent getting used to loose ends.

She glanced at Mrs. Quinn's grave. Lok was yawning and stretching and shaking the dirt from his shovel. He would have been a screeching bundle of joy at around the same time. Two hopeless fathers in charge of two helpless babies. It's a wonder anyone survived.

"I recollect the day you first started to run," said Annie, chuckling at the memory. "You were barreling down the banks of the Arrow and Pandora was playing in the sand. And you picked her right up and carried her off. After that, Lottie would have needed oxen to pull you apart. You were lost in your own world, speaking in secret languages."

"Cathedral," prompted Jenny.

"Poison oak," said Pandora.

Sudden as sundown, Gentle Annie began to cry.

"I'm sorry, I must seem a contradiction," snuffled Annie, dabbing at her good eye and wiping dark streaks down her cheeks, "but it's the way the pair of you talk to each other. Long ago, I used to chat with Lottie like that."

"If you were such a good friend, why didn't you come and visit her when she was dying? Or give her a loan to buy vegetables?" demanded Pandora. "You could have made her cheerful."

"I tried to," said Annie through her tears, "truly I did. But she told me to save my tainted money and keep away. After she got sick, Lottie wanted nothing to do with the Rush."

It took a few minutes for Annie to finish crying. When she was through, the two young women began to escort her toward the gap in the cemetery wall. Behind them rose the ridge of the Sleeping Girl. Pandora tugged at her plait.

"I don't understand how I'm supposed to feel now."

"How so?" asked Annie.

"Mr. Polk said folks should be sad and sob and tear their clothes off at funerals. Like you did." Pandora tugged harder. "I don't want to tear my clothes off. And I don't feel sad. I don't feel anything."

"It's like your foot being numb," explained Jenny.

"Yes," said Pandora eagerly. "Is that wrong? Is it because I'm odd?"

"No." Jenny smiled. "Everyone feels like that when someone you love dies. I think it's to stop you from hurting so bad."

Watching the Lum brothers tamp the final mound of dirt on the grave, Jenny remembered what Pandora had said to her in the Gorge about being afraid. Maybe the hurt of loving was why she kept running away. Maybe she wasn't afraid of caring for Kam in particular. She was just plain scared of caring.

"We're finished," said Kam, walking along with his shovel cocked at a respectful angle. "And I like the carving and epitaph you put on the headstone, Miss Annie. I'm sure the words will be a comfort."

"Little acts of kindness are the best sort of physic," added Lok.

"You've been reading too much philosophy, Lok," teased Annie. "Be sure to work the rest of your muscles."

"Yes, ma'am."

Lok's tug on his hat reminded Jenny that her father had probably forgotten to protect his scalp on his trip to the coast. For some no-account reason, in the plumb of her soul, she felt an unusual urge to run after his wagon and shower him in shade.

From the first pull of her breath, Hapless had been a mess of a parent. A trudge and a trial and a tribulation. But he had always loved his daughter for who she was—for the thorns and the bloom. It's not often you find a man like that in the mountains. And it's not often that other men are wise enough to recognize his worth.

❧

Taken together, Jenny was experiencing a fine piece of growth that day. Which was all the more reason for her to resent the appearance of an interloper. On a fast-moving horse.

"Jenny Burns! I want the whole of the story!" King Louis slipped off his mount. His spurs were shining and his boots rich as blood.

Jenny nipped behind the stone wall. Louis didn't appear to be carrying a firearm, but she wasn't taking any chances.

"Look, Louis, you deserved what you got."

"I could have you up for assault." Louis rubbed his broken chin. "And I'm using those silver dollars you won to pay for my mirror. But that's not why I'm after talking to you."

Spying the dust cloud, Mr. Polk pocketed his laudanum and came over to see what was happening.

"Something wrong?" crunched the banker of Eden's molars.

"Have any of you seen Mr. Grimsby today?" asked Louis.

"We've been a bit preoccupied this morning, Louis," said Annie, tilting her head toward the gravestones.

"Oh," said King Louis, yanking his top hat off his brilliantined head. "Yes. Very sorry for your loss, Miss Quinn." The sight of Gentle Annie in black linen seemed to be having a sobering effect on his temper.

"You've got more curls than a merino," noted Pandora.

Louis chose to keep his cool and ignore this comparison. "*No one* has seen Mr. Grimsby today?" he demanded.

"Why?" asked Kam.

"I've just come from my back room. Someone has been at my safe."

Jenny's fingertips began to tingle with pins and needles. "You said there wasn't anything in the safe!"

King Louis had the decency to look sheepish. "Well, with respect to a nugget, that was absolutely true."

"In other respects?" asked Kam.

"There might have been a piece of paper," conceded Louis.

Spit, luck, and polish! thought Jenny. Was there anyone left to tell the truth in this territory?

"Did someone steal the paper?" asked Lok.

"No," said Louis. "But I stepped out for a few minutes this morning, and when I returned, the door to the room was ajar. I've seen many a sight in my career, but this is the first time I've seen a page that can pick itself up and walk five inches."

"And since you knew the four kids would be busy with me and the funeral . . . ," said Annie.

"I reckoned there was one person left in their posse who had an interest in my back room," completed Louis.

"Oh, for the love of money!" yelled Jenny. "Why didn't you tell us before?"

"I'm a gambler, Miss Burns. I hold my cards until they're needed. Besides, I thought it was another of Mike's jokes." King Louis frowned. "Only thing being I can't determine how in the good green earth Mr. Grimsby was able to crack the padlock. Magee and myself were the sole men who knew the combination."

Lok raised his head.

"Forty-two, fifteen, twenty-five, eleven."

King Louis lost his color. "Say that again."

"Forty-two, fifteen, twenty-five, eleven," repeated Lok.

"Oh, lordy, lordy," exclaimed Jenny. "We've all got rocks for brains."

Pandora's tongue had been stuck out farther than a ledge for the past five minutes. "You keep talking about the wrong things!" she yelled.

The crowd around her fell silent and stared.

"The schoolmaster has been to the hut and he's seen the clues and he's chasing the nugget," rattled off Pandora, "so now we need to know what he knows! What did the paper *say*?"

"Can you remember, Louis?" asked Annie.

"It was pretty simple. A children's rhyme." Louis grasped his forehead and hummed to himself. "Went like this:

"Priceless riches
Housed in stone.
Vault unopened,
Key unknown.

"What with Mr. Grimsby's actions," Louis continued, "I'm beginning to think that your dream of a nugget might actually be real."

"Oh, no," said Kam.

"What is it?" asked Jenny.

"The card game," prompted Kam. "The fight in the bar."

"It was the first time we didn't have a watch on the schoolmaster," finished Jenny. She turned to Pandora. "How much do you want to bet your skeleton map is now sitting in his pocket?"

"This is absolutely the worst day of my life!" shouted Pandora, ripping open the collar of her dress and sending her buttons flying.

"See?" said Mr. Polk. "What did I tell you about mourning women? No control."

"Oh, stuff a doily in it, Mr. Polk," said Gentle Annie, watching Pandora beginning to keen. "She's suffering."

Of all the mourners present, it was Jenny who found revelation that day. She suddenly saw, with the sharpness of a blade, what a fortune really meant to her. It meant a home for Pandora, and a garden for Kam, and a country for every living creature—butterflies and all. It wasn't enough to be part of the mountains, Jenny realized; she needed to protect them, too.

Our high-country girl was finally cured of her fever. And she wasn't about to let the schoolmaster win.

"Pandora! Pandora!" Jenny grabbed her friend and held her close. "It doesn't matter. Listen to me! It doesn't matter." The harder Pandora flailed, the closer Jenny hugged her. "We're even with Mr. Grimsby. We've both seen the skeleton map and we both know the riddle. We can beat him to it. The solution is right there in front of us. But I can't do it without your smarts." Jenny whispered into Pandora's ear. "You've got to make sense of things."

Jenny took a deep breath, willing Pandora to breathe

with her. She took another and another and another. Finally, her best friend's heartbeat quieted.

"Give her some pacing room," commanded Jenny.

The crowd retreated, and Pandora began her ritual: two steps forward, two steps back. Jenny watched with a tender kind of pride. She was certain that Pandora would solve the puzzle. Her friend was the least ordinary person in the world.

In the middle of her third march, Pandora stopped. "I know where the nugget is."

Jenny let out a wild yodel of celebration.

"But we've got to get to Magee's office," she continued.

"Can't. Emptied," interrupted Mr. Polk. "Contents being shipped to a hospital overseas."

"What?" yelled Jenny.

"Order to the bank came through yesterday. Your father's delivering the goods now," said Mr. Polk.

"Jiminy crickets!" Jenny turned to her friend and lowered her voice. "Pandora, don't worry. My dad only left for the coast road this morning, I'm sure we can catch him. But what are we looking for? Where's the gold?"

And for the fifth time in her life, Pandora smiled.

"In the skull."

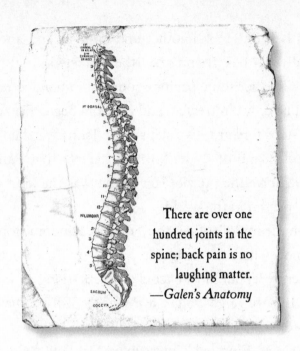

There are over one
hundred joints in the
spine; back pain is no
laughing matter.
—*Galen's Anatomy*

CHAPTER 24

"Dr. Galen's letter told us where it was at the beginning," shouted Pandora over the thunder of hooves and the rumble of the phaeton's rig. "We weren't looking hard enough."

"What do you mean?" yelled Jenny, registering the jolt of the ground in every rung of her spine. They were headed for the Wise Women, where the road ran along the foothills, then swerved west toward the Alps and the coast. Kam was leaning over her left and Lok was peering over her right, and the four of them were bouncing like hailstones on the seats. For a genteel lady, Gentle

Annie drove like a charioteer with her bum on fire.

"The letter under the medicine bottle," bellowed Pandora, "said to pay attention to the hands."

"So?"

"We thought it meant the right hand. But it didn't."

Jenny summoned the image of the reclining skeleton in Magee's office, his right hand over his heart and his left hand resting . . .

"Holy skulls and crossbones."

"Right," yelled Pandora. "The crossbones on the poison bottle were telling us where the nugget was buried. That's why we kept finding patterns. The leaning pillars of the Sleeping Girl's hand and the pattern on the rosewood box and the triangles at the tailrace and the number five on the die. It was saying—"

"X marks the spot!"

"And the riddle?" asked Lok, smashing his jaw against Jenny's shoulder. "What about that?"

"The answer is the brain. It's the gold in the center of all the mountains," shouted Pandora. "Mum always said that the mind is a temple. . . ."

"So the stone means the bone of the head . . . ," said Kam.

"The vault is the space inside the skull, which is round . . . ," said Pandora.

"And the key is . . ." Jenny stopped. "What about the key?"

"How would you unlock a brain?" asked Pandora.

Jenny shrugged. It was hard enough finding the secret places in her own mind, let alone anyone else's.

"Annie!" cried Louis from his horse. "We're taking the turn on the right, the toll road. Be ready for it."

"I've driven more buggies than you've had baths!" answered Gentle Annie. "Keep a watch on your own reins and let me drive!"

They came around the corner on two wheels and hit the toll road at a run. Henry Hicks, who was ushering the last of his flock over the straightway, shook his fist as they skimmed the wool off the backs of his ewes.

"Louis! I ought to set the law on you!"

"Sorry, Hicks, don't want to linger—bridal night with Annie is tonight!" called Louis.

"Oh," said Hicks, hugging his hat to his chest and blushing in the dust. "I'm sure I hope you'll both be very happy!" he called out.

A few minutes later they were through the worst of the gorse and the prickle bushes. Up on this wide stretch of ridge, the earth was littered with the black scrub known as Wild Irishman. Away toward the Alps stretched the curves of the land and the gold of its hide. The phaeton's wheel hit a rabbit hole and Jenny nearly lost her balance.

"We must be close," called Louis. "I can smell money in the wind."

As I've said before, fate tends to take your wishes at your word. No sooner had Louis spoken than they crested the climb at a settlement called Atlas.

"Settlement" is a big word for the place that I'm mentioning. It was a shack or two and a barbed wire fence. Most of the time it was populated by carpenter ants.

Except for today.

❧

"You grow tedious, varlet! A fractious, railing fool!" The man threatening Hapless swung his revolver in the air. "I have charged thee thrice to give over the contents of your shipment. If you do not acquiesce, I shall pall thee in the dunnest smoke of hell!"

"Mr. Grimsby," said Hapless, scratching at his scalp, "what *are* you going on about?"

"I am not Mr. Grimsby," cried Mr. Grimsby, pulling his slipping bandanna back over his nose. "I am Willy the Kid, a notable bandit and rock-mountain thief."

"I don't seem to be able to grasp the tail of this," said Hapless, shifting in his wagon seat. Then he spied his daughter clambering out of the phaeton.

Jenny's heart was throbbing from the thought of another cross being added to the cemetery on the hill.

"Oh, Jenny, thanks be. Can you tell me what your schoolmaster wants? I haven't been able to get a sensible word out of him for the past half an hour."

"You ill-roasted egg!" screeched Mr. Grimsby. "You spineless crustacean!"

Jenny had heard of trains running off tracks, but the sight of the schoolmaster dressed up like a highwayman was a disaster all its own. He was wearing chaps, for pity's sake.

"Settle down, Kid," said Jenny, trying to divert Mr. Grimsby's attention from Hapless. "You'll hurt yourself."

The schoolmaster still lacked his glasses. He squinted at the dark shape in front of him.

"Jenny Burns. I know you of old."

"Yes, you do," said Jenny, taking a cautious step forward, "and you were with me by the river. We're good friends."

"Friends!" railed Mr. Grimsby, firing a bullet into the sky. Jenny froze. "We shall never be friends."

"She gave you a slice of ham," argued Pandora. "And you made her laugh. That's pretty friendly."

"I was performing a part, Miss Quinn!" The barrel of the revolver slewed toward Pandora. "An act, a charade, a scene. You cannot fathom how many times I itched for my switch on that interminable journey. For a man of my breeding to play at games with curs and strays. How are the mighty fallen!"

You'd think Jenny would be spewing hot oil at this

kind of language, but she wasn't. For the first time in her life, she was weirdly calm. Standing in the road, with lives hanging in the balance, she was seeing the whole of the man in front of her.

Sure, Mr. Grimsby was a selfish, snobbish, boot-licking piece of work. Sure, she would never forgive him for calling Pandora a degenerate. But Jenny was also aware that this small, mediocre man was frightened and broke and alone.

Adults, she had come to realize, aren't just a collection of tics or an assemblage of nicknames; they're complicated, contradictory things. There was worth in the schoolmaster's soul; Jenny had glimpsed it, and she was certain—in a place beyond the Rush—he might have led a happier life.

The trouble was, he'd practiced so much for his role as a villain that he'd forgotten himself in the process.

"Mr. Grimsby, I understand you," said Jenny. "Believe me, I do."

"You understand?" cried the schoolmaster, waving the revolver in her general direction. "Atlas himself couldn't knock out your brains, Miss Burns, for you appear to have none. Where would you be without my guidance at the tailrace or Gam Saan? That gold nugget is rightfully mine!"

"What nugget?" asked Hapless.

"Quiet, vile goat!" Mr. Grimsby fired off another

round. "Your breath stinks of French cheese!"

If you can't argue a man out of his madness, you'd best be ready with an alternative. With the second shot from the schoolmaster, Jenny knew there was no reasoning with him. Fortunately, Kam was one step ahead of her.

Actually, he was about three steps beside her, quietly skirting his way past the back of the wagon and around the schoolmaster's right flank. Lok was with him, his crinkled smile more crinkled than ever.

"Now, now, Mr. Grimsby. You'd best be sensible," said King Louis.

The schoolmaster took aim at the figure of Gentle Annie. "One more phrase out of you, Louis, and I'll rid you of your companion."

"You can't be killing Gentle Annie," said Jenny. "Or me and my mates," she added, as the revolver ticked back toward her.

"Oh, heaven, spare a prayer for the friendless man and the motherless child!" wailed Hapless from the wagon.

"Mr. Grimsby, it's time you learned that life is a gift," said Jenny, fixing her gaze on the schoolmaster. His whole arm was shaking. "And we've got to give back. You can help or keep quiet, but you sure as hell-fire can't stop us. Put the gun down. Play's over."

The schoolmaster's index finger was quivering

madly. It curled around the trigger. It hesitated for a hair of a moment then . . .

"*Volcano!*" screamed Pandora.

It was all the distraction they needed. Lok threw his arms around the spine of the schoolmaster with the hug of a vise. Kam grabbed with two hands at Mr. Grimsby's wrist and tugged and twisted until the revolver broke free and spiraled away. Together they wrestled the bandit known as Willy the Kid to the ground.

"A pox on all your houses!" yelped the schoolmaster.

"Kam, are you okay?" asked Jenny, sprinting toward the pair.

"We'll keep him pinned, Jenny Girl. You see to the wagon."

Lok bounced a few times up and down on the schoolmaster's rear. "Be still," he said, "or I can't guarantee the safety of your private parts."

Jenny veered left, scooping up Pandora along the way. "C'mon," she said. "We'll search for the nugget together."

To the wagon they ran, and over the sides they climbed. It was stacked to the skies with crates bound with ropes. This was going to be harder than Jenny had imagined.

"Lordy, lordy, Jenny, what's happening?" Hapless wore the look of a newborn trying to establish the place of his thumb.

"Long story, Dad," said Jenny. "I'll relate it to you later."

"You'd better write it down," said Hapless. "Or I know I won't be able to follow it."

"How do we decide where the skull is?" complained Jenny, kicking at a crate. "And how do we get this open?"

"Here," said Gentle Annie, bustling over to the side and handing her a crowbar. "Use this."

"Annie," asked Jenny, "what in the Arrow's own name are you doing with a crowbar?"

"I find it's helpful to have on moonless nights and deserted byways," said Annie, fluttering her false eyelashes. "A lady is liable to solicitations."

"Start with the crates marked 'fragile,'" said Pandora. "The packers probably decided that bones were breakable."

Shoving the crowbar into the first box of that kind, Jenny pried off the top and riffled through the straw. "Jars and vials so far," she said. "You check the next."

Puffing with effort, Pandora followed instructions. "Frog in a bottle."

"Eyeballs in a case. I think I'll keep hold of those."

"Skeleton!"

Jenny scrambled over the crates. "Can you see the skull?"

Pandora shoved her head over the side and kicked

her feet. For a moment, the whole of Jenny's world ceased to spin. Then, with a grave gasp of breath, her friend resurfaced, hay clinging to her plait. In her arm, she held the head of a man.

"Holy sin of sinners," cried Jenny, "it's bigger than I remember."

"Alas, I knew him, Horatio!" whined the schoolmaster.

"Shut it, Willy!" commanded Jenny.

"It looks like it's been cracked and glued again," said Pandora, running her palm over the bumps and lumps. "We're going to need a hammer."

"We'll use the curved side of the crowbar," said Jenny, fetching the tool. "Here, you hold the skull still."

"Ladies, if you could glance my way . . ."

King Louis was standing near to the Lum brothers. In his left hand, he grasped his ebony walking stick. In his right, he held the schoolmaster's revolver. It was trained at Kam's chest.

"No hard feelings, Miss Burns, but as you know, the law and myself . . ." He allowed the rest of the sentence to hang in the air.

"Louis!" screeched Annie, "what are you driving at?"

"Now, now, Annie, I'm a rational man. I'm not going to kill him. Not if I don't have to." He tilted his goatee at Jenny. "Miss Burns, you have something *I* want and I have something *you* want. An exchange is in order, don't you think?"

"Ignore him, Jenny Girl," shouted Kam. "He's bluffing again!"

"You should think about clamping your mouth shut," said Louis, cocking the revolver. "I can't be responsible for muscle memory."

Jenny was scared right and proper. The schoolmaster was crazy; Louis was sane. He was a veteran of the Rush and the sharpest of shots in the territory.

"Come now, give me the skull, Miss Burns, and we'll both sleep sound for the night."

Would it surprise you to learn that Jenny was more than willing to give this lazy opportunist what he wanted? She was. She was ready to hurl it—and the devil—straight at Louis's smooth, smirking face.

Pandora was the one feeling contrary. "You're a mean, mangy man who wears too much perfume!"

"Pandora," muttered Jenny, "don't rile him. We've got to agree."

"No, we don't," retorted Pandora. "If we hand him the skull, he'll still have the gun. That's a stupid trade."

"On my honor bright," called Louis. "You and your mates will walk away safe. All I want is the gold."

"Liar!" yelled Pandora.

"Have you been planning this the whole time?" asked Jenny, trying to defuse the powder keg of emotions with talk.

"It did cross my mind at Magee's office," said Louis, "that I might want to keep a watch on you both. And after the bank and your story about the map, I figured I'd wait and see what you made of the wooden box. But I swear on my oath that I didn't expect a pair of misfits to get anywhere. I'm very much obliged for your efforts."

Finally, Pandora recognized the sting of sarcasm. "You're a real big pain in the butt!"

King Louis tapped his cane on the air. "Yes, I am."

"Louis, stop this fooling immediately!"

If Gentle Annie's command was meant to jostle King Louis into a mistake, it failed. Her scolding brought him right back to business.

"Enough," said Louis. "I'm not fooling, ladies, and I'm not willing to bide any longer. Bring me the nugget, Jenny Burns, or I'll arrange for flowers to grow over the Chinaman's grave."

It was Louis's final insult that did it. In that moment—and forever after—Jenny would have given anything to save Kam. She plucked the skull from Pandora's fists and made for the road. Her feet had just touched dirt when a massive paw reached around Louis's neck and closed over his carotid artery.

"Drop the gun, Louis. One squeeze is all it takes."

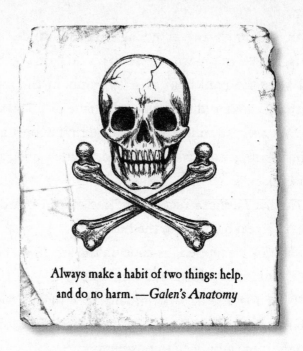

Always make a habit of two things: help,
and do no harm. —*Galen's Anatomy*

CHAPTER 25

Louis dropped the revolver with a thump.

"Fetch the weapon, Kam," said the mysterious stranger.

Kam scrambled for the gun.

"Wind him up, Annie," the man instructed.

Gentle Annie pulled a length of rope from the phaeton and tied it round and round King Louis until he was completely cocooned.

"Right then, are we comfy?"

"Silent Jack!" yelled Jenny. "What in the blue-sea hills are *you* doing here?"

From inside his chrysalis, Louis began to laugh uproariously.

"That wasn't funny," said Pandora.

"You had me for a moment, Mike. Thought you were some mythic beast that stumbled down from the Alps. But your eyes give you away. I know a fool when I see one."

"Mike?" asked Jenny. "Don't you mean Jack?"

"No," replied Louis. "That walking mass of a woolly mammoth right there is my old friend Michael Magee. Doctor, prankster, sage."

Jenny gawked in astonishment at the man known to her as Jack. Could it be possible that the twinkling irises behind those caterpillar eyebrows belonged to the legendary owner of the nugget?

"It's a very good disguise," said Pandora in an admiring way. "But I think you need to work on the accent."

Magee winked.

"Why, my darling boy," said Gentle Annie, charging forward and pressing ten pounds of matted beard to her bosom, "then you didn't fall off a mountain!"

Doc Magee attempted to nod. "A little air, Annie!"

Gentle Annie released her prisoner.

"You were playing with fire with that neck trick," said Annie. "You could've killed your best friend."

"One," said Doc Magee, "King Louis is not my

best friend. Hasn't been since he refused to let Jack into our lives."

"Jack was a foreigner," blasted Louis, "and I didn't care for his horning in on my territory."

"Two," said Magee, ignoring the interruption, "I couldn't have killed him with the grip I had. Not immediately, anyway. The worst I might do is make him faint." He gave King Louis a look. "And wouldn't that have been a tragedy."

"Why didn't you use your own gun? The one with the X?" asked Pandora.

Doc Magee opened his coat and pulled out the bone-handled revolver. "Well, I'll tell you, Miss Quinn. I don't fancy utilizing another person's property. Besides," said Magee, spinning the cylinder to show it was empty, "I took an oath to save souls. Whatever their merit."

"You borrowed the revolver from Silent Jack," said Jenny.

"Correct," replied Magee.

"Then he's still alive?"

"Certainly. He's sitting pretty on his family's farm in the old country right now. Growing medicines. I lent him money for the voyage home right after I dug up the nugget. He offered to linger awhile and protect me, but I told him I had another plan in mind."

"Silent Jack is the one who put the nugget in the skull and shipped the skeleton to your office!" yelled Pandora.

Doc Magee smiled. You've heard of grins that go ear to ear? His went straight from temple to temple.

"That he did, Miss Quinn. Wrapped it tight as a baby and sent it to me with his best attempt at a Galen scrawl. I'm impressed you could read it."

"And I was right!" shouted Jenny, hopping up and down. "*You* put together the hunt. *You* hid the clues in the office."

"And the huts and the jail and the tailrace," noted Doc Magee. "It didn't take long—I asked Jack to deposit the rosewood box at the bank before he left. Then I snuck into town one night to plant the letter and fix up the bones. And tidy the mess those miners made of my books."

"Why create a hunt in the first place?" asked Lok, adjusting his seat on the schoolmaster.

Doc Magee shrugged. "A pleasant way to pass the winter?" He stroked his beard. "Besides, I was getting tired of the Rush. When I found gold, I figured I'd waste it, resent it, or end up losing my life for it. None of those options seemed palatable."

"So you went roaming instead," said Jenny.

"Not very far," said Magee. "I've been up at Troy

for the past decade or so, with the trout and the game and my gardens. It's pretty much a paradise, if you don't mind talking to trees."

"You must have burned the roses, too," said Pandora.

"My, but you are sharp." Doc Magee had lost his smile, but his voice had gained a note of respect. "Ever since your visit, Miss Quinn, I've been thinking about you and your friend. Two spheres of the same brain, I reckon. Yes, I set fire to the rose hips. I planted them; they were mine to destroy."

"You were angry with the world," said Jenny, more to herself than to the doctor.

"I was furious with it. So I decided to murder my old life and start anew."

Jenny didn't need to ask why. She could see the way of it—the first days of Doc Magee's glee, pleased as punch with his practical joke, expecting someone to come to Troy, ready to evaluate the treasure hunters on the merits of their case. Then months of waiting and watching and thinking.

Thinking mostly on greed and stupidity and suspicion, Jenny figured. What was it Mrs. Quinn had said? Pandora couldn't see past the nose on the end of her face? Thanks to their gold fever, the men of the Rush couldn't see straight to begin with. They had glory made flesh all around them, and the only thing they cared about was ripping it—and one another—apart.

And Magee had sat alone in the palm of creation. Year after year of seeing the sunrise and watching the sweet grass grow? Jenny was surprised he hadn't torched the whole of Eden.

There was one person in this conversation who had not yet contributed. That was forgivable—he was wedged under a twelve-year-old.

"Who gets the gold?" wailed the schoolmaster, rearing his head like a tortoise. "In case you are not aware, Dr. Magee, I was instrumental in the process of detection. Those girls wouldn't be here without me."

"The nugget," said Doc Magee firmly, "is mine. And I'd defy a court of law to say different."

Jenny had to repeat her thoughts of the last hour to stop from choking. Money never matters, until it does.

"After watching the ladies argue with each other at Troy, I was quite willing to write to Mr. Polk and instruct him to ship the skeleton back to Jack," continued Magee. "Only, I've been musing on something that Miss Quinn said to me up in the back blocks about understanding. So I'd like to ask her now—what would she do with the nugget?"

As you're aware, Pandora was apt to tell the truth, the whole truth, and nothing but the truth.

"I'd give it to Jenny," said Pandora, "so she can stay in her mountains."

"And I'd give half of it to Pandora," said Jenny, "so she can care for herself and go to school. And give the other half to Kam, for Little Eden."

"And I'd give it right back to them both," said Kam, "because best friends should be together."

"And I wouldn't care," added Lok. "Because money doesn't change anything. People do."

"And I'd say you're all more tedious than a weary nag and a railing wife!" yelped the schoolmaster.

Doc Magee smiled again. "Strong answers from the younger generation; I might argue a point with the elder. If those are your decisions, I have a proposition. We split the nugget three ways. Miss Burns gets half, Miss Quinn gets half, and the Lums get half."

"You can't have three halves," said Pandora.

"Three parts, then," said Magee, acknowledging the correction. "An equilateral split."

The schoolmaster whimpered.

"No, Mr. Grimsby, I haven't forgotten you." Doc Magee gave the sole of the schoolmaster's boot a nudge. "But I've seen enough scars from switches to loathe your length and breadth. What do you say, friends? Shall we turn him over to my mates in the constabulary? I know one or two who owe me a favor."

Hapless raised a tentative hand.

"Yes, Mr. Burns?" asked Magee in surprise.

"I'm not much for thinking," said Hapless, pawing

forlornly at his scalp, "but I hear tell that the territory is sending a bunch of convicts to bushwhack trails to new goldfields in the Arctic. Maybe a schoolmaster would like to help them learn their lessons. Most of them can't read their ABCs."

If Jenny hadn't known better, she could have sworn her father was grinning.

"Hoist with my own petard," muttered Mr. Grimsby.

"That sounds like a peach of an idea, Mr. Burns," said Doc Magee. "I'll make the arrangements when we get back."

"But what about Louis?" asked Kam.

For a man wound up like a bobbin, King Louis appeared unseasonably cocky. "Don't worry, Mike. I'll be booking passage on the same ship as Mr. Grimsby. Business is bad as it is. A new Rush means new blood, and pickings will be ripe. Will you come with me, sweet Annie? We'd make a crackerjack team."

"Not on your Nellie," retorted Gentle Annie.

"And what's to stop me from binding you to hard labor?" challenged Doc Magee.

King Louis winked. "Friendship."

Mike Magee frowned.

"You know, Louis, twelve years ago I might have been willing to grant you that favor. But the girls here have taught me something about the truth of one's actions." Magee directed those strange gray-greenstone eyes toward Jenny. "I was wrong to give up on trying," he said. "I should have stayed in Eden and cared for her spirits. Nothing is gained by ignoring the problems of existing."

He turned his attention back to the ghosts of the past.

"We failed them, Louis. We were supposed to protect the earth for the next generation, and we ruined it." King Louis opened his mouth to speak, and Magee cut him off. "Nope, you don't get to spit any more of your venom. You're heading for prison and I'm going to work with the children on reviving Eden. For *everyone* in it." Magee raised an ominous finger. "Squeak one more word and I'll make sure the judge doubles your sentence."

Jenny was pleased to observe that King Louis was looking dazed and disquieted. And obediently silent.

Pandora coughed.

"Right," said Doc Magee. "Who wants to crack open my skull?"

⤸

I was pondering the virtues of leaving the story there; only, Jenny insists there are a few more things you should know. I asked if she'd prefer to write the last words herself, but she said no—she was a hardworking farmer and I was an idle doctor, and the whole point of this tale was to keep me busy in my dotage. In the years since we first met at Troy, Jenny hasn't lost her winning ways. So I'm going to do my best to phrase the ending as she would like.

For example, holding a gleaming hunk of gold is as magical as you might expect. Jenny could almost forgive a man for craving it. But after you've tossed it around for a while, the nugget becomes a rock, the glow becomes a glimmer, and the clean cutting wind reminds you of home. There was sheep dung and sunshine and grass and good earth in that wind, and she was eager to return to Eden.

She was an older Jenny, and a wiser one. Her mountains might be laced with fevered dreams and petty greed; but they were also bursting with beauty and sorrow. Let men dribble their drivel and snigger their hatred. They were no match for the sky or those who were willing to dance with it.

And so she led the way. With the two bandits trussed tight in the phaeton, and Hapless and me taking it slow with the horses, most of the party was able to walk out in front. Pandora had requested it.

"How can we be sure King Louis and Mr. Grimsby will be leaving town?" asked Kam.

"Mike has always been tight with the law," said Annie, dreamily twirling her follow-me-lad curls. "And he's good at arranging things."

"Do you love him?" demanded Pandora.

Gentle Annie smiled. "Don't know if I could find most of him at the moment. But when he's had a wash . . ."

"You didn't answer the question."

Annie patted her comfortable posterior. "Now more than ever. I don't care if he's been away for ten years or two hundred, I'll always have room in my heart for his shenanigans."

"Well, that makes no sense," said Pandora.

"You're right," answered Annie, "because love doesn't make sense. Some loves bloom and wither in a day; some put down roots to the core of the earth. I've known love that with a little tending might have grown to an oak, but it died at the sapling. Others simply run wild and free. It's always a surprise."

"Then how do you know if a love will survive?" asked Kam. Jenny did her best to keep an eye on the horizon.

"Stay patient," said Annie, smuggling a smile to me. "And keep weeding your garden."

Walking along with the group, Jenny was beginning to appreciate that this was the kind of love she felt for her dad. No matter the season, it would always require endless patience and fertilizing and care. It was quite unlike the love she felt for her mum—that was a plant that grew fierce of its own accord.

But you know, and I know, that there was another love in our Jenny Girl, one that went deeper and stronger than any she'd care to acknowledge. Hit it with a hurricane or fire it to the ground, and it would always grow back better than before. Jenny knew it, too, and she decided it was high time she did something about it.

She turned to her friend. "I just want to say I love you."

"Okay," said Pandora.

Jenny nodded. It was enough for the moment. She snuck a look at Kam. The rest of it, she told herself, would come when it might.

"Lok, you've been very quiet," noted Annie. "What's the first thing you'll be doing with your riches?"

"Not sure," said Lok. "Sleeping more, I hope."

"You'll be helping me plant trees," said Kam. "Now that the soil has some wet to it, we'll have to squeeze as much work in as we can before the snows."

"I'll help!" said Jenny. "After I get some of the stuff done at our place."

"What place?" asked Lok.

"I'm going to buy Old Randolph Scott's station up on Reed's Terrace. You're welcome to stay with us. I've bagged the room in the turret and Pandora gets the room off the orchard, but there will be plenty of corners left over. I'm thinking we'll start with fifty sheep and see how we go from there. I don't want to worry Dad overmuch." Jenny paused. In her haste to leap mountains, she had forgotten to consult her partner. "Is that okay with you, Pandora?"

"I don't mind," said Pandora. "As long as we're not close enough to hear each other snore."

"And what will you do about school, Miss Burns?" teased Annie.

"Oh, I doubt I'll be needed at school."

"I wouldn't be too sure of that. I heard Mike talking about plugging the gap until they can find a new teacher. He'll be taking a muster every morning."

Shivers and quivers, thought Jenny. Just when you think you've got life sorted . . .

"Once I finish studying, I'm going to open a private detective office," said Pandora.

"Come again?" asked Gentle Annie.

"Like Mr. Grimsby was talking about when we were in Gam Saan. Private detectives solve puzzles and capture outlaws. I'm going to be one of those."

"Pandora," inserted Jenny gently, "there won't be many folks who need a girl to catch jailbirds."

"Yes, there will."

"Why?" asked Jenny.

"Because I'm a lion. *Phwarrr*," roared Pandora.

"Sorry, you're a what?"

"It's a joke!" Pandora waited for the reactions. Kam smiled. Lok attempted a chuckle. Gentle Annie seemed bewildered.

"You said jailbird," insisted Pandora.

"Yes," said Jenny.

"So cats like to catch birds."

"Yes."

"And the lion is the biggest cat in the world." Pandora looked from face to face, then crossed her arms. "Ah, to heck with you all."

At that, her best friend nearly cracked her ribs with laughter. "Pandora," said Jenny, snorting back her tears of joy, "that's the best darn joke I've heard in my entire life."

"Good," said Pandora.

"You know what I always say, Miss Quinn," I interrupted from my perch on the phaeton. "As soon as you've made a thought, laugh at it."

We were coming to the end of the ridge, where the road curved north toward Eden and the river. From her spot on the rise, Jenny told me she could see the whole of the valley in front of her: Lake Snow, the Arrow, the top of her Cathedral tree, and the face of the Sleeping Girl. A wide-open world in the trust of a kid. She would guard it with her life.

"There's one last thing I want to know . . . ," began Pandora as I brought the horses alongside her.

"How can I enlighten you?" I asked.

"If you're here and Jack is alive . . ."

Pandora paused.

"Yes?" I prodded.

"Whose head did we just crack open?"

"Well, now, where do I begin?"

AUTHOR'S NOTE

This book is a love letter to Central Otago. Like so many areas around the Pacific Rim, the South Island of New Zealand was inundated with treasure seekers in the nineteenth century. In the Wakatipu Basin, you can still find remnants of their quest in Arrowtown, the ghostly buildings in Macetown, and many lonely places along the rivers.

The geography, the culture, the immigrants, the idioms—my aim was to capture the flavor of the Otago goldfields. But, contrariwise, I also wanted *Magee* to be a universal tale—a cock-and-bull adventure in the spirit of Banjo Paterson and his bush poetry. Which is all by way of saying I have taken considerable liberties with dates and details. Eden and its inhabitants are my own invention. Some of the mountain ranges are fictitious. And many of the descriptions are open to your imagination. In my head, the islands of Jenny's mother are the Marshall Islands of my cousins, Lau and Tony, but this area of the world and this time period are filled with fascinating people and places. I encourage you to explore them, as I have, and to make Jenny and her home your own.

It has been an honor to write this book, to talk it over with a new generation, and to draw information and inspiration from the generous experts of diverse backgrounds who helped me in the process. And if you are a Jenny or a Pandora or a Kam or a Lok, I hope I've come within a country mile of having this story ring true to you.

ACKNOWLEDGMENTS

Every adventure involves collaboration, but this one was a true team effort! I'd especially like to thank:

- My mum, Dr. Rita Teele, a pioneer in pediatrics and immigrant extraordinaire.
- My team of expert advisers—Meha Littlewood, Caroline Teele, and Sophia Thompson—who provided invaluable insights into Jenny's experiences.
- Lau Almeida, who lent her smile and spirit to our girl of the mountains.
- My ever-patient editors at Walden Pond Press, Jordan Brown and Debbie Kovacs, who urged me to go deeper and think harder.
- Forrest Dickinson, an incomparable illustrator and all-around mensch.

• Amy Ryan and Joel Tippie, designers of taste and discernment.

• Claire Caterer and Renée Cafiero, who turn copyediting into an art.

• Charlie Chin, a master storyteller, children's author, and American treasure.

• Shenwei Chang, who enriched and emboldened Kam and Lok.

• Jack Lyons, Ronan O'Rahilly, Fabiola Müller, Stanley Carpenter, and Rand Swenson. Their section on "The Origin of Anatomical Terms" in *Basic Human Anatomy* was a key resource.

Finally, I'd like to add a special thanks to all the folks who are working to preserve and protect the earth for future generations. If you believe in Jenny's creed, please consider donating to the Royal Forest and Bird Protection Society of New Zealand or an environmental cause of your choice.